Secluded Summer at Hidden Havens

Secluded Summer at Hidden Havens

Wendy Black Farley

New Harbor Press

RAPID CITY, SD

Copyright © 2020 by Wendy Black Farley

All rights reserved. No part of this publication may be reproduced, distributed or transmitted in any form or by any means, without prior written permission.

Black Farley/New Harbor Press
1601 Mt. Rushmore Rd., Ste3288
Rapid City, SD 57702
www.newharborpress.com

Publisher's Note: This is a work of fiction. Names, characters, places, and incidents are a product of the author's imagination. Locales and public names are sometimes used for atmospheric purposes. Any resemblance to actual people, living or dead, or to businesses, companies, events, institutions, or locales is completely coincidental.

Secluded Summer at Hidden Havens/ Wendy Black Farley -- 1st ed.

"The head of a literary agency swaps places with a writing teacher for a summer, and both find love and intrigue."
—Kirkus Reviews

"Black Farley's book is a lighthearted romp, offering a modern, less-serious spin on a campus novel … The dialogue is often flirtatious, and the gossip between characters is downright infectious . . . Readers will be charmed by the author's descriptions of the Adirondacks and by Benita's beloved Hidden Havens, with its rich history and its feeling of midsummer whimsy"
–Kirkus Reviews

"A fun tale of two women's summertime adventures, featuring compelling dialogue."
– Kirkus Reviews

"Season" Your Reading

Also by Wendy Black Farley

Season's Stranger

(Cori Sellers, Book One)

Season's Shadows

(Cori Sellers, Book Two)

Five Stars, Readers' Favorite Book Reviews
Readers' Favorite Book Award Winner
Finalist, Indie Excellence Book Awards and American Fiction Awards

Connect with Wendy Black Farley on:

Facebook: Season Your Reading

Wordpress: wendyfarley.com

Twitter: @Wendy_Farley1

Acknowledgements

Illustration for Secret Trust
Amy Hall
Chestnut Hill Vintage

Editor
Diane Kane

Special Thanks
Peggy Fuller
Pam Williams

Chapter One

Adirondacks

I don't know what I'm doing or why. Bridgett had forty-five minutes left in her lunch break and decided to find out what all of the chatter was about. She knew nothing about this new application for reading books on the internet. In fact, she knew nothing about old applications for reading books on the internet.

Most of her young co-workers read the novel on their cellphones. Bridgett had a flip phone. She borrowed a laptop from the office and was surprised how easy it was to follow the login directions for the app, "imprinTABl." She located the book and opened up Chapter 1 by clicking on the novel's cover.

Secret Trust - Chapter I

"Next up, the Power Lotto numbers. Right after this." The purchases Isaac Anderson made at the Brook Crossings convenience store the day before nearly slipped his mind. But the announcement on the network affiliate television station for the Adirondack Region that the Power Lotto numbers would be announced right after a commercial break reminded him to check his numbers.

He rushed to towel off, dress, grab his ticket and park himself in front of the TV. "Isaac, don't you be late for the bus on the first day of your senior year!" His mother shouted from her bedroom. Muriel Anderson was the definition of a helicopter mom. *I hope putting on her make-up takes long enough for me to catch the numbers.*

Isaac's heart started racing. He could feel his pulse down his arms, up through his neck and into his temples. He choked and tried to thwart a cough by clearing his throat. He checked the numbers on the screen again, and then his ticket. *Am I transposing numbers?* Isaac's dyslexia was most pronounced with numbers. The diagnosis had defined him for the last decade and confined him to the 'sped' population at school. The loving over-protection of his well-meaning mother was just a bonus. Long before his diagnosis, his Kindergarten teacher, Mrs. Kinder, had kept him for an extra year because he couldn't set up simple math problems.

"I'm ready mom. Leaving soon." He tucked the ticket into his pocket. He needed to check it again later.

"Good. I'm off. I have an early meeting at work. Why are you sweating?" Muriel emerged from her bedroom and gently touched his forehead with the back of her hand. "Do you have a fever?"

"No. I'm fine. I think the shower was too hot for a day like today." He was dazed and would have said anything to get her to leave as planned.

"Okay. Just get your stuff and get going."

"I will." And Isaac planned to leave. Otherwise, the neighbors could report him to his mother. It had happened before.

I need to check the numbers again. It can't be true. He tried to remember everything he had heard about the downside of lottery winning. *Secrecy. I have to keep it a secret. I have to plan. But I probably didn't win at all.*

He didn't want to do a search of the winning number; his mother kept track of his browser history. Just as he was about to leave the house, the winning number was reported again. *They don't give me much time.* But he read it forward, backward, middle to end both ways. *It looks real!*

He clutched the ticket. *I've heard I should sign it right away. But then if I lose it, anyone can turn it in. If I take it with me, I could lose it. If I leave it in the house, my mom could find it. I need a lawyer.*

Isaac fetched his travel belt from his room. He placed the lottery ticket in the belt, tucked it under his clothes, and left the house. He had no car and no license. His mom made him promise to wait until he was 18 to drive, which was yesterday. He was signed up for the driver's education class this semester at school.

He had no money except his birthday money, and he spent some of that yesterday for the cola and the lottery ticket he bought on a whim while his mom was chatting with a friend.

I can walk to the Library. I'll do some research. No. I can't do that. They'll tell my mom. They can keep track of my browser history. I'll walk over to the church. Anything I tell the Pastor is confidential. No. That's a priest.

Isaac kept walking, all the time trying to be invisible. *This town. I can't let anyone see me. I can't talk to anyone.* Flint Loch was teaming with joggers and others trying to enjoy the outdoors before the late August mid-day heat.

Isaac took the back road to Flint Lake, which served as his refuge. He sat in a shaded area; not only protected from the sun but from view of any who might come by. It was still early, but he had very little time until his mom got reports of his absence from school, including the resource room, and that random resident unnoticed by Isaac who saw him walking the streets. He recited scripture verses silently looking for direction.

A half hour passed. By some miracle, his cell phone had some bars. It wasn't a smart phone; it was pay as you go. There was no data connection, but the only good thing was that it wasn't tied to his mother's phone. He dialed information for a taxi number in the next town. Directions to the Lake were difficult. His left/right orientation often failed him, and the driver wasn't invested in understanding what he was trying to say.

It was over an hour before the taxi arrived. "I want you to take me to the largest attorney's office in the Capital Region." Isaac was nervous.

"That's gonna cost you a pretty penny. Are you good for it? I've invested a lot of time in this fare as it is." The driver said nothing to gain Isaac's confidence.

"You have no idea." Isaac's sheepish tone belied the implication of his words. He got in the back seat of the dilapidated sedan.

The driver took off without comment. It was late morning by the time Isaac gave the driver the last of his money and entered the tallest building in the vicinity. Birney-Finn-Lansner & Rockney occupied most of the towering building, which was a combination of steel and windows. There was a directory, but Isaac had no chance to read any of the names or locations before he was interrupted.

The lobby had a receptionist. "What building are you seeking?" She made it obvious that someone like Isaac would have no business in such an elite practice.

"I need a lawyer. Someone who is good with finance."

The receptionist didn't know whether she should laugh or be angry. He must be pulling her leg, but she played along. "Do you have an appointment, sir?"

"No, but I need to see someone right away."

"Why don't we make an appointment?"

"I'm serious."

"Why, sir. You make it sound as though it is a matter of life or death." She thought she made her condescension both clever and gentle.

"It might be."

Chapter Two

Miami – Three Weeks Earlier

Benita Sotolongo jolted when she heard a faint click of the hallway door to the office suite. *Who would try to get into the office in the middle of the night?* Before she could reach it, the door closed shut. Fearful but curious, she opened it up and peered into the hallway to the sound of another door closing. That sound came from the direction of the stairs. *Odd and scary.*

She glanced around the moonlit office and quickly shut down the computer. *It's nearly daylight. I can't let anyone find me here.* Her state of exhaustion made her escape from the office seem as if in slow motion. She sighed with relief when the elevator door closed with her as the only occupant. With a quiet whirr, it descended the ten flights to the ground floor.

Safely deposited in the vast lobby, she began to relax and craved her favorite breakfast. She determined she wouldn't be noticed at the Café La Leche, which was the restaurant on the ground floor of the massive Basin Quay building. The Basin Quay was more of a city block than a building.

Benita purchased a café la leche, along with a Cuban tostada. As she turned toward the exit, she was surprised by a voice behind her, "Busted!"

Startled, Benita turned to see the woman she wanted to avoid. Celeste Wentworth, the administrative assistant at Soto Literary Agency, was constantly keeping an eye out for Benita. Celeste had warned Benita the day before that she would check to ensure Benita would not "pull an all-nighter." Benita was Celeste's boss as well as owner of the agency. Celeste considered Benita's well-being to be a part of her job description.

Benita's mouth opened, but nothing came out before Celeste spoke again. "So, you just couldn't resist #Pittmad tweets all night, could you Beni?" Celeste's words stung, but the use of the childhood nickname given to Benita by her father soothed the rebuke to a caring declaration.

Yvette, the barista who had served Benita, saw the pseudo attack and was watching the two with interest. "You literary types have your own language. What in the world is pittmad?"

Celeste looked around Benita at Yvette and apologized. "Yeah. You learn not to take us 'literally.' Sorry; bad pun. Also, sorry--I didn't intend to create a scene. There are designated days during the year when authors pitch their WIPs, or 'works in progress,' to agents using Twitter. Beni can't resist reading them until they stop. Despite the designation of 'a day,' it can go on for many days. It's exhausting, and I warned her not to work all night."

"Oh. I get it." Yvette went back to her customers. There was no need to doubt Celeste; Benita was a known workhorse.

"So, what is your excuse?" Celeste was not finished chiding her boss.

"You will soon find out. Please call a staff meeting for noon today. I'll be back by 11:30, and I want to meet with you alone first, then Kendrick, followed by the rest of the staff for a working lunch. I'll order food before I leave. Ahem. I would like to sit and enjoy my breakfast first, now that I'm exposed."

"Were the pitches that good?"

"I'll let you know. Now, you've come to work at the crack of dawn for nothing. But I do appreciate that you care."

"You mean to tell me there's no work waiting for me after your nocturnal marathon?"

"Oh. Yes. I guess there's plenty to do. But it could have waited."

"Sure it could." Celeste smiled, patted her boss's arm, and proceeded to get her own coffee.

By the time Celeste received her coffee and headed to the elevator, Benita had devoured her breakfast and proceeded to place the lunch order. "Yeah. It's me again, Yvette. Is it too late to order lunch today for the entire staff?"

"No. It's fine. What can we get for you?"

"Oh, good. Cuban sandwiches, please. Would you add some soft drinks and sweet tea? No fries. You'll deliver as usual?"

"Sure will. And we'll send the warming tray to keep the sandwiches hot."

"You're the best!"

"Lo se. Lo se."

"Oh, and please, put it on my personal account. Por favor?"

"Si."

Benita obtained a Lyft to take her the twelve blocks to her condo. Though a perfect time for walking before the scorching heat of the day, she was in a hurry. She needed to be rested and fresh for the impending staff meeting.

Benita punched the entry code to her building and entered the lobby. She decided to quiet her guilt about taking the Lyft and took the high road to her condo, the stairs. Her place was only four flights. Unless she was carrying groceries, it was the best way to get in her steps without sweltering outside.

Benita took a quick shower and nearly fell into bed. After about four seconds, her alarm sounded. Or so it seemed. It had been three and a half hours. She arose, reapplied her makeup, which was custom-ordered for her light tan complexion, and dressed in a sheer-lined short-sleeved blouse with slits at the shoulders and a white pencil skirt with blue hydrangea's cascading down the front. Benita easily managed her wavy black hair in her current style — wispy shoulder-length cut in long layers.

Before returning to work, she called the front desk. "Hi, Carlton. I was wondering if my luggage could be delivered from storage to my apartment today?"

Chapter Three

Adirondacks

Maren Scott strained to hear much of the conversation at the table where she was enjoying the rare occasion of a restaurant lunch with her colleagues. The celebration was in the outdoor covered terrace at the nearby Adirondack Park Golf Course's restaurant. They were teachers celebrating the last day of school. It had been a half day.

Maren settled her portion of the bill and headed back to Clear Lake Central School to finish grades by the 3:00 p.m. deadline. As she approached her classroom, Maren saw one of the math teachers, Rex Jacobs.

"Hey, Rex. I wish you had joined us for lunch. It's so seldom we have the opportunity to eat out, and drink, in the middle of the day together."

"The eating and drinking would've been okay. No need of getting together with a bunch of people I see all of the time."

"Fair point, but not for the rest of the summer."

"Did you forget? We're teaching summer school."

"Actually, I'm not."

"Why not?"

Principal Jeanine Gawl appeared from around the corner. She had a knack for interrupting and taking control of the conversation.

"Maren, how did your students take the news that you wouldn't be teaching the writing workshop at summer school?"

"Well ..." Maren attempted to phrase her thoughts without success. The one-word statement conveyed more than a little hesitation.

"Well?"

"I didn't tell them."

"My office. With me, please."

After settling in, Principal Gawl glared at Maren. "Do I need to say another, well? These kids are going to be furious. Humble though you may be, you know how popular you are with the students. The ones who had you as a teacher are looking forward to learning with you again this summer. The students who haven't studied with you consider you a legend and feel so fortunate to spend the four-week summer session with you."

Maren was a word maven, under normal conditions. But a sensible response to Principal Gawl escaped her now.

Maren stumbled along, "Well. Sorry. Oh, I said it again. I humbly acknowledge that my failure to follow through on summer school could have an impact. That said, I fear students could convince their parents to withdraw their enrollment while they can get a partial refund for the workshop. Absent that, I believe once they have some time in the workshop, they're going to realize how fortunate they are to have the benefit of someone as a facilitator who is involved in writing as a profession."

"Oh. Yes. You have a point. Do you feel this is at all unethical?"

"Do I feel deceitful in not informing the students of the teacher change? Yes. I do. But we discourage our students from teacher shopping, do we not? Teacher changes occur as a routine. They are more determined by qualification and contractual compliance. It is my understanding they are not student driven. Do I have this right?"

Chapter Four

Miami

Benita was back in the offices of Soto Literary Agency promptly at 11:30. She gathered up Celeste in her whirlwind, and they closed the door behind them in her office. The office had a water view of the Intracoastal. Benita gazed at it almost as if for the first time, "This view is so beautiful."

Celeste was quick to respond. "Isn't it? How often do you slow down enough to enjoy it—or even notice it?"

"Not very," she said with a slight touch of sadness. "Right now, I need to get to the point. Kendrick will be coming in a few minutes." After what she thought a cowardly sigh, Benita blurted out, "I am taking a break."

Celeste moved forward in her seat. "What do you mean?"

"You know the agency was my father's passion. I've learned to love the folks I work with, the agency and what it stands for, and even the work. But despite the legal documents identifying me as the owner, I feel as though the agency owns me. I need time away."

"You're telling me! So, a vacation?" It was Celeste's attempt to strike a balance between panic and treading lightly.

"I need to be honest. It isn't a vacation. It's part retreat, part volunteer experience, and part exploring my future."

"Are you saying your future might not be here?" Celeste still tiptoed in her quest for answers that she might not want to hear.

"Not necessarily. Yes. Possibly."

"I know my time is almost up before Kendrick comes in. What part is the retreat, what part is volunteer, and what are you exploring? Just curious. It might help me know where we stand."

"The agency will continue. I will go into that in more detail later, but you do not need to worry about your job. The volunteer experience will be at a high school in the Adirondacks, where I will be teaching a summer workshop on writing and the publishing industry. I'll have limited connectivity where I am staying, and that location will be undisclosed. I am taking textbooks to learn more about an advanced degree in my field--linguistics."

"Does this have anything to do with Kendrick?"

Benita closed her eyes and shook her head gently, "No. Not at all."

There was a knock on the door. Benita turned toward the door with a sudden look of fear on her face. She dropped her voice. "Wish me luck with Kendrick."

Celeste stood quickly. Before opening the door, she said, "Good luck. With everything."

Kendrick let her pass before entering. He examined Celeste's face for a clue of what transpired, but she looked away from him and exited quickly.

"Please have a seat, Kendrick." Benita valued Kendrick Harrington as the most senior agent and former protégé of her father before his death. She continued. "I wanted to let you know about immediate plans that will have an impact on the agency. You have been the Vice President of Soto since before I began working here with my father. You know every aspect of this business. That said, I am hoping you'll accept the position of acting CEO during my upcoming absence."

Kendrick stood. He was visibly agitated, and the fact that he had just been offered a promotion seemed to go over his head. "You make it sound as though this is something imminent."

"It is. I will be leaving right after lunch."

"Benita. How can you do this? I saw all the recommendations you forwarded from #pittmad. Why did you ask for a multitude of manuscripts only to leave us in the lurch? I am finding this quite outrageous. You don't seem to find a need for any more explanation than you're leaving right after lunch? And what about that new application you launched?" Kendrick took out his handkerchief and wiped his eyes. He turned and stared out of the window for several seconds before he spoke again. "Does this have anything to do with our relationship? If you're wondering, I know you are convinced it won't work out."

Benita spoke softly. "Kendrick. You are a wonderful, talented man. We are not destined for romance. As for the firm, you've got this. I've hired an extremely competent high school English teacher for an internship during the summer. She can read many of the manuscripts I requested without breaking a sweat. She will know how to get in touch with me if I am needed."

Kendrick raised his voice. "A high school teacher! Benita, my fears would not be assuaged if you provided the most prominent literary agent in the business during your absence. A high school teacher is supposed to make me feel better?"

"You don't know her."

"Do you? Really?"

"We haven't met. No. If, as you say, I have a unique sense for this business, why not trust me in this decision as well? I think some plans I have during my absence can help with the new app as well. Give this a chance. Please."

"Look. This teacher may be a prolific reader. She may have a sense for good writing and even for what the public wants. But there's the rest of the publishing industry she certainly knows nothing about!"

"Kendrick. I need to meet with the staff, and I really don't want them to see your panic. If there's anything I know, you've got this."

"Benita, you're taking off because you're beleaguered and overwhelmed. Now you're asking us to do this without you. And maybe it's more about 'us' than you're willing to admit." Kendrick exited without waiting for a response.

Shaken, Benita tried not to show it to the staff. They all were present when she arrived in the conference room. Benita composed herself as they gathered sandwiches and beverages to consume while their boss filled them in on why they were meeting.

When they were all making progress on their lunches, she spoke.

"It seems as though it's been a long time since we had lunch together. I met with Celeste and Kendrick just a few minutes ago to inform them of the news I am about to share with you. I have decided to take a leave of absence for an undetermined period. I have a four-week commitment, so I will be away for at least that length of time. It could extend for the entire summer."

There was quiet chatter among some of the agents that quieted as Benita continued.

"This is a pressured environment, and I am sure you all feel it. Due to the access the public has to me, especially via social media—which I especially want to escape, I will be 'unplugged' for the duration. I won't be checking in on any basis, but there will be an individual identified to reach me in an emergency.

"I have asked Kendrick to become Acting CEO in my absence. There will be an intern with an excellent background in writing, editing, and literature who will be joining the firm for the summer. Her name is Maren Scott, and she will be here the day after tomorrow. Please welcome, trust and depend on her.

She'll be especially helpful as we transition from textbooks and nonfiction into fiction genres.

"Any questions?"

There did not seem to be the panic that Kendrick, and to a lesser extent, Celeste had shown. The staff continued with their lunches with several expressions of good luck. Benita sensed that Jett Fellows, Soto's CFO, and Zina Casey, the agent who encouraged Beni's idea to shift the firm to representing fiction, were pleased with her announcement. *Something about them seems odd.*

Chapter Five

Adirondacks

Benita obtained a lease car at her destination airport. The drive from the Capital Region of New York to her summer retreat location was breathtaking, but long. After an hour on the interstate, the mountain peaks became more prominent. In addition to the rolling green heights were the spikes of scar faced ledges rising from the lush mounds. A she exited the interstate, there was a wide mountain river parallel to the wending state route she traveled and mountains rising so high they seemed to be closing around her--almost as an immense tunnel of rock.

Benita had visited the Adirondack mountain home of Adelaide Havens every summer until the summer she turned sixteen, but not since. Memories of this place were surreal and evoked a flood of emotions, especially those of a summer romance.

Hidden Havens, a nineteenth century stagecoach tavern and inn, was worthy of its name. Built by her uncle's ancestors as a shelter for stagecoach travelers along the old northern turnpike in northeast New York state, it had been restored over the years to maintain the original architecture and furnishings. The two-story mini-mansion with its narrow wood clapboards, small, symmetrically arranged windows, and the ornate, hand-carved molding surrounding the entryway was classic for its time.

The access road and long driveway had never been paved, and the pines created acres of beautiful groves. The tavern occupied a large area where the forest was cleared to accommodate it. Floral and fruit trees adorned the front, while sectioned vegetable gardens and an edging of flowers followed the east side to the vast backyard. On the other side of a low stonewall on the west side of the yard was a road leading to the pristine lake front. *Plowing this road must be a chore, but it has to be made passable for fire prevention; even though Aunt Dilly has used it as a summer home as far back as I can remember.*

Adelaide Havens, Aunt Dilly to Benita and Adele to everyone else, who was now a widow, had married into a wealthy family. She was the half-sister of Benita's mom, Leonie, and was her mom's senior by more than a decade. Her aunt greeted her at the front door along with a friendly, yapping dog called Rackie. Rackie was a bronze-colored cocker spaniel and was Adele Havens' companion whether at her permanent home in White Plains, New York, or here at Hidden Havens. *I think his real name is Racket! I see why.* Benita stooped to give the dog attention. It soothed his curiosity, and he sat back as if to watch the next act.

"Beni! Welcome, welcome, welcome. Come in. You must be exhausted. I have some tea ready to serve in the east parlor." A quick hug, and she was on her way to fetch the tea with Rackie patting behind her. Hot tea would not be an appropriate offering in Miami at this time of year; but the hot summer sun had yet to assail the cool Adirondack mountains. Her aunt also used the nickname, Beni, picked up from Benita's father.

"That sounds wonderful, Aunt Dilly," Benita called after her as her aunt was already on her way for tea. "But I can't bring myself to sit again for a few minutes, and I have been looking forward to a reunion tour of the grounds and cottage."

Her aunt returned to the parlor. "Of course! I'll come with you. Just let me get my hat."

As the two walked arm-in-arm, Benita was at once doing a real tour and a tour down memory lane.

"Oh Auntie, I don't know why I have stayed away so long. This is so gorgeous. We have plenty of fresh fruit in Miami, but I still savor the memories of fresh cherries, plums, and pears from these trees!" A sweet scent filled her nostrils. "Oh, look at the late flowering rhododendrons on the other side of the stonewall! And I can see the purples and pinks of the lupines growing wild in the woods near the lake!"

They didn't walk as far as the lake, but instead veered back toward the vegetable garden on the southeast side of the house. Adele was humble about the garden. "It's nothing like it used to be, but I like to keep it going. Whatever I can't use I can give to the church food pantry."

"No need to be modest, Auntie. I don't know how you keep up with everything!"

"My sense is that I do very little. I spend as much time arranging for professional help as I do tending to the grounds myself. I miss Uncle Havens in many ways, but he was especially attentive to the landscape and produce."

"I miss him so much. He made almost everything fun. Even his nicknames. Yours stuck, didn't it?"

"Yes. He called me Deli for a long time. But all it took was one time referring to me as a 'Dilly,' and there was no turning back!"

"I remember he called me "Itty" when I was very little. He claimed it was a good derivation of Benita! I'm so glad *that* didn't stick! You both were so different from my parents. They were obsessed with their own pursuits—mostly their professions. You and Uncle Havens lavished me with attention during the summers here *and* when I visited you near the city."

"Oh, I'm glad you had that impression of Havens. Although, he was quite a bit like your parents, really. But he doted on you. When you were around, his other obsessions faded."

"Were you jealous of his work in New York City real estate?"

"Oh, a little. Sometimes I developed a bad attitude about it. But if I needed him, he was all in. I loved him so much my focus was on the time we could have together rather than our time apart. I'm glad he was happy in his job. Just as I am happy that your mom loves her job. I wish she hadn't felt she needed to give up living with you and your father in order to stay focused on her work. Speaking of your mom, is she still an integral part of referring textbook business in the direction of Soto? And, do you see her when you're in the city?"

"Not much. You know her. So busy! To answer about her involvement with Soto, that avenue of print books is slowly changing to digital due to the use of tablets in schools. It's still a big market, but we're doing what we can to make a transition to digital and delving into fiction at the same time."

"How about your dad's passion, the Cuban political voice? Has someone taken up the mantel since his passing?"

"Kendrick did for some time after father's death. He and I decided their voice could and should be heard, but there are many more avenues available to them. So, not so much lately."

"Lots of changes."

"It gets overwhelming at times."

"Speaking of Kendrick, how is he? I always wondered if you two were a possible item?"

Benita smiled and shook her head. "No. Well, in a way, we tried. But it just wasn't meant to be. It was more than the age difference—that seems to run in the family! He's more like an uncle to me."

"I see. I recognized my stepson also had a crush on you, but you did nothing to encourage him. I didn't know if it was the age difference or that he was family."

"Both. Yes. I know he wasn't related by blood. His own mom died, and after you and Uncle Havens married, you were like a mom to him. So, he is family." Benita looked at her aunt to see her response and was surprised to see a smirk on her face. "What?"

"Oh. I was just thinking about how he visited for a weekend that last summer you spent time with us here. We all knew you were in a fog of sorts when you finished that week at Chain Mountains Extreme Camp. He might have been a little jealous and was the first to notice. We surmised it was a camp romance. Do you remember that? First love, maybe?"

I haven't forgotten … or at least, never for too long. My first kiss, and the best one yet!

"Beni?" Aunt Dilly summoned Benita back to the present. "That's exactly how you were after camp. That trance!"

Benita blushed. "Oh, I'm sorry Auntie. I do remember. I won't deny it."

"Did you stay in touch with this crush?"

"We did. Until letters went out of style and emails changed to texts and cell numbers changed and college and career pursuits all conspired to make us lose contact."

"That's too bad."

"It is. And it is what it is."

Arriving at the back of the Inn, Benita gushed over another treasured aspect of the building and grounds. "Oh, this sweet porch. We've spent so many hours out here: the porch swing; picking over peas, beans and blueberries; competing with the peepers as we chatted late into the evening!"

They entered through the back door and proceeded to the east parlor. Adele disappeared for a few moments and returned with a silver tea set on a matching tray with antique china cups.

"That is such a beautiful service, Aunt Dilly. Is it antique?"

"It's safe to assume everything you see here is an antique, including me, dear." She chuckled and then took the conversation in another direction.

Adele put down her teacup and clapped the top of her knees with both hands. "So, what about you?" Tell me about your summer plans!"

Chapter Six

Miami

Humidity glommed on to Maren Scott even though the transition outside from airport to limousine was brief. *How do people stand this? Maybe spending the summer in Miami wasn't such a great idea.* It was a momentary lapse, for she was grateful to Benita on many fronts. She offered Maren the opportunity to be immersed in the literary world for the summer and took over her teaching duties to boot. Then there was the generous offer to use Benita's apartment, which Maren seized without hesitation.

After another brief exposure to the blanket of wet heat that enveloped her between the limo and the lobby of Benita's building, Maren stood in awe of the entryway. She remained enamored of the surroundings as she entered the apartment. The modern, open kitchen/living/dining area was large yet inviting. If someone had described the hard-surface waterfall island and the grey cabinets with the sparkling white subway tiled backsplash, she would have thought it cliché. But it was stunning.

A wall of windows with a view of the city ran along the right side of the U-shaped sectional sofa, facing a gas fireplace with a large television installed in the wall to the right. The black dining room furniture provided a stunning accent behind the white sofa. She decided she could be comfortable here.

The apartment revealed very little in the way of personal belongings. There was ample closet and bureau space for Maren to unpack her wardrobe, and there was space in the bathroom for her items she needed daily.

She mused over the variety of make-up, which Benita seemed to have overlooked. It was the brand and tone Maren used. She hadn't met Benita in person, but she guessed her own skin tone was several shades darker than Benita's. *Of course. She left it behind because she didn't need or want it.*

***

It was not apparent to Maren on her first day of work how she should go about locating the Soto Literary Agency's offices within the Basin Quay Block. There were numerous directories located throughout the maze of a lobby. She decided to get a coffee in the Café and ask if they could direct her from there.

"How can I help you?" Yvette ceased wiping the counter and looked up at her.

"Many ways, apparently! I would love a cup of coffee and directions to the Soto Literary Agency."

"Just coffee?"

"Yes."

"Cream and sugar?"

"No thank you." Maren received a strange stare, but Yvette quickly filled her order.

"You're not from around here, are you?" Yvette took a chance.

"No. It's quite different where I come from. But we do have exotic coffees. I like to keep it simple."

"Uncomplicated is good. The quickest way to the agency is down the corridor to the right, take the Basin Quay elevators, and exit on the tenth floor. You'll be able to take it from there. Do you know Benita Sotolongo?"

"Sort of. In a long-distance kind of way."

"Oh. I see. I think you'll fit right in."

"Thanks?" Maren was not sure how to take the last comment, but she would remember it. She sensed Yvette kept score. And she gave directions well enough to get Maren to the offices. As soon as she entered, Celeste greeted her.

"Hello. May I help you?"

"I'm Maren Scott. I'm here to help with fiction acquisitions for the summer."

"Oh! It's nice meet you. Let me show you your office. Be sure to keep me informed on what you need here at Soto or anything about Miami you need to know. We tend to move fast and independently around here! Don't hesitate to slow us down when you have a question." Celeste was wary of this arrangement, but she wanted to be gracious all the same.

"Thank you. Between you and Yvette, I think I'll be okay!"

"You've met Yvette. Good. And you have her sized up, too! Let me introduce you to a few folks."

"On the left is your office, bequeathed to you for the summer by Beni. To the right is Kendrick. He's the acting CEO and has been here for years. He helped Beni's dad build up the business until they received added help from Beni when it was obvious her dad's health was failing."

She knocked on the door jamb to Kendrick's open office. "Kendrick, do you have a moment to meet Maren Scott?"

Kendrick stared at his screen for several seconds before responding. Slowly he turned to them, leaned back in his seat and said, "Welcome. And I mean that. We are drowning in made-up stories! Are you ready to help?"

"Yes. Should I meet the rest of the team?"

Celeste stepped in again. "Sure. There are a few others working on fiction. I'll take you to them, then get you set up in your office."

After quick introductions to Polly, Reece, Marshall, and Zina, she was shown to her office. Benita had set Maren up with passwords and left instructions on the best ways to get started, which mainly involved reading the manuscripts requested by Benita during pittmad.

Maren's day was perfect. She read all day. *What a gig. Even the worst bagatelle was okay with her; she was reading!*

Deep in thought, she was startled when Kendrick knocked on her open door. "Oh, Kendrick. Hi! How was your day?"

"I should ask you, but I was wondering about something else. How would you like to have dinner?"

"How nice. I would. Very much."

"Great. What do you like?"

"Well, we don't have much for street food where I come from."

"Any food you want, you'll find it within a few blocks from here. Street food works for me. What would you think of Aunt Sarah's Soul Food Deli?"

"Real soul food?"

"You bet."

"You're on!"

"I have a quick errand. Meet me in the lobby in a half hour?"

"Sure." She almost said, 'it's a date.' *Was it?* Maren hadn't been attracted to a man since—she didn't know, exactly. Her divorce was a long time ago. She was happy. Happy to be reading all day, happy about the authentic soul food, and happy to be thinking about an interesting man.

Still caught up in her reverie, she scooped up her bag and exited her office. Though the rest of the office looked dark, she thought she would say goodbye to anyone else who remained. As she entered the section of the suite where she had met Zina, she noticed her entering the office occupied by someone she hadn't met. Maren didn't intend to spy, but she stopped so not to startle anyone.

Maren thought she overheard a man's voice say, "So. Any more fakes?"

Chapter Seven

Adirondacks

Benita was more excited than nervous as she entered Clear Lake Central School. She found the Main Office right away, where her cheerful "Good morning" received a monotone "Hello" by a detached, stereotypical northeast greeter who remained seated at a perpendicular angle to a counter that represented her fortress from the public.

Benita remained warm. "Is Dr. Gawl in?"

"She's in the building. Have a seat until she returns."

"Thank you."

A thirty-something man emerged from an adjacent area of the office with a pile of papers. Benita looked up and greeted him. He barely grunted and continued out of the office.

"Don't mind him. He's always like that."

"He's fine." Benita remained friendly and was a bit surprised that the receptionist felt the need to explain his actions—or even noticed anything was out of the ordinary given her variety of reception. Several minutes passed when a well-dressed woman rushed in without noticing Benita.

"Dr. Gawl. This lady is here to see you."

Dr. Gawl took off her glasses and looked at Benita. "Oh. Hello. What can I do for you?"

"I'm Benita Sotolongo. I'm here to conduct the creative writing workshop."

"Oh! Of course! Welcome. We appreciate this. I'll take you to your classroom."

Jeanine Gawl escorted Benita to Maren's classroom. On the way, Benita noticed the man she had seen at the office copier. She decided to try to break the ice. She crossed the hallway, knocked on the open door, and said, "Hello again. I wanted to introduce myself. I'll be teaching across the hall for the next month."

"Oh yeah. Hi. You're going to need a lot of luck."

"I'm sure I have a lot to learn about teaching. I'd like to know your name if that's okay."

"Rex Jacobs. Math." Rex Jacobs didn't make a move from where he was writing on the whiteboard.

"Good to meet you. Maybe I'll seek your wisdom on the tricks of the trade as we go along."

"Not likely."

"Okay. Well. Good to meet you. Talk to you later."

Her training had taught her that there was far more to Mr. Jacobs than what presented as sheer rudeness.

She shook off the encounter and returned to become acquainted with the classroom and its resources. She studied her outline, read the student roster, scarfed down a sandwich, and awaited the afternoon arrival of her students. The schedule allowed for long weekends for families and staff since Monday class was afternoon only; Tuesday through Thursday were morning classes and afternoon adventures; and Friday classes ended at 11:30 with no afternoon session.

It was finally time for the students to arrive. They trickled in, each looking more confused than the next. It seemed like the most awkward moment of her life, but she couldn't decide what was wrong. She tried to engage each student as they arrived, asked questions about their summer experiences, computer games, and the latest mall attractions. Nothing worked. When everyone seemed to have arrived, she gave them her name and a little about the Agency and her work. She took attendance and got to the point. "Okay. Something is wrong. What is it, and is there anything I can do?"

The students glanced at one another. The young man who had responded to the name, Jake, finally said something. "We thought Ms. Scott was teaching this class."

"What? You mean, she didn't let you know I was guest teaching?"

"No. She's a really popular teacher." Benita thought Riza was the name of the second student to respond.

"I think most of us took this course because she was the teacher." The students were getting braver.

Benita allowed a brief silence and said, "I'm sorry to disappoint you. Your teacher is talented and insightful. Though it might upset us to be in this situation, I think we should trust her judgment. Undoubtedly, she had a good reason for keeping this information from us. Can you trust her along with me and give this a chance?"

They shrugged, but there were no overt protests.

"Let's get started. I hope your interest will be piqued by what I have planned."

Benita struggled through an outline of her plans and gave out her first assignment. It was an in-class writing exercise where the students were to create their ideal comfort animal and write a quick children's story about the animal.

When the session ended, most students simply left without a goodbye and half without handing in their papers. Benita collected the papers left behind on the desks. Despite her belief that it was an engaging exercise, most students had written between two and four sentences. It took her a few minutes to read through all of them, and none had any potential as an interesting read.

Chapter Eight

Miami

Kendrick suggested to Maren that he introduce her to some of Miami's attractions over the weekend. He called her on Saturday morning to make their plans. "How would you like to see Miami on a motorcycle?"

"I think I would love it."

"Have you ridden on the back of a motorcycle before?"

"Yes. Quite a few years ago."

"You'll do fine."

By some miracle he found a parking spot on the street in front of Benita's apartment and was buzzed up to meet Maren. They both enjoyed the entanglement encountered as they deciphered their individual roles in mounting and sharing the two-wheeled vehicle.

He motored down Biscayne Boulevard by a Mediterranean Revival building with a Spanish-style cupola on a tall tower. He slid into a parking spot where they could see the building and talk. Without dismounting, he asked "Did you know Miami also has its own Freedom Tower?"

"I don't think I did," Maren responded. "It's extraordinary."

"I think it dates back to the nineteen-twenties when it housed the *Miami News*. You know, back when print media was all the rage."

He continued, "The newspaper moved in the late fifties, and the federal government used the building for over a decade to process Cuban refugees. It's changed hands a few times, as I understand it, but is now a museum and cultural center that's part of Miami Dade College."

He headed toward Ocean Drive, down shifted, and putted for a long distance in a lower gear so that she could take in more of the beauty that Miami had to offer. He explained he would take her by some of the Art Deco buildings nearby. They stopped in the Art Deco District and enjoyed a late lunch.

"How about an interesting stroll after lunch?" he asked as they finished their seafood platters at the Beach Club.

"The beach?"

"Maybe later. I was thinking of the Tropical Botanic Garden. I've only been once, but I recall it's remarkable."

"I would love to. And a walk would feel pretty good right now."

He smiled but was too much of a gentleman to ask if she feared the development of saddle sores.

They walked hand in hand and at times arm in arm as they enjoyed the lush tropical setting when they arrived at the gardens.

It was late afternoon when he said, "I don't want the day to end, but I have some work I have to do at home this evening. Plus, I don't want to be a monopoly on your time and dictate what you should see while you're here."

"Kendrick, I've had a perfect day. Thank you for everything."

They motored back to Benita's apartment and Maren said. "Please, don't park. I can see myself inside the building."

He was reluctant but agreed and gave her a quick kiss on the lips. "I'll call tomorrow?"

"I'd like that."

He was a man of his word. They planned to get together again on Sunday, and, at his suggestion, enjoyed a swim in the Venetian Pool.

***

On Monday evening, they planned another dinner together and spent a romantic evening watching a boat flotilla on the bay. Sitting on the water's edge and holding hands had led to a series of tender kisses at the end of the evening.

Chapter Nine

Adirondacks

Benita's emotions deflated. She wanted to video chat with Maren and ask her, "What were you thinking?" She wanted to go home, or anywhere. She was still wound tight after her hour-long drive back to Hidden Havens.

Maybe a run will help. Aunt Dilly was out with friends, so she quickly changed, got Rackie's leash, and headed out toward the logging road that extended west beyond the Havens property. She ran well beyond her normal distance and realized it would be a challenge to keep up the pace on the return trip to Hidden Havens. As Benita moved to reverse direction, Rackie made an abrupt stop and began a low growl. Benita tried to coax him along, but he held fast even as Benita nudged him a bit with a gentle pull of the leash. Rackie was focused on the trail just traveled. Benita saw it too.

She whispered, "Holy moly, it's a bear! Thanks, Rackie." She kneeled beside him and rubbed his side. She couldn't decide whether there were any options. If she waited it out too long, it would be dark. She knew the road eventually joined a county road, so she quietly kept going in the direction she had been traveling. She had no idea what she was getting herself into, nor how far from Hidden Havens she would land. *Are those rain clouds?*

She ran more than a mile when she thought she spied a building. She continued toward it and soon saw a Jeep with someone approaching the driver's door. She shouted, and the person turned toward her just as the first drops of rain splashed her face. The Jeep's owner saw her and summoned her to continue.

As Benita approached, she began to get a clearer picture of the individual. She was a female in a ranger type uniform. Breathless, Benita came close enough to speak to her. "I am so glad to see you." She was breathing too hard to say more.

"Let's get you both into the Jeep before it starts to rain harder." The ranger made sure they were loaded and belted before asking for more details. "Where are you going?"

"I was taking a long jog. When I went to circle back, a huge bear was in the path."

"Ah. I don't blame you for continuing on! Where are you from?"

"I'm spending the summer at Hidden Havens. Do you know where that is?"

"Oh, sure. I garden for some of the folks in the area, including Hidden Havens. I'll take you back. Are you family?"

"Yes. Mrs. Havens is my Aunt Adele."

"Nice lady."

"She is. I'm Benita Sotolongo."

"I'm Pala Onatah."

"I can't tell you how glad I am to meet you, Pala. Thank you so much for this."

"It's also what I do. I work part-time as a ranger. I usually head out to do rounds just before dark to make sure all is okay. Especially with a storm threatening."

By then, it was raining. When they reached the inn, it was a pelting rain.

"Please, come in and wait out the storm." Benita wasn't familiar with mountain weather, but the atmosphere seemed rife for hail.

"I think I will. Thanks."

Benita invited her to the West parlor, provided her with a towel to dry off a bit, and set the log in the fireplace ablaze. The temperature made a precipitous drop. She then said, "I'll get us some tea."

While she was gone, Pala picked up a couple of textbooks that were on the sofa table. When Benita returned with the tea, Pala decided to settle her curiosity. "Are you a linguist?"

"Yes. I plan to do some studying this summer. I'm exploring the possibility of an advanced degree."

"Are you planning to study any of the Iroquois languages? Is that why you're here?"

"Are you interested in indigenous languages?"

Pala replied with enthusiasm. "I am. In fact, I think I can say I'm fluent in Mohawk."

"Really? How? Have you studied on your own?"

"Yes. Summer workshops got me started."

"I don't think I would be taking much of a chance in asking if you are Native American."

"Very much. So, are you studying any of the languages?"

"I'm interested. I spent time studying many language structures as an undergrad. But my area of linguistics is in communication—especially the social aspects of communication."

"Like speech impediments?"

"Well, of a sort. But not articulation, per se. My studies and the first few years of my career centered on the neurological challenges that impact the ability to understand social language."

"Oh."

"I really appreciate what you're doing. Every native speaker brings us that much closer to retaining the language. It's my understanding that four of the five Iroquois languages are now considered extinct."

"Yes. Sadly."

"Would you like to pass along your knowledge?"

"I would. I think about it all the time. Uh, I must get back. Some time I'd like to talk to you about social language. I think I've come across some people who could benefit from that kind of help."

"Sure. Let's talk again."

"I'll be back later this week to work in the garden. Maybe you'll be here."

"Maybe I'll help you in the garden. I won't be running again soon. It recalls something a friend said to me when she saw me going into the gym. "You don't have to join a gym. There's plenty of work to do!"

Chapter Ten

Miami

Before beginning work on Tuesday, Kendrick asked if Maren would attend the performance of a local dance troop that evening. She readily agreed.

Maren worked without a break until 2 p.m. She chose to get in a little movement by going to the Café and decided to get something more interesting than black coffee. She splurged with a caramel macchiato. A little people-watching was in order, so she stayed in the café to enjoy imbibing and spying on people as they moved about. She noticed Zina was there with a nice-looking older man and wondered if he was the one who asked about the fakes.

Off and on she had thought about that comment. Fake what? It probably was nothing and almost certainly none of her business. She wanted to mention it to Kendrick, but she also wanted to give their relationship a chance before giving him a reason to think of her as a gossip and even worse an office spy.

She took her tray back to the busing station, and Yvette caught her eye. Yvette gave a nod toward Zina. Maren wasn't sure how to respond, so she simply raised her eyebrows and shook her head yes. And took the elevator back to Soto.

She settled back into reading. The work was becoming more intense because the time had come to contact authors and to begin deciding which ones to offer a contract. Instead, she decided to read one more manuscript. As she read, something seemed off. She continued and realized she had read this work before.

Tracing back the origin of the manuscript, she discovered that this particular one wasn't requested by Benita. It was one of the documents uploaded to Benita's account as part of a random review of the selections by other agents. Knowing that this was not an original work made her question what was going on at this agency.

She needed to talk to Kendrick. She was about to text him when she received a text from him. "I'm sorry. I have to cancel tonight."

She immediately sent a text back. "Hope everything is okay?"

He didn't get back to her before she left that evening.

***

Nor did she see him the next morning. She emerged from her office. "Can I ask you about something, Celeste?" Maren approached Celeste's desk.

"I didn't know you were here, Maren. Sure. Here, or your office?"

"My office please."

Maren closed the door to her office behind them and then sat on the edge of her desk close to where Celeste was seated. "I feel as though Kendrick has ghosted me, and I'm right in front of his nose?"

"I won't pretend I haven't noticed. If you're going to ask me what's going on, I don't know."

"Oh. I was hoping he said something. Have you ever known him to act like this?"

"Not like this. Kendrick is a private person. But I got the impression he was not only comfortable with you, but fond of you as well."

"There were definite vibes. Maybe he feels as though we were moving too quickly?"

Celeste took a moment and a cleansing breath before responding. "Possibly. I think the only thing you can do is to break through the ice some way. You have to work together."

"We do. I can keep reading, but the time has come for me to begin negotiating with authors and publishers. Even if I could do that on my own, I want to stay well within company guidelines and practices. Is that something you're comfortable doing?"

"The theory part, yes. But not in practice. I do no formal negotiating."

"Though I have no doubt you would be very good at it, it isn't up to me to put you in that position for the first time."

"Agreed. Thank you." Celeste paused for a moment and then said, "Talk to him. It's all you can do. That's what you have skills for!"

Maren chuckled, despite how inadequate she felt in the situation.

Maren quashed the pirated work, yet she worried that there could be others. She was thankful for the program that allowed her to discover the 'fakes,' but it didn't indicate which agent had it up for review. *Could it be Kendrick? Whoever was responsible should notice it was rejected.*

Maren did as Celeste suggested, summoned up her pluck and ability to ply words, and knocked on Kendrick's door. "Hey, do you have a minute?"

Kendrick was rigid as he rose from his desk. "Yes. Please have a seat."

"I hope everything is okay. I'm sorry last night didn't work out. I was looking forward to another nice evening."

Kendrick cleared his throat. "Yes. I am sorry it didn't work out."

Does he mean the evening or the friendship? She returned to the conversation. "I think I'm at the point where I could use a primer on how to approach authors and how to proceed from there with a manuscript that I think is worthy of representation."

Kendrick, who never stuttered, stuttered a response. "Yes. Well. Here's what we need to do — a step at a time. Please forward any under serious consideration to me. I'll then work with you to make contact and proceed on those that are worthy of negotiations."

Maren mumbled a barely audible, "Ok," as she rose and exited the office. She was mulling over all the possible implications of what he just said. The more she thought about it, the more confused she became. Her only conclusion thus far was that his actions made him highly suspicious to her with regard to whether the agency was trafficking in 'fakes' and, if so, if he was the huckster.

Should I tell Celeste? Benita? Maybe I should just get out of here and teach my summer course. She sent a text to Benita.

Chapter Eleven

Adirondacks

Benita arrived early for the second session of the writers' workshop. Despite the shaky start, she felt confident in her revised plans. She was reviewing her notes when she saw a shadow pass by the open door to her classroom. The shadow moved back toward her door and morphed into a person--a very handsome blond male person who was familiar. In the split second she was about to say his name, he said, "Benita?"

"Troy?"

"Yup. It's me." He rushed over to her, and as she rose from the desk, he gave her a bear hug, so to speak. His was much more welcome than the furry variety she escaped on the day before.

"What are you doing here?" Benita said with surprise in her voice.

"Manipulating my way in to see you!" He sat on the student desk in front of her.

"What do you mean?"

"Well, the story starts way back at Chain Mountains Extreme Camp. Do you remember?"

"Yes. I remember well." Benita had no reason to be coy.

"Here are two takeaways from Chain Mountains Extreme Camp: First, my career as an outdoor adventure leader; and two, knowing that the Benita Sotolongo on the teacher roster for summer school at Clear Lake had to be you."

Her heart was pounding, but her curiosity allowed her further inquiry. "I think I need you to give me more than just the abridged version!"

He chuckled and sat on a desk in the front row. "I direct the Outdoor Adventure Program at Cliffside Community College. The college's summer session deploys the students to internships in the elementary and high schools that also have summer sessions. When I saw that you were replacing Maren Scott, I took this assignment myself. Not only did I want to see you, I want to spend time with you. How about helping with our hike up Craggy Rock Peak this afternoon?"

Benita was trying to take it all in. She defaulted to the familiar. "I don't think I'm dressed for it."

Again, he chuckled. "We'll find a way. I'll be back after your session. I have to catch Rex before he starts teaching. See you later."

After a quick peck on the cheek, he was off. Benita was a bit rattled, and students were about to arrive. She took a quick walk around the room, breathing in and out, and pondering what just happened. And then the students started coming in.

She welcomed them and told them she hoped that they had a chance to think about what she had suggested the day before: That Ms. Scott probably knew what she was doing, and could they give her a chance?

She paused. They gazed at her. They said nothing.

There was nothing left to do except share her new and improved ideas developed during her harrowing run the previous day. She went to the whiteboard, picked up a dry erase marker, and turned back to them. "I have two major projects for our focus this summer, and we're going to start on them right away.

She turned her back to them and put the two ideas on the board.

She placed the marker back on the tray, turned around, and faced a transformed, animated group of students.

***

Troy came by to take Benita to lunch and to problem solve her wardrobe issue for the afternoon. In the meantime, she remembered she had access to Maren's apartment, which was near the school, whenever she had a use for it. Troy picked up sandwiches at a drive-through and waited in the car while she gathered some appropriate clothing and footwear from Maren's belongings and changed into them. She felt guilty about the footwear, but she would replace them.

Troy ate while he waited for her, and Benita ate on the return trip to the school. They arrived just in time to catch the school bus to Craggy Rock—twenty-five miles away. Benita, Troy and Rex were the only chaperones. Rex was reading in a front seat when they boarded and nodded when they greeted him. Troy led Benita to a seat as close to the students as possible.

When they were seated, Troy quietly said, "It's not a pleasant thought, but it's best to be suspicious in every way when on a bus full of teenagers."

"And take attendance?"

"I hope Rex already has. I'll check."

He returned holding the manifest with all of the names checked.

That settled, Troy turned to Benita. "This isn't a very romantic setting, but I need you to know that you were my first real crush."

"I know I'm a red as a beet right now. And that isn't easy given my skin tone. At the risk of making it worse, I need you to know something too. You were my first kiss."

"I hope it still rates with those that followed."

"Are you prying into my romantic life?"

"If I can."

"It's not my place to inflate your ego, but I am a truthful person. I dare say, it remains the most memorable. In the best way."

"Did you say best?"

"I said the word best. But the modifier for kiss was 'memorable.' The word best modified the category of memory." She paused and smirked. Then she confessed, "And yes. It is among my best kisses. I think of it often."

Troy seemed breathless. He muttered a rather hoarse, "Dinner tonight?"

"Yes."

When they arrived at their destination, the students took off as if they had been cooped up for months. The chaperones struggled to catch up. They had given instructions on the bus, so they trusted the students to be well and stay on the path.

It wasn't a long hike, and it led to one of the most sparkling mountain lakes Benita had ever seen—even in all of her summers in the Adirondacks. The kids were not to be dissuaded from swimming—clothes and all.

Benita turned to Rex and Troy. "I wonder what kind of trouble this will cause us with parents. I am a certified as a lifeguard, but not in New York. I trust you both are."

"Of course." Rex had said very little to Benita. It was good to hear his voice, even if his answer was terse.

Their attention was turned to the waterfront. Two students who Benita didn't recognize were running out of the water. "Hey. We found a piece of clothing caught on a log out in the deeper part of the lake."

Troy grabbed the manifest. He whistled twice, and the shrill sound got everyone's attention. He motioned everyone to shore, and the response was immediate. He handed the manifest to Rex and was on his way to where the clothing had been found. Benita followed.

Both dove several times throughout the middle of the lake and along the surrounding banks. They found nothing and returned to shore.

Rex provided some assuring news. "The students are accounted for. This is part of the Park, so we should let the Park Service know. They may want the dive team to search, but there isn't any rush. No one would survive if they've been under this long." Blunt, but to the point. Anyone who knew Rex wouldn't be surprised at his statement.

The sun was hot, and the slight wind dried everyone by the time the bus drove off. As soon as there was a cell signal, Troy called the Park Service to inform them of their find and said he would drop off the shirt at the nearest Ranger Station.

After they returned to the school, and the last student had left with a parent or guardian, Rex drove off in his black SUV, leaving Troy to turn to Benita. "Alone at last!"

"We were alone for lunch!"

"But in a hurry. Are you in a hurry now?"

"No. I'll call Aunt Dilly and tell her I'll stay at Maren's tonight. Want to pick me up there?"

"Yes. As soon as possible."

"Six o'clock?"

"Not a second later, please!"

Benita laughed. She called Aunt Dilly's landline from Maren's landline, then decided to pick out an outfit from Maren's wardrobe rather than changing back into the clothes she had been wearing. *This is getting to be a habit. I'll call Maren when I have a chance and tell her I'm ravaging through her clothes.*

Chapter Twelve

Miami

Kendrick was in a panic. *What a chump I am. Falling for the first attractive woman of color that I have dated since—well, in some time, and she turns out to be a purveyor of plagiarized text. I hate to think it, but it has to be her.*

Kendrick's computer access was far different from Benita's, but he still received manuscripts for random reviews. He wasn't accustomed to auditing the novels. Though an avid reader, his time at work and pleasure was involved in nonfiction almost on an exclusive basis. He was a movie viewer, but one with a rarefied taste. A pirated version of fiction could go unnoticed by any agent except Benita.

Maybe this could have been going on for a long time. Maybe it isn't Maren. But his panic remained. His only access to Benita—anyone's only access to Benita, was through Maren. *What a stupid plan.* He was irate; too irate to be still. Kendrick closed down his computer, left his office, said, "Have a nice evening" to Celeste, and left the building.

Kendrick drove to his home in Miami Shores. He changed his clothes, unlocked his garage, took the canvas covering off his motorcycle, and took off toward North Bay. With the wind whipping his clothes and the dominance he felt over the elements as he veered through the streets, he expected the tenseness and strain to abate. It wasn't working. He couldn't shake the memories of Maren holding him while they traveled around Miami on the bike.

He didn't stop until he had ridden through Surfside, Bay Harbor and finally stopped at Indian Creek Village for a bite to eat. He returned home and mulled in front of his television until time for bed.

***

Celeste was confused. She knocked on Maren's door, but walked in without being invited. "Kendrick just left. He barely said good-bye. He never leaves in the middle of the day. If he eats, he orders delivery. If he has errands, he fits them in near the end of the day—and usually only on Fridays! Something major is up."

Maren was unsure how to respond. "I'll see what I can do."

"Like what?"

"I'm not sure, but I'll work on it."

Chapter Thirteen

Adirondacks

Troy had forgotten to ask which apartment belonged to Maren, so he had no choice but to remain in the car and hope that Benita would appear. It occurred to her by five past the hour what was the problem, and she met him in the parking lot.

"You can tell I am out of practice! I failed to tell my date my exact address and exchange cell numbers; which we should have shared prior to taking kids on an outing, by the way."

He cowered and said, "I think I've lost my head; it's all your fault, you know. It makes me wonder, why haven't we been in touch?"

"I think the best explanation is the one I gave my Aunt Dilly the other day. We kept up with technology, but we didn't keep our technology up."

"You were talking about me to your aunt?" He was grinning. Not an evil grin, but one that showed his pleasure at being a topic of one of her conversations.

"Well, not by name."

"By what, then?"

"By virtue of her noticing I had been smitten at summer camp."

"Are you still?"

"We'll see. I'm too hungry to know," she deflected.

"Then let's get you fed. Do you like Native American cuisine?"

"I may not be that familiar …"

"Let me introduce you."

"Fine with me."

The Summit restaurant was very pleasant, and they had a wonderful time getting reacquainted. The first course was enough to satisfy Benita. The Three Sister's Soup accompanied by Acorn Bread was delicious and filling. Yet, Troy wasn't satisfied until she tried the Pine Nut Catfish and Baked Pumpkin. She relented, but only if they shared an order.

Sharing was the right move. It set the stage for some playful intimacy as they ate, fed each other, and talked about old times and how often they thought of each other through the years.

By the time they walked hand in hand to the car, it was clear that enough time had been wasted between kisses. Troy drove to a nearby mountain overlook, and to their delight, they were alone. They sat together on the bench overlooking a striking view.

They talked, but the more they stared at each other's faces, and watched each other's mouths for words, the more they started brushing lips. The soft touches became full kisses. Within a short time, their kisses became passionate and even demanding.

Neither wanted it to end, but they both had early obligations. When they arrived at Maren's apartment building, they were reluctant to part. Benita was about to exit the car, when she chuckled.

"What's funny?"

"We still haven't gotten each other's contact info! And we wonder why we weren't in touch for over a decade!" She took out her phone and her voice changed from playful to serious, "And I haven't even turned on my ringer since I left school. Huh. Must have been preoccupied."

As Benita turned on her volume, Maren's ringtone sounded. Then it sounded again. "Oh my. I hope all is okay with Maren." She turned to face Troy. "She was only going to be in touch in emergencies. I wonder if I should call back this late. I'll send back a text and tell her to call the apartment if she needs to talk now."

Troy simply shrugged. "In any event, let's get our numbers added before we forget again."

They did. "I'm coming with you." Troy opened his car door and circled the SUV to open hers as well. He continued, "I need to know where Maren's apartment is so I can meet you inside the building—in the event you bunk here again."

Benita smiled. "I have to get her clothes cleaned and returned. So, I'll be back at some point!"

It was wonderful and miserable to say good night.

"I'll be in touch." It was the best whisper Troy could manage. He wasn't good at whispering.

"Good. Very good."

Chapter Fourteen

Miami

When Maren sent the text to Benita, she knew a response would be after school closed the day before. She was surprised that a text wasn't sent until very late evening, but Maren decided not to call at that point. The topic wasn't conducive to a late-night discussion.

In the meantime, Maren continued reading and went beyond waiting for random manuscript confirmation. She accessed the document files for all the agents who had agreed to review fiction. She dreaded what she might find and the repercussion of her "snooping" on them. *But I want the truth. And I want Kendrick not to be involved. But his behavior made him so suspicious.*

Finally, Benita's ringtone sounded again. "So sorry for the delay. I'll be in touch as soon as the session is over today when we have time for a long conversation. Send a text back if it's an emergency. I think it's going well here. The first day was almost tragic."

Almost tragic. I wonder what that means. And join the club.

Maren told Celeste she would be out of the office for long enough to get a coffee and a snack. *No. I'm going about this all wrong.* She returned again to Celeste and said, "Tell me about Kendrick. What's his story?"

"Most of what I know isn't firsthand knowledge." Celeste looked around as if trying to decide what she was willing to divulge. "I understand Montez Sotolongo, Beni's father, hired him out of college with no experience. I think he was the consummate protégé. Kendrick was engaged to one of the agents who emigrated to foster the Cuban political publications, but her work visa expired. Mr. Sotolongo worked hard to get it renewed. She was deported despite his efforts.

"They both were heartbroken. The agency hit rock bottom and remained there for several years. Beni's mom brokered innumerable textbook acquisitions, which I think saved the agency at the time. The residuals don't hurt, even now.

"Things were going well until Mr. Sotolongo's health became compromised. That is when Benita gave up her work as a speech pathologist and came to work here. It wasn't soon after she arrived, maybe even recently, that I thought there was a spark between her and Kendrick. If so, it didn't last. I wondered if it made it awkward for them, but they didn't let it impact the Agency, at least that I know of."

"Thank you, Celeste. Have you ever wondered about his loyalty or integrity?" "No, not in the least." Celeste seemed taken back by the question. "You may notice I like idioms. So, let me say 'he's a straight arrow.' No doubt in my mind."

"Good. Do you have concerns for any others here?"

"It's a workplace. You know. People can be so peopley. Some can get on my nerves. Though, I don't know if I question anyone's honesty in their work. I'll think on it and get back to you. Oh, and talk to Yvette. Her intuition has yet to be off." Celeste paused. "Wait, is there something going on?"

"Please don't say anything, Celeste. I don't know. That's all …"

Celeste's cell sounded, and from the look on her face, she needed to check it immediately. "It's from Kendrick. He has an appointment in New York City. He'll be in touch in a few days."

Chapter Fifteen

Adirondacks

Benita greeted a lively group of students. "It's so good to hear your enthusiasm!" They were working on their first project: Nominating Maren Scott for a teaching award with the Frederick Foundation for Excellence in Education.

Benita continued, "The network coordinator at Clear Lake put a notice about our plans on gradeCorrect, the report card webpage, and grades were posted a few hours later. Great exposure. Dr. Gawl will forward any emails supporting the nomination. We have to move quickly; everything is due on Monday. Any questions?"

"Ms. Sotolongo."

"Call me Benita. Please."

"Ms. Benita. When will we know about the award?"

"Good question. Finalists will be announced in a month. They'll allow additional supporting information at that time. Runners up will be invited to a banquet in New York City in late July, at which time the order of awards will be given."

"May we attend if she gets that far?"

"I would say yes. I'll do what I can, even if we must stand up through the dinner and ceremonies!" She saw the confusion on the students' faces. "I'm kidding. I hope that won't be necessary. Any other questions? So, today we'll identify her innovative teacher methods and organize the comments according to the category each comment supports. First, let's take a few minutes to hear your thoughts on our other task for the summer?"

"You mean the Wattpad idea?"

"Well, yes. My intention is for us to create a serial piece of fiction using an internet application. There are several choices including Wattpad, but also Bookmate, FanFiction.Net, Fiction Press, AO3, Scribd. It's a long list at this point. And at Soto, we have developed one called 'imprinTABI'."

Jake broke in. "I really like this idea. It's good for even the TL;DR guys."

"Just in case, Jake. Could you tell us what that means?"

"Oh, yeah, sure. Too Long; Don't Read."

"Thank you. We need to work on the teacher award nomination, but let's spend five minutes brainstorming about the focus of our serial fiction."

Nikki Copeland spoke for the first time. "Why don't we publish our recommendations for Ms. Scott!"

Riza Lucas was the first groan and commented, "That's a big Facepalm."

Most of the students slapped their palms against their foreheads. Benita couldn't help but smile, then quickly added, "I think everyone would be thankful for a period where we brainstorm without judgment! Nikki, thank you for your thoughtful suggestion. It is going on the board. Anyone else?"

Jake was never shy. "Spit-balling it is! We want to call it 'Clear Lake Spills the Tea.'"

Benita caught his drift immediately. "Something along the lines of "Gossip Girl?"

Jake was impressed. "I see you're woke! At least when it comes to Gen Z terms. Must be your background in linguistics."

"You've done your homework."

"We have."

"Okay. Any other ideas?" There was a pause. "Well, since I know the content of the teacher nominations, let's hear a little about the potential content of 'spilling the tea.'"

Jake, ever the spokesperson, read from a list:

- Cecile Forest, daughter of sports columnist Chip Forest, is celebrating her plans to attend Four Columns University in the fall. Cecile, who was accepted at all eleven of the colleges to which she applied, wishes to thank her father for writing the application essays.
- Doug Ainsworth is proud of his summer job at South Valley Farm and expects his vegetables to outperform any other farm's produce due to his genius idea to create compost using the manure reclaimed from the dog park.
- Regina Bixby, the lead bully of Clear Lake Central, had her spies stalking prom queen apparent Sally Weil so that she could purchase the same prom dress as Sally and show up to the prom five minutes prior to Sally. (The spies also kept her informed of Sally's impending arrival.)
- Coach O'Dell, to be sure every member of the girls' softball team made the list of Academic All-stars in the *Clear Lake Crier*, had Sylvester Knight hack the gradeCorrect system at Clear Lake Central to change any deficient grades.

Jake paused.

Benita had been struggling not to laugh. "Do you have more?"

"Oh yes. What do you think?"

Tongue-in-cheek, Benita responded. "I trust these aren't real people and real situations."

"Well ... I knew this might be a problem IRL. A guy can hope." Added to his spirited nature, Jake was also quite winsome.

"My suggestion is that we put a pin in that idea in all of its brilliance and proceed with another one that makes you enough money to hire a lawyer before we start 'spilling the tea'." Benita made a mental note to avoid the South Valley Farm.

"Facts," Jake replied.

"That leaves us with one suggestion. Are there any others?" Benita inquired of the group.

"I think I have one. Want to hear it?" Wesley asked.

"Totes." This reply was from Brynn Stevenson.

"I think about what it would be like to win the lottery." Wesley spoke, and everyone was listening.

Riza added. "You're too young, though."

"I know. Maybe it could be a senior who is 18 already," Wesley suggested. "And, maybe he wants to keep it a secret."

Brynn added some ideas. "Yeah. Especially from his parents. Can you imagine how they would take control?"

Riza Lucas was the first to become enthusiastic. "Oh, oh, like *It Could Happen to You* meets *Waking Ned Devine* meets *Trains, Planes and Automobiles*!"

"Yes. Something like that," Wesley responded since the initial idea was his.

"Noice," Jake commented.

"Great reference to your namesake, Jake." Benita recognized the hallmark comment of the character from *Brooklyn Nine-nine.* "And Riza. Very nice comparisons to existing pieces of work. Literary agents like that."

"Hey, let's vote!" Jake also liked to retain control. "Who wants teacher award recommendations? No one. The rest want 'Serious Senioritis!' Right?"

It was unanimous. Even Nikki voiced her support.

"Now that's settled, we can go back to finishing up the teacher award nomination. By the way, did you get together to prepare for today?" Benita asked.

In unison, "Yes."

This is good; scary, but good.

Chapter Sixteen

Miami

The ringtone for Benita sounded on Maren's phone. "Is this a good time to call? BTW, how do you have the stamina to teach every day? I'm exhausted!"

Maren responded. "LOL. It takes years of practice. Many fall by the wayside! Yes. This is a good time. Video chat?"

Within moments, they were face to face … digitally. Maren spoke first. "So, what are you doing with them that is so exhausting?"

"Are you on Wattpad? Or anything like Wattpad?"

"Really? What a great idea! Are they down with it?"

"They are. What a creative bunch."

"Yes, they are. Scary good. I can't wait."

"You'll know as soon as we're live. Probably by the end of next week."

"I'm impressed, Benita. Well done."

"Well, we haven't done anything yet. But I sense they'll come through. So, how are things at Soto?"

"I don't know. That's the truth. But I have suspicions that I don't want to keep to myself."

"Oh. Have you told Kendrick?"

"Kendrick mysteriously disappeared from Soto and reappeared in New York City."

"Wha … What? Did something happen?"

"I'll try to explain as well as I can. He and I were working well together and even got together outside of the office."

"As in dating?"

"Yes. At about the same time as I found a pirated manuscript through the verification system, he cancelled plans about five minutes before we were supposed to get together. Then he was gone."

Maren continued to explain what she had found thus far.

"I think I need to come down." Benita was crestfallen.

"I know I would feel the same way." After a long silence, she reconsidered her response. "Benita, it sounds as though you are just getting started with the kids. You made me think that there are a few steps I've missed. I should look into them before you disrupt what you're doing."

Benita wasn't at all sure she should postpone going back to Soto, but it would be so much better if she could finish the teacher award nomination before returning to Miami. She and Maren then could easily switch places. "I'm going to agree, tentatively. But let me know everything that you find out. Even if we have to get an IT firm involved."

"Agreed." Maren was relieved she wasn't left alone with the decisions.

"I'm going to try to get in touch with Kendrick." Benita acknowledged it was the least she should do.

"Good idea. I hope he hasn't left the country."

"I can't believe that. Any of this would be so out of character for him."

"I got that from Celeste, too." Maren said.

"Does Celeste know about this?" Benita was worried about losing control of the information.

"No, no, no. I simply asked for her assessment of Kendrick when he disappeared. No doubt she suspects something, but she has no idea what's up."

"Okay. I'm so sorry about all of this."

"I am as well." Maren's voice showed how perplexed she was.

They were reluctant to end the call, and there was more that could be said. But nothing more could be done via telephone.

Chapter Seventeen

Adirondacks

Benita wondered when the note tacked to the door jamb of her classroom had appeared. She glanced at the clock and she rose from her desk. It was one-thirty in the afternoon. The students were already on their adventure, so it was obvious she wouldn't be helping today. She plucked the note from the frame.

"*You were very involved in a video chat when I came by. Sorry I missed you, but you picked a good day to skip the afternoon adventure. We're going to the mall to their new Escape Room. It might get a little claustrophobic. I know you'll probably head up to your aunt's. I think I can find her landline number and call you there. I imagine there isn't a cell tower in proximity to the Hidden Havens! Miss you. Love, Troy*"

Benita thought about the message. *I think I'll wait until they get back. I'd hate to miss Troy, and I have plenty to do.*

She decided she had time to launder Maren's athletic clothes and drop off the LBD at the dry cleaners. She returned at 3:30 just as the bus was leaving the premises, but Troy's red SUV was still in the parking lot. She drove close to it, but he wasn't near it. She parked and found him exiting the building.

He smiled when he saw her. "I was hoping you still would be here." He grabbed her hand as they walked toward the cars.

"I see you made your escape."

"They're a creative bunch. There were three teams, and we timed them. It was close. The attendant said they did better than most."

"What I've seen from my group shows they are very creative." Benita said.

"So, how are you?" Troy's tone became a bit seductive.

"Just so very glad to see you."

"Are we having dinner?"

"I would love to, but it would be a long drive home. I'm so tired, but I can't tell you why." She winked. "I want to see Aunt Dilly. She and her friends are leaving on a vacation to Hawaii tomorrow."

"Oh. I didn't know she would be away."

"Two weeks!"

"Why don't we drive a half hour in the direction of the Havens? Then your drive home from dinner won't be so daunting."

"Good plan. I have a call I want to make before I lose a cell connection. I'll meet you, where?"

"Let me see. There's an inn near Schroon Lake. It's nice. I'll give them a call to be sure they will be open while you make your call."

She left a message with Kendrick, revealing her number, her aunt's number, and the school number. She told him it was urgent. Troy was waiting outside of the car.

"Everything's a go with dinner. I wrote down the address. Let's not drive in tandem. I don't think it's the safest way to travel. See you there," Troy said.

"Sounds good."

He had driven off when her cell sounded. It was a text from Kendrick.

"Do you have a connection?"

She sent a text back. "Yes. Now is a good time." She knew she would be later to dinner than planned, so she sent a text Troy hoping he would get it before losing a connection.

She answered her cell. "Hi, Kendrick?"

"Yes. Is everything okay?" Kendrick was fishing to find out what Benita knew.

"I was calling to ask you. I understand you are AWOL! People are worried." She laughed a bit so that he would know she wasn't chiding him.

"I have business in New York City."

"It came up suddenly?"

"You could say that. Is that why you're calling?"

"That's part of it. Some irregularities have been discovered at Soto. I might have to return. Of course, I wondered if you knew anything about it."

"Have you said anything to Maren?"

"She's the one who told me about it."

"When?"

"Today."

"Why didn't she say something to me?"

"I wasn't there, Kendrick. I can't answer that with any degree of accuracy. But I think you disappeared before she had anything tangible."

"I see. I really need to get back and help. I have an important appointment tomorrow. I'll be back on Friday."

"If I need to, I'll join you over the weekend."

"Okay. Are you worried?"

"Very. But I trust Maren, and I told her to get our IT specialist in, if she needs to."

"Good plan. Sorry I jumped ship."

"We'll work through it."

"How are things where you are?"

"Good. Quite good. But I can't enjoy any of it until this is settled."

"I understand."

Chapter Eighteen

Adirondacks

No amount of time in the Adirondacks makes one immune to the abundance of unique vistas encountered at unnumbered venues. The Schroon Lake Inn was no exception, and Benita found Troy outside drinking in the beauty of the mountainside lake just below the Inn's property. He received her message earlier, so he wasn't surprised by her delay.

He kissed her on the nose, then held her chin as he kissed her lips. They embraced and kissed again. He breathed the scent of her hair and whispered, "I've been waiting almost twenty-four hours for this."

Benita took a deep breath to compose herself and took in the stunning surroundings. "It's wonderful." Then her attention turned back to Troy. "How are you?"

"Perfect. How about you?"

"Better now. You're the elixir I need."

As they walked up the stone steps to the Inn's entrance, he probed. "Is everything okay at school?"

"Actually, that part of my life is going quite well."

"How about in the romance department. Is that going well?"

"Very well."

"Problems with your business, then?"

"Yes."

"What's up?"

"Don't know. Possible manuscript forgeries. Maren noticed, and the acting CEO went AWOL."

"Do you suspect him?"

"No, but Maren had to. I finally connected with him, and that's why I'm late."

"Sounds suspicious."

"I still don't think so."

"I hope this doesn't mean you have to go back, though I wouldn't blame you." Troy's voice dropped on the last phrase.

"I'll try to wait until this weekend," Benita said.

"I'm so sorry. I'll go with you if you would like. I want to do something to help."

"Isn't the weekend peak time for outdoor adventurers?" Benita sounded skeptical.

"Priorities. Meaning, you." Troy teased despite situation.

"Thanks."

The hostess seated them in a beautiful rustic dining room. A buffet was a dining option, and they helped themselves after connecting with the waitperson.

Seated with their full plates, Troy provided what he thought was good news. "It takes a lot to impress Rex, but he thought highly of your diving abilities and especially your 'diving in' to help."

"Oh. I wonder whether he will find me worthy of a friendly greeting now and then."

"He's different. I don't know him well, but things have been especially hard since his wife disappeared." Troy sounded sympathetic to Rex.

"Disappeared?" Benita asked.

"Well, yes. I never met her. I think she was a biology teacher at Clear Lake. She submitted her grades at the end of the previous academic year, emailed a resignation to the principal, left a note for Rex, and disappeared. She told him not to look for her." He gazed at her for a response.

Benita put her fork down and stopped chewing. "Did he look for her anyway?"

"I think so. The obvious ways," Troy said.

"My sense is that social situations are difficult enough for him. This would compound it." Benita said.

"I take nothing he says personally." It was Troy's way of acknowledging Rex's differences without judgment.

"Good choice. You know you're very special." Benita wasn't teasing. Her comment was genuine.

He gently took her hand in his. "Oh yeah? I'm glad you think so."

They finished their dinner and went down by the lake. It was dusk, or a little beyond, so they ended the evening in a far too brief caress.

Chapter Nineteen

Miami

The landline in Benita's condo rang as Maren came out of the shower. She saw the caller ID as The Havens and picked up.

"Hi Maren. How are you?" Benita greeted Maren.

"Good enough. But I haven't made any progress since we last talked."

"That's fine. I wanted to report that I spoke with Kendrick. He has an appointment tomorrow, but he'll fly back as soon as he can and will be in on Friday. I don't know what was or is going on for him, but I don't believe he's involved in the situation at the office. I'll plan to come back for the weekend."

"Should I plan to go home to New York?"

"No. I need you there … if you're willing. If I can't make it back for Monday's afternoon session at Clear Lake, we'll get a substitute. By then, the kids will be in the driver's seat. If one of us needs to return to review their work before they publish, we'll decide that later."

"Okay. I'm feeling better. It was tough going it alone!" Maren's voice was strained.

"I can't imagine. Thank you for noticing something was amiss. In my shock, I don't think I said that. Try to get a good night's sleep."

"I'll try, Benita. You too."

***

Maren arrived at the Café at the crack of dawn, knowing that is when she would be most likely to find Yvette and have the possibility of a conversation.

"What can I get for you?" Yvette said it before looking up. "Oh. Hi! You're early!"

"Any chance you've earned a break?"

"Not hardly at this hour. But I'll take one anyway. I'm going to have a macchiato. What about you?"

"I'll have one too!"

They found a seat. Maren spoke first. "I need your intuition, if you're willing."

"Okay. I'll try." Yvette appeared intrigued.

"Do you have anything to say about Zina Casey and the guy she was with the other day? I sensed a signal."

"That guy she was with is the accountant for Soto, Jett Fellows."

"Oh. I feel so ignorant."

"Don't be silly. How long have you been there? Like, ten minutes? Are they up to something?" Yvette asked.

"I was going to ask you," Maren said.

"They meet here often. I don't sense there is any romance, so I have to suspect no-good."

"Why not romance?" Maren was curious why Yvette would make that judgment.

"He's married, and she plays the field of younger guys. I can't see her in a May-December romance."

"Have you ever overheard any conversation bits?"

"What I presume are titles of books. Not catchy titles; probably textbooks. I've heard them mention percentages, royalties. None of it was out of place for people in a literary agency, but I wondered why he would have so much to say about manuscripts, which I have heard them discussing. And I definitely heard her start a conversation with, 'while she's away,' but then what she was saying trailed off."

"If you hear anything else, will you let me know?" Maren's interest was piqued.

"Of course. I hope you can tell me more about this at some point."

"I hope so too."

Chapter Twenty

Adirondacks

"I didn't think I was going to see you before my trip, Beni." Aunt Dilly looked at Benita with a curious upon her late return to Hidden Havens after the dinner at Schroon Lake. Benita had just hung up the telephone extension in the East Parlor.

"I know, Auntie. I'm sorry. I hope the last couple of days have been going well for you."

"They have. I think I'm ready. I took Rackie to the kennel this afternoon. My neighbor acts as caretaker for the property when I'm away, and his children are good with Rackie for short periods. But I think the kennel is best for such a long absence."

Benita's aunt continued. "Rena is picking me up at seven in the morning. Probably just after you leave for school. How have things been for you?"

"Aunt Dilly, so much has happened in the last forty-eight hours, it sounds made up." Benita sounded incredulous.

"You're into fiction now, aren't you? Sorry. You're serious. What is it dear?" Her aunt had a good sense of humor.

"No need to apologize. I love humor. It helps! I think you're going to be sorry you asked. We both need to go to bed at a reasonable hour, yet I know the details will be important."

"Let's try."

"The best first. I reconnected with Troy, the dreamboat from Chain Mountains Extreme Camp."

"What? How?"

"What did I say about details?!

"But Beni!" Aunt Dilly held her hands out like a child asking for more candy.

"He coordinates the outdoor leadership program at Cliffside Community College. His students intern with summer schools to provide adventure experiences. He saw my name on the roster at Clear Lake, so he took that assignment."

"That's better than fiction."

"Right? Moving on. The kids seemed to love my ideas for the class projects. It really turned things around."

"Oh, I'm delighted dear, but not surprised. But tell me more about that when I return, go on now with the rest of your story."

"This is the bad news. Something is going on at Soto. The teacher who changed places with me, Maren, noticed it. And Kendrick disappeared."

Aunt Dilly sat down and looked very sheepish. "Oh my. What are you going to do, Beni? Just when things are going so well here."

"It's hard to know. I don't think I suspect Kendrick. But I don't know what's up with him. We've talked. Maren will continue to investigate the irregularities, which are with manuscripts—possibly some forgeries. I have from Friday afternoon until Monday afternoon to fly down and investigate without missing any teaching. But if I need to, I can stay longer. I must. I can't let people besmirch the reputation of the agency."

"No. Oh, dear. I am so very sorry. It's so disheartening that people would do this and are using your absence to further their nefarious enterprises."

"I'm sorry to worry you with this. Please don't. That's why I'm paid the big bucks, right?"

"I hardly think the bucks are big enough for this."

Chapter Twenty-One

Miami

Maren succumbed to a case of homesickness. It was an accumulation of things. The heat, the fraud, the disappointment and sadness over her relationship with Kendrick. It felt as though there was no vision or sense of purpose at Soto, and she longed for home. Fiction lost its luster for the first time in her life. *Maybe I need to tell Benita that the experiment failed.*

Despite the hopelessness, she arrived at Soto and ordered black coffee hardly making eye contact with Yvette. Her poise had disappeared, and she was loathed to negotiate contracts without help. Yet, she arrived at her desk and began reading. Soon after her arrival, Celeste knocked and entered Maren's office.

"How are things, Maren?"

It was hard to pretend. "Okay."

Celeste wasn't convinced. "Has anyone spoken with Kendrick?"

"Yes. He and Benita spoke. He's coming back on Friday."

"There's a lot you're not telling me."

"About Kendrick? Even Benita doesn't know what's going on with Kendrick. I hope we can find out. I don't know if I did something to make him take off. It could have been planned, but if so, he didn't mention it in all of the time we spent together."

Celeste was convinced there was more, but let it go and returned to her desk.

A video chat call came into Maren's office. Her door was open, and Celeste didn't resist the urge to hover unobserved outside the office.

"Hi Benita."

"Hey. How are you doing this morning? It seemed weird for Benita to make small talk.

"Eh. You know." Maren's response confirmed Benita's sense that it was no time for levity.

"I would understand if you want to abandon ship. I'm about to start class, but I think I know what I have to do. I have some business in New York City, so I'll drive down after the Friday morning session and catch a flight from Kennedy or Newark. I haven't made reservations yet, though."

"Okay. Should I come North? Let's put it this way, what would you like me to do?"

"I still hope we can follow through with our plans for the summer. That said, I wouldn't blame you if you bag it all and leave Soto. But please stay until both Kendrick and I are there. Use your access privileges to check the accounts of every agent; don't just rely on the random submission reviews. I know it's boring."

"No. Not at all. I'm happy to help. Do you have a plan for when you arrive?" It was a stretch for Maren to say she was happy to help. She hoped if she said it perhaps it would become true.

"I'm still working on it. I will meet with each staff member over the weekend and hope I have a sense of what to pursue from there. After our call, I'm going to contact Celeste to call in our IT expert for clarification on log-in information."

"Good. I can see if anything is happening live; but I don't get how to go back in time or anything of the sort."

"No. I'm sure I won't be able to uncover much information from the past either. It's disconcerting to think it's a member of the staff. But I can't imagine another scenario."

"So, would you like me to go to a hotel while you're here?"

"Of course not. I'll stay on the daybed in the den. Stay right where you are. I should mention that my friend, Troy, probably is coming too."

Maren threw her head back a bit in surprise. "Oh. Your friend Troy. You've struck up a friendship already." Maren knew from her brief time with Kendrick that it was possible.

"Old romance rekindled."

"I see. No, I don't. And I can't wait to hear more. Even more reason I should vacate the apartment, though."

"No, no. There are guest services at the complex. I'll reserve a space for him there."

"Are you sure?"

"Yes, Maren. That is how I want to do things. Please believe me."

"Okay. I'll get to work. Our pupils are about to storm your room, I'm sure."

"Yes. Talk to you later."

Celeste had returned to her desk as soon as she heard her name mentioned in the conversation. Her office line rang a few minutes later with the caller ID showing a blocked number.

"Hi Celeste. How are you?"

"I'm well, Benita. Good to hear from you. I've missed you."

"You as well. I've even missed you constantly keeping tabs on me." Benita cleared her throat. "Very quickly, as students are entering my classroom as we speak, I need you to schedule someone from our IT agency for the weekend. Maren will be there to supervise, and she can authorize any payment methods they require."

"Okay, Benita. I have her signature authorization on file."

"Let Maren know if no one is available."

"Got it."

"Thanks, Celeste. You're appreciated."

The conversation ended, and Celeste was more confused than ever. And offended. *Why is Beni concealing her contact information from me and the fact that she's coming back for the weekend?* She was hurt and getting angrier by the moment.

Chapter Twenty-Two

Adirondacks

"Good morning! We only have two morning sessions to get our teacher award nomination written and the supporting data collected and organized according to our categories of excellence for Ms. Scott's teaching! Are you up for it? Benita wasn't surprised at the enthusiastic responses.

"Let's list the categories on the Board, and then we'll review the write-ups we've prepared as well as those submitted in response to our notice on the gradeCorrect program. Ready?"

The students shouted out their ideas as Benita tried to keep up.
- Flipped Classroom
- Literary Circles
- Music Integration
- Visual Art Integration
- Media Integration
- Students as Experts
- Concept Attainment
- Teacher Centered
- Mnemonic Devices

"These are excellent categories. That you know these concepts alone illustrates the good teaching and educating that happens here at Clear Lake. The recommendations I've read so far should fit well into these categories. So, let's divide into pairs. Dr. Gawl's assistant has integrated your comments and the comments received from the community into a document on a drive created just for our class. Please review each comment and place any that conform to your category in a document with your teaching method as the heading.

Jake raised his hand at the same time as voicing a question. "When is this due?"

Benita answered, "Monday by 9:00 a.m."

Brynn asked, "Are you sending them overnight express or something?"

Benita pursed her lips and then answered. "I'm not trusting any method other than myself. I'm going to take them to the headquarters in New York City. I'll leave right after tomorrow's session, so the document has to be polished and printed by the time you leave."

Jake queried, "What if you don't get there before they close their office for the weekend?"

Benita was ready. "I called. They have a secure drop off, and the building is open until seven in the evening. If I don't have car trouble, I'll be okay. If so, then I'll have to do the express mail."

The students paired off easily. There was no jockeying for positions, and the work flowed smoothly until the session was over in what seemed a very short time.

Upon the students' departure, Benita began her work of reviewing the documents they had created. She was engulfed in reading when she heard Troy's voice.

"Hey. How are things?"

"Good. The best now that you're here. I'm fretting about the agency. If it wasn't for this teacher nomination, I would be there. It's hardly something Maren can step in and complete!"

"Agreed. So, what are your plans? I don't imagine you're coming with us to rock climb?"

"No. I'm sorry. Will you have enough help?"

"Yeah. We're starting off in the gym. We'll move on to the real thing next week after a little practice. Then you're in, right?"

"I'll give it careful thought." Benita's tone was skeptical, but hopeful.

"What are the plans?" Troy asked.

"Are you sure you want to come?"

"Yup. I'll make a good bodyguard if things get dangerous."

Benita shivered. "I hope those particular services won't be necessary. Besides, ripped though you may be, your blond good looks are hardly intimidating. More along the lines of inviting, I'd say."

Just then, they were interrupted by Dr. Gawl's hurried entrance into Benita's classroom. In her typically frazzled manner, she said, "Oh. I'm sorry. I didn't know I would be interrupting."

"Dr. Gawl, this is the Director of the Outdoor Adventure Program at Cliffside Community College, Troy Bradshaw."

"Oh. I think we might have met before. I wondered when I first met you whether your parents were fans of Troy Donahue, one of the heartthrobs of the 1960's."

"It might be, but I don't see the resemblance." Most of the time, Troy was upbeat and unflappable. He showed just a little that he was perturbed.

Benita noticed the change in his demeanor and changed the subject. "What can I do for you, Dr. Gawl?" I just wanted to make sure everything is organized for Maren Scott's teacher award nomination."

"I'm hopeful. We're on schedule from what I can see. I'm reviewing the student's work so far."

"Is there anything Sylvia can do to help?

"I don't think we would be as far into the project as we are without her. She's been collecting supporting comments and samples of students' work. Could you spare her for the last hour of the session tomorrow? She could integrate the students' papers, proofread, and organize everything into a final document?"

"Yes. I'll tell her right now. Can you get it submitted on time; do you think?" Though asking pertinent questions, Dr. Gawl came across as a nervous Nelly.

"I'm going to hand-carry it to New York City tomorrow afternoon."

"Oh my, is that necessary? Can't it be submitted electronically?"

"We haven't time to scan all of the student work, and some of it isn't conducive to scanning. Besides, I want a receipt in hand for its submission."

"So much for the digital age. I guess that should do it! Nice to meet you, Troy." Dr. Gawl exited.

Benita mocked. "Named after a movie star? And you bear his resemblance? How could your parents know that when you were first born?"

"I think I said that I don't see it. But I used to get that from a lot of female boomers when I first meet them. My dad was a Troy Donahue look-alike, I understand. It became his nickname and my real name. Now, can we drop it and not mention it again?" He tried to muster up an annoyed look.

"Have you seen any of his movies?" Benita wasn't about to let the subject go.

Troy scoffed.

"Well, have you?"

"Okay. I watched Parrish." He was reluctant to admit it, and his statement was terse.

"I'll have to see it sometime." Despite his discomfort with the subject, Benita continued the taunt.

"Don't.

She was still amused but agreed to drop the subject. "Do you want to know the plans for the weekend?"

"I assume a drive to New York City is involved."

"Yes. Let's leave from school. I'll arrange a flight from as near an airport as I can on Friday evening. You can stay in a guest suite at my apartment complex."

"I'm in. I have Friday afternoon and the weekend off. I do have to teach a class on Monday morning, so I should fly back on Sunday."

"I'll get to the arrangements right away and text you when they're confirmed. I'll see you in the morning?"

"Yep. Now, I need to get going."

He kissed her with a peck on the lips. She stood, and they kissed for a long time before he made himself part from her.

Chapter Twenty-Three

Miami

Maren was weary of sitting after her day reviewing the manuscripts accepted by other agents at Soto. She wasn't reading for pleasure; and it felt like the chore it was.

Deserving of a break, she treated herself to an evening walk on the beach. The sun was beginning to set, and it gave off a warm glow on the water. The royal palms were her favorite, and they swayed in the sea breeze as she trudged along the sand.

The sand was warm from the heat of the day, but not too hot. She took off her sandals and enjoyed the feel of the fine, white grains between her toes. She became more mindful of the beauty and began to stroll leaving behind the determined steps that were more about her angst than enjoyment of her surroundings. The visual beauty and the grainy foot massage worked its magic. Suddenly, she felt hungry for the first time that day.

Maren made her way to the food truck recommended by Kendrick. *Kendrick. How could I have been so happy with him just a short time ago? Why am I here? Benita will understand if I abandon this plan.* Suddenly, she wasn't hungry. She threw her food away in a nearby receptacle and walked back to Benita's apartment.

***

Kendrick arrived at the Miami International Airport early in the evening. Time away from Miami had only confounded his thinking. He took an Uber to the beach for a cleansing walk before dinner. He had no illusions of truly clearing his head, but he felt a measure of relief in returning to beautiful surroundings and familiar territory.

He walked to his favorite food truck in time to see Maren exit the area. His impulse was to call out to her. At present, events in his life were turbid and how he felt about Maren and why he felt that way was the most muddled part of everything going on.

***

Chapter Twenty-Four

Adirondacks

Pala Onatah was working in the cold-weather crops of Hidden Havens when Benita arrived back for the day. Though emotionally exhausted, Benita felt some physical labor would calm her system.

"Pala! Thanks for all you do here. Could you use some help?"

"Only if you're inclined."

"The last time I gardened was the last summer I was here. I would love to renew my acquaintance with the good earth. I'll be back after I change."

They worked for a half hour in silence. Tilling and hoeing used a different set of muscles than those engaged when jogging or circuit training.

"I won't be so proud of my labors tomorrow, I'm afraid." Benita decided a little conversation was in order. She wanted to get to know Pala better.

"It takes a long time to get used to this kind of exercise." Pala validated Benita's comment.

"Have you always done this kind of work?" Benita inquired.

"Off and on. My degree is in science, so I will always be interested in plants and animals. I have a nice balance going on right now working as a ranger and landscaping. Sometimes on weekends I work with the farm about a half hour from here that recycles compost materials."

"What kinds of materials?"

"Food refuse and paper ... mostly."

"Is that the soil you've used here?"

"Yes. They keep me informed on research. For instance, did you know there is a wax worm that can eat plastic? The excretions are biodegradable."

Benita didn't hide her surprise. "Oh. Really? Although, I doubt they can devour enough to help with the disposal of the tons left in transfer stations. Not without creating an inordinate number of wax worms!"

"Exactly. And wax worms are known for destroying beehives." Pala and Benita both made facial gestures to show their disgust, and Benita noticed for the first time Pala's wry sense of humor.

Benita ventured a question. "Have you lived in the area for very long?"

They had started gathering up the gardening tools, loading some into her truck and the others in the gardening shed.

"I've been in this area since my husband and I split."

"Oh. I'm sorry."

"My decision. Thanks for your help! I think I can get to one more farm before dark. See you another time."

"Thank you. I don't think my aunt would be able to stay if it wasn't for you."

Following Pala's departure, Benita explored some of the property and buildings she hadn't seen since her visit years ago. The stone carriage houses were unlocked, which surprised her. These structures were beautiful with their hipped roofs and arched door openings. She glanced inside of one and was surprised by its contents. The stagecoach should not have looked out of place. This is where it belonged—until about a hundred years ago. Benita walked all around the stagecoach. *Imagine the stories it could tell.* With a gentle touch, she explored the curves and angles of the antique structure. She looked inside and marveled at how well it was maintained yet worn with age. *I wonder if some saddle soap would bring luster back to this interior.* She also examined a surrey with the proverbial fringe on top.

She entered the second carriage house, and, by stark contrast, it contained a very lovely motorboat. It was a Bowrider that had been retrofitted for solar power and mounted on a trailer. Nearby, was waterskiing equipment. *I hope this business in Miami can be settled. This is really where I want to be.*

Chapter Twenty-Five

Miami

Kendrick picked up a cup of tea in the Café before making his way to Soto early the next morning. He seemed to be the first one to arrive, which was his plan. He sat at his desk for a full minute before he tried to overcome the dread of discovery and logged on to his account. Once access was achieved, he couldn't decide what to do next. He was still in a fog when Celeste appeared at his door.

"Hi Kendrick. Good to have you back."

Kendrick lied. "Oh. Yes. It's good to be here." He hadn't expected anyone this early in the morning.

Celeste wasn't one to pry. She hadn't needed to in the past. She was kept apprised of anything that was of interest—until now. *Nothing makes sense. Benita takes off and is incommunicado except through someone none of us know. Kendrick follows suit but is back now. Benita is returning but thinks it needs to be a secret. Maren isn't leaving. What could possibly be going on?* She had returned to her desk and was about to sit down when rage overpowered her.

Celeste marched back to Kendrick's office and loomed in the doorway. "Kendrick. What on earth is going on? You can't act like it's normal to take off for New York City without telling anyone. And you can't pretend that you and Maren weren't getting involved romantically. That followed Benita's flighty job exchange and now there's her apparent return this weekend she's keeping secret from me. Explain, please!"

Kendrick was calm in his response. "I can't, Celeste. I will when I can, I promise. You'll hear it from me first if possible."

"Really. You don't know why you went to New York? Are you looking into a job exchange too, Kendrick?" Celeste felt entitled to her sarcasm.

"No. Just a job. Possibly. Since you insist, I've had a standing offer from a small publisher of textbooks. When things got a little shaky here—those are the details I can't go into right now—I decided to interview."

"Are you leaving?"

"I don't want to. Not if this gets sorted out."

"The 'this' you can't tell me about."

"Yes."

"Is something wrong with the agency?"

"We intend to find out."

"Is it Maren?"

"No. She and I suspected something at the same time, so we suspected each other. I know it wasn't me, and it doesn't appear she is suspected either."

"Can I know what it is?"

"No. I've told you too much. If you say anything, you will hamper our ability to get to the bottom of it and you may become a suspect yourself. Those are the only reasons you have been kept in the dark."

"What if I have information that can help?"

"Do you, Celeste?"

"How do I know until I know what seems wrong?" Celeste thought he deserved the run around; at least a little bit. "Don't gaslight me."

"I'm not. Really, I'm not."

"Then, we'll find out what you know when the time is right."

Celeste left his office, and Kendrick leaned back in his chair to think. A foreboding thought crossed his mind at about the time he heard Maren's voice in the outer office. Unwelcome as he knew he would be, he jumped up from his desk and approached her.

"Maren, can we talk?"

She glared at him, unable to respond.

"Please. I think the problems may go deeper than we thought. Can we talk in your office?" Kendrick held out his hand, palm up, toward her office.

She still couldn't speak to him but motioned for him to follow her. He closed the door to the office behind him. "I'm so sorry for what I've done. I'll come back to that later, but I think we need to check the financials."

"Why?" Maren was alarmed.

"Manuscript forgeries are—pfft—ridiculous. What could they accomplish? I think it might be about money, and the forgeries were just a practice run at hacking our accounts. We need to log in and check."

"Wouldn't the accountant notice? And say something?"

"One would think. But this just occurred to me, and I want to know what I'm talking about before I pursue it with anyone else. It's been difficult for me to know who I can trust." He had been leaning with his hands on her desk. He looked at her to gauge how his statement was received. "I trust you."

Maren's response was a sheepish, "Thanks." She logged in. Together, they spent two hours on scores of accounts.

"The pattern is clear. Active accounts are fine. It's the accounts that are almost dormant. The ones that have minute royalties with minor quarterly payouts in the near past. At least fifty of them have multiple transfers in the last week. Quick calculations—it amounts to twenty-five grand!" Kendrick spoke as he stood and paced the floor. "Where would Benita be right now?"

"Just arriving in her classroom. The students will be there in less than a half hour."

"Call her. Please."

Maren dialed the school and asked for Benita's classroom.

"Hello, It's Benita Sotolongo."

Maren and Kendrick were on speakerphone. He spoke, "Benita. It's Kendrick and Maren."

Benita was silent. It took a minute to adjust to hearing from him and to hear he was with Maren.

"Hi. Is everything okay?"

"No. I know you're about to start class, but we've found problems that are worse than manuscript forgeries. It involves money."

Benita gasped and stood up. "Oh my gosh. What money and how much?"

Maren interrupted. "Benita, it's Maren. We don't have much time. Go and see if Rex is there and asked him to come to the phone. Tell him I need him."

"Ah, okay." Benita did as she was told and was surprised when Rex came immediately. She put the phone on speaker and said, "Rex is here."

"Rex. It's Maren. We have an emergency that involves financial accounts. You used to be an accountant, right?"

"Yeah." He glanced at Benita. "What's up?"

"This question is for both of you. What would you say about an account that has been receiving royalties, monthly, and payouts on a quarterly basis? Both minute. For the last few weeks, there have been numerous transfers out. Small ones."

Benita spoke first. "Is it just one account?"

Kendrick answered, "No. There are many of them."

Benita asked again, "How many accounts and how much are we talking about?"

They told her. Rex whistled and asked, "What are these accounts?"

Benita answered, "My guess—these are textbooks that have been revised a number of times over the years and now are digital as well."

Kendrick responded, "Yes. That's true, for the most part."

Benita asked, "Where's Jett Fellows. Please get him if he's in."

Maren left the room and returned a moment later. She waited for a lull in the conversation. "Celeste said Jett's not in today. He's on a beer flight."

Rex quipped, "Lucky guy. For my part, since I'm not there, I can just say this does sound dodgy. That's an understatement."

Benita agreed. "I really need to get down there." She was torn. There was Maren's nomination and theft at her agency. "I'll see if I can change my flight to right away."

Rex had gotten wind of her plans for the teacher nomination. He understood her predicament. "We'll talk about it and call right back." They hung up.

Rex turned to Benita. "Let's go to the empty classroom while our students get settled in our classrooms." They moved to an empty classroom. Rex spoke again. "I've heard talk. I know how important it is for you to be at school this morning and now you need to be at your agency. Can I do something to help?"

Benita wrung her hands. "I don't know. I wonder if what's happening in Miami is even beyond me. I want to call the police, insurance and our IT experts."

"Then do that. If you can focus on the nomination for the next three hours, then we can talk again. You okay?"

"I think so. I'll call Kenrick and tell him to get in touch with those folks." Benita was calmer with a plan in mind.

"Good. I'll make sure both classrooms of students settle in."

Chapter Twenty-Six

Adirondacks

"This is a valid piece of work." Jake commented to the class on the teacher award nomination they were preparing for Ms. Scott.

"Is that your way of saying it's high quality, Jake?" Benita was faking normality and tried to stay focused on the nomination.

"You know it is. It slaps."

"But are we going to finish in time?" Wesley seemed jumpy.

"Ms. Townsend will be here shortly to proofread and make sure it is all pulled together into a cohesive submission." Benita tried to stay focused.

"But isn't that our job as writers?" Aaron had said very little during the process.

"The more eyes the better. That is true for any author. We won't be asking Ms. Townsend to do any writing or restructuring. Those are our tasks. She can give it a critical eye, which is an important aspect of writing." The students were clever and excellent writers. She did her best to add to their skill a knowledge of how to ensure excellence in a submission.

Dr. Gawl's assistant, Sylvia Townsend, arrived, and the final hour available flew by. Her stern demeanor was magnified in her criticism of the document's overall appearance. Without changing a word, she worked her magic in making the document organized and presentable. She printed it out, the students attached the supporting sample assignments she and the students had collected from the community. It all was sealed in a large box with the address printed on the front along with the school's return address in the corner.

Dismissal brought high fives all around. Rex, Troy and Dr. Gawl all descended on Benita's classroom as the students filed out. Only Rex knew of the emergency. He spoke, "Do you want me to deliver the nomination?"

Troy and Dr. Gawl looked at Rex and then Benita. The confusion on their faces commanded an explanation from her, so she told them what had been discovered.

Dr. Gawl was the first to respond, "I'm willing to help. I can deliver the documents for you."

"Thank you. Rex has offered too. I don't know what to do."

Troy's anguish for her showed on his face. Despite that, he tried to be reassuring. "Call Kendrick. See where things stand."

Benita returned to the group after a quick call. "Kendrick doesn't understand the circumstances here at school, but everyone is willing to meet with me tomorrow. He will cover until I get there.

***

"I really want to try to make things better. Will a kiss help?" Troy was getting into the passenger's seat of Benita's rental.

"There will be time for kissing when we have this document delivered and are on our way to Miami!" Benita smiled and brushed his cheek with her hand. Her tone changed back to reflect the reality of her mood. "The GPS says it will take four and a half or five hours to get to Manhattan. Does that sound right from your experience?"

"You're asking an outdoorsman about the Big Apple?"

Benita thought it would be impossible to banter under the circumstance. But Troy had a way about him. "What? Don't tell me you've never been? You're also a New Yorker!"

Troy laughed. "Yes, I've been. But no more often than I've had to. And then, I didn't drive. I took the Metro North into Grand Central every time if I'm remembering correctly."

"So, what did draw you there?"

"A few Broadway shows and concerts. You can imagine my conference venues are not in a sprawling metropolis like New York City. What about you?"

"Mom lives there--well, in Brooklyn now. But Paris for the summer. I don't spend much time with her. Aunt Dilly's year-round residence is in White Plains. I stayed there a couple of times, but mostly I visited them at Hidden Havens. I have traveled to innumerable conferences and meetings in New York City. I enjoy it, but I can't say I've had a lot of free time to get to know the city as I should. I've done some of the touristy things. I enjoy the theater, and it sounds as though you do, too."

"Yeah. I do."

"Maybe we can go to summer theater in the Berkshires this summer? Or maybe Jacob's Pillow or Tanglewood?"

"I would enjoy that. But no need to go so far. The Adirondacks has summer theater too."

"Yes. It all sounds wonderful to me." Benita had a special curiosity about the Berkshires. She was confident of her ability to convince her handsome companion that the trip would be worth his time. That is, if she came back from Miami.

"This is good. I love being with you anywhere." Troy never seemed to worry about being hokey or sentimental.

"Me too. I wish it wasn't marred by my anxiety to get this nomination delivered and the mess in Miami. I don't know what's going to happen there."

111

To add to the anxiety, the Palisades Parkway was nearly a parking lot, which remained the intermittent situation for the rest of the trip. The lag caused them over an hour's delay, and they arrived with barely enough time to find a parking garage that cost them $50 and a five-block trek to the office on Twenty-Fourth Street. She knew the area since many of the literary agencies were near the Flat Iron district and she felt fortunate that it was close to the entrance of Route 495.

They delivered the package at 6:30, which allowed plenty of time before the building closed. She obtained the receipt she coveted, and they made the return trip to the parking garage. Traffic still was heavy, and Benita gave up hope of having dinner in Manhattan. The drive to JFK Airport would take one and a half hours normally, but on a Friday night, it would be at least two hours. They would be rushed to make it through security to board their 9:45 flight.

They had just taken the ramp onto Route 678 when she turned to Troy in another moment of panic. She caught her breath and said, "I forgot to ask if you have a real ID or a passport?"

He turned to her to set her at ease. "Yes. I've flown a number of times since they became available, but they're not required until October."

"Oh good."

Troy had a way of calming Benita's fears. She was thankful he was with her.

They were rushed to turn in the rental, catch a shuttle to the correct terminal, and get through security. It was a relief to board, and it was good to be on their way; especially side by side.

Chapter Twenty-Seven

Miami

It was 12:30 on Saturday morning when they landed at Miami International Airport. The steamy morning air made their skin gleam. The only good thing about that hour was fewer people to compete with them. The Uber had them in front of Benita's building by 1:15.

Troy wiped his brow as a staff member escorted him to his guest room, and Benita kissed him goodbye, with a promise to send a text when she was ready to head to the Basin Quay Block.

She felt as though she tossed, turned, and dreamed all night of people betraying her in bizarre ways at work. She only was convinced that she had slept due to the dreams and the alarm awakening her. She sent the promised text to Troy right away to be sure he awoke as well. She asked him to give her a half hour and meet her in the lobby.

That meant a quick shower, a little makeup, a brief run through her hair with a brush and the cool hairdryer. A white summer shift was the best choice to be donned in a hurry. She rushed down the stairs in order to be five minutes late.

Troy was reading a newspaper when she arrived, and he smirked at her as she hit the crash bar and bounded through the stairwell door. She wasn't disheveled, but it wasn't Benita's typical look.

They stopped at the Café in the Basin Quay, where Benita introduced him to her favorite breakfast. Yvette was nowhere to be seen, so it wasn't the best version of her breakfast. Troy wanted to like it, but he was honest that it would not become his favorite—nor even be ordered again by him. They refilled their coffees and took the elevator to the tenth floor.

Benita was surprised to see Kendrick, Maren and Celeste all there. She hadn't wanted to disturb Maren, so she had no way of knowing Maren had exited the apartment a half hour before Benita's alarm. "Wow. Hi, everybody. You've surprised me, but thanks for being here. This is my friend, Troy."

Kendrick came forward first to greet Troy and shake his hand. Celeste nodded and smiled. Maren said, "How nice to meet you."

"It's good to meet all of you." Troy was charming, though he had told Benita he suspected one of them.

Everyone stared at Benita. Celeste spoke first. "How are you going to proceed, Beni?"

Troy formed a slight scowl in response to Celeste's apparent insolence and looked at Benita. She blinked once and almost imperceptibly shook her head. "Let's meet in the conference room. Have you all had breakfast or at least coffee?"

All except Troy said, "Not breakfast."

Troy added, "I wouldn't really call what I had breakfast." He looked at Benita and raised his eyebrows. He resisted the obvious but thought it anyway. *That is no breakfast in my estimation.*

Benita called the Café and ordered a variety of muffins and a carafe of coffee. She left her cell for a text when the food arrived since the outer office door was locked.

They all proceeded to the conference room and quickly got down to business. Maren and then Kendrick outlined the irregularities they had uncovered as well as how they had come across the information. Celeste was the only one hearing it for the first time, and she gasped. "Oh. This is so much worse than I imagined."

Kendrick provided an explanation to Benita for his behavior in fleeing to New York. "I was so worried that the reputation of the firm was plummeting, and I wanted 'out' while I could."

Benita was gentle but direct. "Why didn't you talk to me about it?"

"Benita, you had just taken off and left a stranger as our only conduit to you. A conduit I had no idea wasn't involved in the discrepancies. The two coincided so conveniently." He turned to Maren. "I am sorry, Maren. Really, I am."

Maren looked down and then at Kendrick. "I suspected you, too."

"No wonder with the way I took off."

Celeste changed the direction. "So, what is the plan? What are we going to do?"

Just then there was a text for Benita saying her food delivery was at the door. Kendrick rose to collect the food and Celeste went to the conference room closet for cups and napkins. Maren helped with the setup while Benita answered another knock at the door.

"I'm Carson Ambrose. I was contracted through Circuit Security to provide a consultation to Soto Literary Agency this weekend."

"Oh, Mr. Ambrose. Welcome. We're just getting started. Come in. Have a seat and help yourself to some coffee and a bite to eat. Everyone, this is Mr. Ambrose with Circuit Security."

"Thank you." He poured a cup of coffee, black, and took a sip. "What seems to be the need?"

Benita spoke up. "Let me introduce everyone and explain." She gave a brief overview of those around the table and what had been discovered so far.

He had some immediate questions. "Do you know of any password breaches lately?"

Everyone looked around and shrugged their shoulders. Benita offered, "Not that we've noticed, I guess."

"Do you have new employees or other individuals accessing the office that don't normally belong?"

"Maren is the only new person, and we don't suspect her. She was the first to bring it to my attention." Benita was sure to be the first to answer so that no information could be misconstrued about Maren's newness with the agency.

Celeste spoke up. "Darren Granger lost his pass card to the office. But he found it soon after."

Benita's agitation was apparent. "What? When, and why wasn't it reported?"

Celeste offered what she thought would settle everything. "A little over a week ago, I think. But he found it right where he left it. Nothing happened."

Ambrose queried next. "Where?"

"The Café."

Ambrose again asked, "How long before he noticed?"

"When he arrived the next day."

The night I was here scouring through pittmad tweets. The office door opened, but I couldn't see anyone. Benita was annoyed as she moved forward and put both hands on the table facing Celeste. "Overnight?"

"Yes, but he found it right at the table where he left it."

Ambrose, who was as jaded as Benita wanted him to be, commented, "That doesn't mean a thing. I am going to assume an unauthorized individual gained access to the offices because of that misplaced access card."

Maren couldn't help but speak up. "But there still are passwords to overcome. And I overheard the accountant and an agent talking about 'fakes.'"

Ambrose looked at Benita. "You should pursue the agent and the accountant; I'll pursue what I can find on the server. And everyone, please call me Carson."

Benita went into action. "Celeste, would you please get Jett and Zina into the office right away. I'll provide Carson with access to the server."

Carson quickly replied, "I don't think there will be any need for help with access."

Benita looked at him wide-eyed for a moment. *Is that scary or reassuring?*

Troy and Benita retired to her office. When they were seated, Benita turned to him and said, "Is this unbelievable?"

"What's unbelievable is that people call you Beni, and I never knew it!"

"Sometimes, Troy, you are so shallow." She raised her eyebrows, and then her demeanor softened to show she appreciated the humor despite the situation.

He got up from his chair and moved closer to her. "I know. And it bothers you immensely." She arose from her chair and met his kiss. He kissed her for a long time. When they parted a bit, he joked again, "I may be shallow, but I present with very in-depth affection."

"Indeed, you do." She felt a little better—for the moment.

Chapter Twenty-Eight

Miami

"Zina is on her way. I still haven't been able to reach Jett."
"Thank you, Celeste. Even if Jett becomes available, I doubt his ability to be fully present given the nature of his recreation yesterday!" Benita was still trying to find humor wherever she could.

Celeste continued. "Yvette might know something. Ask Maren. She was going to chat with her a couple of days ago."

"About what?" Benita asked.

"I didn't know what was going on, but she asked what I knew about Jett and Zina. I simply told her about Yvette's seeming intuition about people and situations. I didn't think of it at the time, but she might know something about the office pass."

"Oh. I'll talk with Maren and maybe call Yvette at home if it seems like something to be pursued. Please let me know when Zina arrives."

She found Maren in the conference room, and Maren gave the essence of what Yvette said about Zina and Jett. They chatted for a moment until Celeste came by with Zina.

"Thanks, Celeste. Maren, Kendrick and I wish to have a chat with you." Benita addressed Zina. "This is my friend, Troy Bradshaw."

Benita noted that Zina didn't look nervous. *I think I would be nervous if my boss returned to town over a weekend and called me in for a chat. Especially if I had done something wrong.*

All except Troy gathered in Benita's office, and Benita closed the door. Troy stayed in the conference room. "Zina, some irregularities have been noticed in both the accounting system and with some fiction submissions."

"Oh, thank goodness you know. Jett and I didn't know what to do."

"What do you mean?"

"I found the fake manuscripts just about the same time as Jett found the fake withdrawals." Zina looked relieved. "It was just when Ms. Scott arrived, so we didn't know how to get word to you. We didn't want to say anything to anyone else since we couldn't be sure who was involved."

Benita was confused, but she kept her wits about her. "I didn't know you and Jett were friendly enough to confide in one another."

"We were reluctant to tell you, but Jett is a distant cousin of my mother. He originally told me about this job. I hope you're not upset that we hadn't divulged that to you."

Benita wasn't concerned, and it was a good explanation of why they would confide in each other when they could trust no one else.

There was a knock at the office door, and Kendrick opened the door since he was closest. It was Carson.

"I have a question Ms."

"Benita."

"Yes. Benita."

"Go ahead. I think we're all interested in getting this thing unraveled if we can."

"Should employees be working overnight?"

Benita was quick to respond. "I did and often do."

"Alright. Anyone else?"

Celeste answered this time. "Very early in the morning, perhaps, but not in the middle of the night."

Benita made a request, "Everyone, please stay in the office suite until we have exhausted all of the information we can get. I know it will be boring, but don't access your computer until Carson says it's okay."

"Have you found something?" She asked Carson when he appeared in her office.

"There is a login that has been used over the course of several middle of the night sessions. I traced it to Polly Kozol."

"Polly! Polly? As far as I know, Polly could rightly bear the middle name Anna. I can't see her as the culprit."

"It's possible she doesn't log off at night. Whoever has been accessing the office could simply use her station. I'll keep digging without touching her computer. I think you should have crime scene in to check for DNA and prints. Have this Polly come in for elimination evidence."

"I will."

Benita went to the conference room to update Troy. He went with her to her office to make the call to Polly, who came in immediately after Benita's call. She admitted that she hadn't shut down her computer at the end of the day for months. "Have I caused problems?"

"None that you could have been aware of. I won't chide you now. Yes, I will. You know updates are done on the server overnight. I don't know how that has occurred with your computer logged in. I'll check with Carson to see the impact, but we have other things to worry about at the time. You'll need to stay until the police arrive to gather your DNA and prints."

Polly looked appalled. "But what if I don't want to?"

Benita couldn't believe the gall. "I guess we'll ask the police about that."

The police arrived and went beyond what Benita would have imagined. Crime scene dusted Polly's office, the front door, and other places that could reveal evidence such as the water cooler. A detective questioned everyone. Polly never again mentioned an unwillingness to cooperate.

It had been a long morning by the time Benita offered that folks could leave. She expressed a desire to stay overnight to see if anyone tried to break in, and Troy approved of the concept. He objected to her being the one to stay. "You know, with all of the activity, the thief may be permanently scared off."

"That might be the best outcome we can hope for." Benita felt as overwhelmed as she had at the beginning of the day. "We both know the evidence will do no good unless the culprit has some sort of record."

"That might be likely." Troy tried to reassure her. "I'm staying in Miami tonight, but I can't tomorrow night. I would advise getting an off-duty police officer until you can hire a safety officer."

"I guess that would give me confidence enough to finish my summer pursuits, although I don't know if Maren is willing to continue the arrangement. I wouldn't blame her if she feels there is nothing left for her here."

"It scares me to think you might not return to Clear Lake."

"Me too. I care more about seeing you as I do anything else. True, I want to finish the project with the students, and I want the agency to be okay. But what if the system has been compromised beyond the simple use of a particular station that was continually in operation?"

"What are you thinking?"

"What if I have to close the agency for now until this is sorted out? Then what if the damage isn't repairable." There were tears in Benita's eyes.

"You're tired. Don't think about that now. Carson can advise you on that or refer you to someone who can." Troy tried to reassure her.

"Yes. You're right. But I'm not leaving you here tonight."

"What, then?" Troy asked.

"I'll ask Carson what he recommends."

Troy was concerned about Benita. She seemed defeated. He was exhausted, so he knew she had no energy to face the dilemmas. He just wanted her to rest.

Troy left the building in search of some take-out and was delighted with the food trucks. After her breakfast recommendation, he wasn't sure he was in touch with Benita's tastes. He took the low road and ordered numerous burgers. He brought them directly to the conference room at Soto and then circled through the office to let any remaining folks know there was food. Despite Benita's offer for folks to leave, no one had, and the burgers were devoured.

Troy ventured to Benita's office. Benita said, "I have good news. One of the detectives arranged for a temporary security guard to stay tonight. I've placed an ad in the newspaper for permanent security. Kendrick is willing to interview and hire. I'm not sure, but at least I can think about returning to The Havens and Clear Lake."

"That's a relief." Troy said.

The security guard who was going to cover until 5:00 a.m. arrived by 7:00 p.m. that evening. Benita provided his access card and information about the office. She offered to get him food, but he had brought a snack.

She felt guilty leaving, but she and everyone other than the security guard did.

Chapter Twenty-Nine

Miami

Troy, with his positive attitude, tried to convince Benita things would work out with the agency. He insisted that they dine at her favorite restaurant. The hour was late, and it was cool enough to eat on the terrace of the Provence. The city was a vision with its sparkling lights and swaying palms. The beauty of the night and the gentle breeze calmed Benita's inner turmoil. She had forgotten her hunger during the day, but now she was ravenous. The Croque Monsieur was a perfect meal. Since she had a tiny breakfast and no lunch, Benita made room for Profiteroles, encouraged of course by Troy suggesting they share a dessert.

After, they walked along the beach and enjoyed the quiet waves with other lovers strolling slowly, holding hands, arm in arm, or in a full embrace. They trekked to Benita's apartment building in the same manner and reluctantly said good night in the lobby. It was past midnight when Benita reached her apartment. She knocked a warning knock before entering so as not to startle Maren.

There was no answer and when Benita entered, the apartment was empty. Benita showered and emerged in her robe to find Maren just entering.

Maren spoke, "Oh. I'm glad I didn't awaken you. I didn't intend to stay out so late."

Benita voiced her approval. "I'm glad you were enjoying the city. Were you?"

"Yes. I have a beach I frequent when I need to unwind. I went there, and then to a favorite food truck."

"Were you alone?" Benita asked lightly.

"Yes."

"Oh. I'm sorry. I should have invited you to dine with us."

"Not a chance. You needed time with Troy. Did you have a good dinner?"

"Yes. Provence. One of my favorites."

"Are you French?"

"Yes. The distaff side of my family has some French in their background, and my mother embraced the identity. I think she needed the distinction since my father was such a prominent member of the Cuban community in Miami. She is always in competition with someone or something; even with herself."

Maren chuckled.

Benita ventured a question. "May I ask you about Kendrick?"

"It depends on what about Kendrick."

"Is there something between you?"

"For a minute. I think our mutual distrust got the best of us."

"No road back?"

"I can't imagine."

"Is it too soon to ask about your plans?"

"Under review. What about you?"

"Probably the same. I want to follow through with the students' fiction project. But we both know you could do just as good a job if not better. The irony is that the summer getaway was to clarify my stance with the agency, but the getaway may force me back to the agency. I'm venting. I'm so sorry I got you into this mess!"

"What a story! Who needs to make them up, right?"

"Benita laughed. Let's get some sleep. We'll plan a week at a time after we get a night's sleep. Troy could only obtain a morning flight, though he wanted to stay late into the day."

"Sounds like a plan. Good night."

Chapter Thirty

Miami

Benita was awake before Maren. She took her time dressing, applying make-up and then sent a text to Troy. He was at her door within ten minutes of her text.

"Can we have a redo of breakfast?"

She giggled. "I can't tell you how much I missed my favorite breakfast when I was away."

"Ugh. Sorry for you. Really sorry for me. Any ideas of alternatives? French again?"

"New Orleans doesn't have a corner on beignets. You should taste the Miami variety. But, another time. We should probably just have pancakes and attempt to get you to the airport on time."

"Just pancakes. How can you say, just pancakes?"

They were quiet at breakfast. Both were sad they had to part without knowing how long it would be.

Tearful as she drove away from the airport, Benita decided to walk along the beach before the heat precluded any enjoyment. She parked at home and walked to the beach. She was in a fog when she heard her name and turned to see Maren.

"Hi, Maren. Is this your favorite beach?"

"Yeah. And the only one I know down here!"

"Got it. Have you had breakfast?"

"Yes. The food truck over there. It's becoming a staple."

"You could do worse. Let's walk together. I think Kendrick is covering the office until I arrive. Any thoughts about our week?"

Maren sighed and looked at her feet while she continued walking. "I know this sounds ridiculous, but I wouldn't mind staying if you're here."

Benita was silent. Maren thought she wasn't going to respond. Finally, she did. "My motives for returning to The Havens are Troy, the serial fiction project, and The Havens; in that order. They are purely selfish. My immediate responsibility is here, though. I should arrange for an insurance claim, coordinate overnight coverage, and make your experience worthwhile by working with you on offers to authors. A couple of days could make a huge difference. I just need to get my heart out of New York, contrary to the TV ads!"

Maren smiled. "Can we put the class in the hands of a substitute for a few days?"

Benita scoffed a bit, but in a good-natured way. "What a good idea. The kids will be fine; Dr. Gawl won't be, I'm afraid."

"If we're going to do this, we need to give her as much notice as possible. I think I have just the candidate. If he's interested, it will stand us in good stead with a partial solution when we have to hit Dr. Gawl with the news."

"I love the way you craft sentences!"

"And we can have a video chat with the kids to explain what's going on. They might as well know about the drama. If you're okay with that, Benita."

"Let's go to the office where it's quiet and cooler. It's getting hot out here already."

On their way, Maren explained about the candidate to fill in for them. "He was a regular substitute, or guest teacher is the term preferred by Dr. Gawl, and a former English teacher. He retired early to care for his father and write full time, though he has yet to publish." He sounded like a good candidate to Benita.

Maren went into the conference room to make the call and emerged with good news. "Dirk Blodgett is available and excited to take the class, now if we are able to convince Dr. Gawl."

"Good. We better contact her right away. Does she video chat?"

"Ah, no. I'll call her. Be right back."

Benita paced while Maren went back to the conference room. She had sent Kendrick home for the rest of the day and told him that if all worked out, she would take the early morning duty the next day.

Maren reemerged a full hour later. She looked drained. "That was a hard sell. For all her flighty behavior, she can tackle an issue with the tenacity of a bloodsucking leach."

"Poor you. Sorry to put you through that. Final answer?"

"She agreed to it. She's going to talk to Dirk. She said a video chat in the morning is a good idea, though she wanted no part in setting it up."

Maren continued. "I'll let Dirk know and go over the schedule. He didn't know anything about Wattpad or similar apps."

"The kids will figure it out if he's willing to supervise."

"He will. His has mad skills in classroom management." Maren raised both hands in a gesture that indicated she was stepping out of character.

Benita smiled. "That reminded me of Jake!"

Maren chuckled again and changed the subject. "Could you get me a guest room in your apartment building?"

"Please don't, unless you're uncomfortable with me in the apartment. I want to take a long view of the situation and hope I won't have to be here for an extended time—and that you will decide to finish the internship."

"If it's okay with you. You're the one on the daybed in the den. Let me know if you change your mind."

Now I must tell Troy. I hate this plan, but it is a good plan.

Chapter Thirty-One

Miami

"You've been here for hours, haven't you?" Celeste resumed her protective tendencies toward Benita's penchant for overdoing work.

"I had a lot to catch up on. And I called the insurance company. To my surprise, they're sending over an investigator right away."

"On a Sunday. And you can file a claim so soon?"

"We'll find out."

"Have you had any breakfast?" Celeste was hitting all the protective notes.

"Yes. But I was about to go and grab a coffee."

"Let me. I didn't pick up anything on the way in. And I don't want you to miss the insurance agent. And, I think you must be ready for a snack."

"My usual?"

"How about something more substantial?"

"Surprise me, then. You and Troy! Honestly. What is wrong with a Cuban Tostada?"

Benita unlocked the door to the office suite since she was expecting the insurance representative. Celeste returned with coffee and scones, and Beni invited her into the office to eat.

"Thanks. But I'll stay at my desk in case the insurance representative arrives. I hope you can finish your morsel before you meet with him."

"Very thoughtful."

Benita devoured the scone and rid her mouth of the dryness by gulping the café au late. She was finished when Celeste knocked. "Ms. Leslie Perreault is here representing the insurance company."

"Yes." Benita stood and exited her office to greet her. "I'm the owner of the agency, Benita Sotolongo. Pleased to meet you; do come in. Would you like coffee?"

"I'm fine. Thank you. Good to meet you as well." Leslie Perreault was young, but confident. She removed a tablet and asked Benita for an overview.

When Benita paused, Perreault asked if there was a location where she could work.

"Yes. The conference room. Right this way."

Benita returned to her desk and found Maren seated in a guest chair. "I guess we didn't sort out the use of the desk!"

"No. Awkward." Maren looked away.

"No need to be. I haven't even logged in. Let's, and we can go through some of the information on representing authors."

"Sounds good."

Their work was interrupted after a couple of hours by Leslie Perreault's appearance at the doorway to the office. "Ms. Sotolongo."

"Call me Benita."

"And I'm Leslie. I've put together a tentative plan when you have a moment."

"Now is fine."

"Should we meet in the conference room?"
"I'll follow you."

They were seated around a corner of the table from one another. "My plan is three-fold. One, reimburse you for the loss thus far. Two, stop the graft. Three, catch the thief and recover our reimbursement."

"How will you proceed?"

"With your permission, we're going to migrate your software to a server we maintain for these breaches. Your current server will become a fake server. Any logins will be traced to the IP address, and we'll arrest the culprit."

"Celeste, who isn't a suspect, has a limited knowledge of the overall plan. She will sign in and sign out thumb drives daily that will provide access to the new server. We'll hire an overnight security guard to see if anyone tries to gain access to the suite. If so, the attempt will be thwarted. I've ordered an access change to the suite immediately and a hidden closed-circuit camera that will be monitored in the insurance office. Any questions?"

"Many, but I probably wouldn't understand the answers! It sounds impressive. I guess I'm okay for now."

"Okay. I'm off. But I'll be in touch. At the end of the day, I want you to personally access every computer, exit the programs and log off. I would keep the inner workings of this plan a secret—the new server and all. Their access cards to the suite will be reprogrammed. Celeste knows to ask for them; she and they will only think she's checking to see that they're all accounted for."

"What if one of the agents signs into the old server by mistake rather than using the USB drive?"

"We'll be alerted and give you a call so that it can be investigated."

"What should I say about the USB drive?"

"Something innocuous. You could tell them you don't understand, but it is required by the insurance company. All of this can be blamed on the misplaced access card. Any questions?"

"Not right now." Benita's confusion wouldn't go away with a quick question.

"Oh, a reimbursement check for your loss thus far will be sent by messenger," Leslie responded and headed toward the door.

Benita worked in a thank you in between Leslie's brisk dialogue.

"You're welcome. I think you'll be satisfied. We have a good clearance rate. That keeps your rates down." Leslie winked at her.

Chapter Thirty-Two

Adirondacks

Dr. Gawl made an abrupt, but characteristic entrance to what had become Dirk Blodget's classroom before the class was about to begin in the afternoon on Monday. "Oh good," Dr. Gawl addressed the students. "You're all here. I have some announcements. Sit, please."

The students gazed from Dirk to Dr. Gawl while settling into random seats.

"You all know Mr. Blodget from his guest teaching during the school year. Well, he is going to be here for perhaps a few days. Ms. Sotolongo had to return to her agency in Miami to settle some problems, and Ms. Scott is needed to assist."

The classroom erupted with chatter,

"Now, settle down. They want to explain the situation to you themselves and discuss your assignment. Jake, we were wondering if you would be willing to use your cell phone to conduct a video chat. Would that be acceptable to you?"

"Totes, uh, I mean, totally okay with me." Jake accepted the challenge suspecting that neither adult in the room would have experience with a video chat.

"Good. Here is the number you should dial. Are you all prepared to participate?" Typical of Dr. Gawl, she did not notice that everyone was more relaxed about the situation than she was.

Jake prepared the call, and Maren quickly answered. "Hello? Is this Jake?"

Jake replied, "Hey, Ms. Scott. This must be one of your most modern teaching methods yet!"

Brynn was standing closest to Jake and nudged him. For her part, Benita rolled her eyes at Jake behind the back of Maren, hoping she wouldn't find it curious that he was talking about her teaching methods.

Jake realized his slip and spoke again before Maren had a moment to respond. "Whazz up?"

"I think I'll let Ms. Sotolongo explain." Maren handed the phone to Benita.

"A lot is up, so it seems! How are you all?" Benita waited while Jake held up the cell and a few students responded with greetings.

Benita continued, "We're attempting to settle some problems here at Soto Literary Agency. In my absence, Ms. Scott uncovered some irregularities in acquisitions and in the accounting system as well. We both are working with the authorities and hope to see some resolutions in the next day or so. Our goal is to make sure the source of the problem is identified and stopped." Benita paused, and the inimitable Jake piped up.

"Hey. Our teachers are kick-butt gumshoes. You go!"

Others cheered until Dr. Gawl tempered their enthusiasm.

A bit embarrassed, Benita spoke again. "We discussed your project, and we know you'll put your skills to work and start a draft of a serial novel. What you need to do first is decide on the internet application to be used. Everyone should participate in writing the first episode; I will leave it up to you to define your approach. Each of you should take to social media to build hype around the debut."

Jake interrupted, "When will that be?"

Benita asked, "Do you mean the debut?"

"Yup."

"I was thinking, once we debut, perhaps this Friday, we would publish almost every day for the remainder of the summer session."

"So, we should plan on fifteen episodes?"

"Yes. Create your story arc accordingly. Does that sound reasonable?"

"Yeah, that slaps." Jake's way of saying it was high quality.

Maren asked for the cell. She took possession and added, "I hope all of you will welcome Mr. Blodget."

Unanimous applause greeted the announcement. Mr. Blodget humbly nodded and added, "Could I be Dirk to everyone from now on?"

Chapter Thirty-Three

Miami

Benita's cell rang in the middle of the night. She answered automatically without checking the caller ID.

"Benita Sotolongo, please."

"Speaking."

"The police are on their way to arrest a man trying to access the office suite of Soto Literary Agency. I am retaining him based on his attempted use of the old access code and his lack of ID associated with any of the staff names provided." The caller didn't give his name.

"I'll be right over." Benita was on autopilot regarding her responses.

"That would be best. We don't want to have him arrested if you cleared him for access to your suite."

"I'll be there soon. What is your name, sir?"

"Pardon. Charles Richardson, madam."

"Thank you."

***

Benita notified Kendrick, and they both arrived at Soto as if together. The police had arrived, but the man who had attempted to enter the Soto suite refused to answer questions.

Benita stood a short distance away from the perpetrator. "I don't recognize this man. I know of no reason for him to be entering the offices ever, especially at this time of night. How about you, Kendrick?" Benita turned to see Kendrick's response.

"No." Kendrick had nothing to add.

"Could I talk with him?" Benita asked about the would-be intruder.

"He's not talking to us," a police detective responded.

"Maybe he'll talk to me. Privately."

The man shook his head, no.

"Give us a minute anyway," Benita said.

The all-male group was reluctant to leave Benita alone with this stranger. She insisted, so they moved just far enough to be out of sight.

Benita took a commanding stance. "I don't know if you have a record, but there's no doubt your DNA and prints will be taken and matched to what we have already. There is no need for a confession; they've got you. You're holding the bag, so to speak. The restitution alone is enormous; not to mention the jail time. If it's all you, then fine. If someone else helped, from what little I know, it might be better to share the brunt. That's all." Benita asked no questions, but from the look on the face of the accused, she felt she got her point across. She called for the others to step back in.

Chapter Thirty-Four

Adirondacks

On Dirk's first day with the students, they filled him in on what they had accomplished the prior week in preparing a teacher award nomination for Maren Scott. They made it sound like quite a caper, and Dirk was impressed.

On the second day of their new adventure, Dirk said to the students, "How shall we get started on your novel?" There was no answer.

Dirk switched to another question. "Let's start by creating an account. What name should we use as the user for the account?"

Wesley said, "I think we should use Benita's name. She's the best known, especially in the publishing business."

Aaron countered, "I think we should decide on a catchy identity for our group and use that. We can push it on social media using that name."

Dirk asked. "What does everyone think?"

Jake was the first to speak up. "Our own name. Let's think of one." Everyone agreed.

Dirk asked, "As I see it, there are several decisions. Tell me if you agree. We need a title for the book as well as a cover for the book. A login for the internet site probably should represent the group rather than the title of the book. Who knows, you may go on to more books!"

"Yass!" Jake was referring to the last statement. He continued, "If only Aaron drew more than anime. We could do an illustration for the cover."

"I can draw more than anime when I want to." Aaron was matter of fact and accustomed to Jake.

"I am thankful that is settled! Now, let's talk titles," Dirk said.

"That Ticket Is Lotto!" Nikki was the first to speak.

"No Time for High School," Wesley was an old movie buff, so they asked if there was a reference.

Dirk ventured a guess. "Have you seen *No Time for Sergeants*?"

"Yes!" Wesley was pleased that Dirk validated his knowledge of old movies.

Jake was itching to get in on the action. "Do You Know Who I Am?"

Dirk said. "Let's continue to think overnight and decide tomorrow. We'll then have Aaron work on a cover. Sometimes it helps to think about something else, for instance, what about a name for the group?"

Chapter Thirty-Five

Miami

Maren encountered Kendrick as she entered the reception area, which was teeming with police.

Kendrick spoke first. "Maren. I can explain what's going on, unless you know already."

"No. I don't."

"First, I want to apologize for abandoning you when I should have been helping."

"Thank you for the apology." *Again.* Maren was loathed to say anything more. She was still angry and hurt on so many levels.

Kenrick had a sense about the wide chasm between them and that it would take a long time to repair. "I will work to make it up to you and regain your trust."

"I can only hope that will be possible. I don't know right now."

Benita appeared from her office. "Good morning, Maren. Did Kendrick fill you in?"

"No, he didn't. I just arrived."

"I'm going down for my typical breakfast. Anyone care to come?"

"I would," Maren said.

I would, too," Kendrick said. "It's been a long morning already."

Kendrick and Benita filled in the details for Maren on the elevator. When they reached the Café, Benita was first in line.

"Oh. Mr. Tomas! What brings you to the counter today?" Benita was surprised to see the owner minding customers.

Tomas was fuming. "Just filling in last minute until a replacement can arrive."

"Isn't Yvette usually here on weekdays at this time?"

"Yes, she sent a text five minutes before her shift about an emergency," Tomas said.

Benita gave Kendrick a sharp look, and then spoke to Tomas once again. "We'll take whatever pastries and coffees are easiest. We'll eat them here."

Tomas filled their order, and they chose a table. Benita asked, "Do you find Yvette's absence today an odd coincidence?"

Maren wasn't picking up what Benita was putting down. "Do you see a connection?"

Benita answered, "I think I do. Let me satisfy my curiosity."

Tomas had just been replaced by another barista and was removing his apron. Benita approached him and asked, "Would you mind joining us just for a moment at our table? Bring a coffee if you would like, of course." *That was silly of me. It's his coffee.*

"Of course," Tomas answered as he poured a large cup for himself.

When he had joined them, Benita asked, "What do you know about the men in Yvette's life?"

Strangely, Tomas took her request in stride. "She brought a man to a company picnic once. I think she introduced him as a friend from golfing competitions."

"Would you recognize him?"

"Yes. I think I would," Tomas answered without showing any curiosity.

"I know you have a lot to do, but would you be willing to come up to my office for a moment?" Benita was hoping he would not start asking questions.

"Can I help with something?"

"Yes. It will only take a few moments, and it's best that I explain later. Thank you."

When they reached the office suite, the police presence was obvious still. Benita hoped that it wouldn't impact the veracity of what she was about to do, which she explained confidentially to the detective in charge. "Mr. Tomas, my office is right across the reception area. Could you take a look at the person in there?"

Tomas was confused, but he complied. After a glance into her office, he came back to her with wide eyes. "What is he doing here? That's Yvette's friend I was talking about. How did you know?"

"I'm sorry, I can't explain right now. We have some work we need to do. Please trust me. You may wait downstairs, or you may leave a number where I can contact you later."

"Is there a place where I can wait out of the way?" Tomas was too curious to leave now.

"Yes. Come into the conference room. May I get anything to make you more comfortable?"

"No. Just do what you need to do." Tomas' expression remained puzzled.

Chapter Thirty-Six

Miami

"Hello?" Benita answered her cell while she, Maren and Kendrick waited for the police to finish with the part of their investigation that required their presence at the Soto Agency.

"This is Leslie Perreault, Benita. We've had a login attempt for your accounting program, and we've traced the IP address to the British Virgin Islands. The police have been notified, and I think we'll have a name for you soon."

Benita said. "Thank you. I think I can guess the name. It might be Yvette Martin."

"Why do you say that?"

"We don't know for sure, but she serves in the Café on the ground floor of the Basin Quay, and she didn't come in today. I asked the owner of the Café some questions and he was able to identify the detained man who was trying to gain access to the Agency as a friend of Yvette's."

"That was good thinking. Do you have any other clues?"

"She would have had access to the pass card that Darren Granger left overnight in the Café. She could have copied the code and returned the key to the table where he left it. Probably watching to see that no one else disturbed it so Darren wouldn't suspect anything had happened to it."

"Good work. If you ever want to change careers, you're hired. I'll let you know if your hunch is accurate and if this Yvette is apprehended." Perreault ended the call.

The security guard came to inform the trio that the police were taking the criminal into custody. He had confessed and implicated Yvette as an accomplice. The guard added, "The culprit told us Yvette has a friend in the BVI and intended to move more money to an offshore account. Probably would have been headed to a country that doesn't extradite, if she hasn't already."

"I hope not." Benita's optimism plunged, "Not after all of this. But why was the man here?"

"That he wouldn't say. Making sure he left no evidence? Double-cross—an attempt to transfer funds before this Yvette did?" They were guesses by the guard.

Chapter Thirty-Seven

Adirondacks

"What are you doing here?" Troy walked by Benita's classroom for the third morning hoping for something he didn't really expect. But here she was!

"I hope I'm welcome!" She wanted to be coy for a change.

Troy embraced her, looked around, and seeing no spectators, kissed her long and hard. They were still in an embrace when there was stirring in the hallway.

"Oh my, Benita. Welcome back. Has all of the scandal ceased?" It was Dr. Gawl in her usual flap.

"Things are back to normal at the agency, so I decided to create as much normality here as possible. I am sorry for the disruption." Benita knew that Dr. Gawl could conjure up a panic about any event, and even peripheral involvement in the agency's data breach was, as she had said, a potential source of disgrace for her.

"Oh, dear. Does Dirk know?"

"Yes. But he's coming in for a transition session. My treat."

Dr. Gawl trotted off, muttering something Benita didn't want or need to understand. Troy grinned at Benita. In her frenzy, Dr. Gawl had failed to acknowledge Troy, much to his delight.

Other commotion was overheard, and Rex Jacobs appeared at her door. "I'm glad to see you're back. Does this mean it's all good at your Agency?"

"Yes. Thank you for your help. The culprits have been caught, most of the money was recovered, and the server is safe again. I think the shock is wearing off, and Maren will be able to resume her goals for the summer."

"Good." Rex's tone gave the impression he had heard TMI. He turned and left the classroom just as Dirk entered. Greetings were exchanged and explanations repeated just as the first students arrived.

"What are you doing here?" Several students gathered around her desk, ignoring Dirk and Troy. Troy left on that note.

"That seems to be the greeting of the day! I think I'm back for the duration of our project. Let's start the morning again. Hello. I am happy to be here. I'll take attendance and explain everything!"

The students took their seats quicker than usual. Troy made his exit, and Benita began her explanation. She ended with the latest information she had received early that morning, keeping the students on the edge of their seats. "Her name wasn't really Yvette, and she only pretended to be Latina. She is British and is wanted in Great Britain as well as the British Virgin Islands. My company was not her only target; she has scammed many others. She's a chameleon, of sorts, and a real charmer.

Benita continued to a captivated audience. "Her modus operandi was to pose as a worker in areas where she had a vantage point and await opportunities to hack. She hadn't been caught in the States previously. And the Miami police hadn't checked the international database for DNA or fingerprints until after she was caught."

When she finished, she was surprised that Aaron spoke first.

"Wow. That's a better story than we could make up!"

The class laughed and many agreed.

Benita said, "Speaking of our story, fill me in."

Wesley piped up, "We have a name, we think."

"Oh really, what?" Benita asked.

"Student Stringers." Wesley offered. "Or, for the purposes of the app, studentStringers."

"I like it. What else can you tell me? Benita wanted to keep the momentum going.

"We have a title for the series of chapters," Riza said. ***"Secret Trust."***

"Very good. A little mysterious, straightforward, classy. Anything else?"

"We named the first few characters and have an outline for the first chapter." Riza continued providing information.

In full teacher mode, Benita said, "Great. How about a cover? That's always important. It is what people see first. You know, many believe you can judge a book by its cover!"

Jake offered, "Aaron is working on it!"

"Aaron. Thank you! Are you all set for ideas? You shouldn't have to do this on your own."

Aaron said, "I could use some help." He was a little sheepish.

"Let's talk about our ideas for images." Benita smiled and looked around.

Jake spoke up. "Anything other than a bunch of forms of ID's plastered on the cover."

Others commented, "Yeah." "For Sure." "Not that."

Jake added, "Our guy, Isaac, likes to go to a nearby lake. Our story is set in the Adirondacks, of course. So, also of course, there's a mountain. Maybe the cover could have him by a lake, looking like he's confused. It could mislead people in a lot of ways ... on purpose? Suggesting things like he has amnesia or he's a criminal on the run or just plain lost. Or maybe holding the ticket?"

This sparked some interest from Aaron. He said, "Yeah. I'm picking up a vibe here. I'll work on it. It's okay to come up with other ideas too. I can do more than one sketch."

Chapter Thirty-Eight

Miami

"Do you think we can start over?" Kendrick was at Maren's office door.

"Forgetting the past couple of weeks? Don't I wish." Maren smiled and set him at ease. "There's a lot to process, isn't there?"

He stepped into her office, though she hadn't invited him. "It brought out the worst in me."

"It's still hard to believe it all happened. I thought I was in it for the experience, but I never expected that kind of experience." Maren smiled and a nasal breath escaped her, but it wasn't a chuckle. She was confident she would never laugh about any of this ever.

"Would you consider going out to unwind after work? I would like to try to make it up for running out on you."

Maren considered what he did unforgivable. To her and to the agency. She grappled with something to say that didn't sound vindictive and rude.

"I'm still frazzled, I'm afraid. I'll be better after a few days of my favorite activity—devouring fiction." She didn't thank him, ask for a rain check, or do any of the acceptable evasive techniques.

Maren wanted to go back to the Adirondacks and be with her students. It was for them that she stayed in Miami, however. She believed that Benita's idea for the writing workshop was incredible, so she maintained the unorthodox exchange. She dared to hope her initial passion for the project would return.

She tried to unwind with a walk on the beach into the alluring sunset that evening, trying not to ruminate over her anger with Kendrick. *How could he run off when he was the one responsible for the agency? And, how could he have suspected me when we had started to care about each other? Then leave me to continue to do damage if he thought I was responsible? It doesn't make sense.*

She purchased some food from her favorite truck, waited for the cool of the evening after sunset, and walked back to Benita's apartment.

It was Kendrick's favorite food truck as well, and he had the same thoughts about himself as he watched her from a distance. He had to come up with explanations for himself before he could begin to earn the right to explain his actions to Maren. But he had no intention of giving up.

Chapter Thirty-Nine

Adirondacks

"I've missed you so much!" Benita fell into Troy's arms when the coast was clear. They kissed with no thought of stopping.

"I was afraid you wouldn't be able to come back." Troy's voice was hoarse. "I have to go now." He kissed her again. Waterfront activities today," He said breathlessly. "Mostly kayaks."

"Do you have enough help?"

"Yeah. Thanks. We should be good for tomorrow, too. We'll be in the gym, and the students can spot each other. Have you picked up Rackie yet?"

"No. I'll head there now and bring him home. Poor doggie. I think he'll be so excited to come home even though Aunt Dilly isn't there."

Troy kissed her nose. "I'll let you go. Enjoy! I'm going to drive up tonight to see you."

"Nice!"

***

Rackie ran around the property's circumference in back of The Havens so fast he was almost on his side. He returned to where Benita was watching, barked, and repeated his run.

The excitement of the dog as well as the beautiful vistas of The Havens provided the soothing touch Benita needed in the aftermath of the harrowing few days in Miami. The mountain laurel was lavish as it dotted the wooded areas as far as

Benita could see. She tore herself from the view and fetched Rackie's dish of water, which she placed on the small porch. On his second return trip, he jumped on the porch and slurped up its contents before parking himself with wagging tail in front of the French doors to the kitchen area. Benita unlatched the door and let him in.

The dog trotted through the entire house stopping to sniff along the way. Benita supposed he was searching for Aunt Dilly, who wasn't due until the following week. He settled into his bed in the kitchen and in less than a minute Benita heard the typical doggy snore. *How do they do that? Perhaps if I ran around the property twice?* She laughed and proceeded to finish unpacking.

She heard a noise, peeked out of the guest room window and saw Pala working on some of the fruit trees on the west side of the house. She changed her clothes and went out to chat. "Hi Pala. May I help?"

"Hi. I heard you drive in. I'm almost finished, but thanks for the offer."

"I'm about to have some iced tea. Would you join me?"

"Sure. I actually have some questions for you, if you don't mind."

"Absolutely. I hope I have the answers!" Benita led her to the foyer.

They proceeded to the east parlor, and Benita offered a seat. Pala declined to be seated unless Benita could find a wooden chair to keep her work clothes from soiling the fabric-covered furniture. Benita scoffed. "This throw isn't an antique. I'll place it over the sofa. There. Feel free to relax. I'll be back with some tea and the strawberry pie I picked up on the drive home."

"I'm famished. Thanks." Pala said.

Benita returned with the beverages and the pieces of pie on vintage Noritake Azalea dessert plates. Pala commented on them, "I am not dressed for this occasion! Are these antiques?"

They both laughed. Benita explained. "They're from the 1920's. The stagecoach runs had subsided, and The Havens no longer was needed for a tavern. Uncle Havens' grandmother decided a more contemporary décor was to her liking and invested in the art deco set."

Pala smiled and changed the subject, "You've been away. Was that planned? I knew about Ms. Havens' trip but was surprised by your absence as well."

"No. It was not planned." Benita was emphatic. "There were problems at the agency."

"Can you talk about it?"

"Sure." Benita provided a full rendition of the past few days. They each had two glasses of tea and finished their pie by the time Benita had told her tale.

Pala blew out a cleansing breath and said, "Wow. What a whirlwind! And it's all resolved?"

"Seems so. I have a lot to be thankful for." It was as though Benita thought that for the first time.

Pala put down her delicate dessert plate and stood. "I'm not going to bother you with my dopey questions."

"Nonsense. I'm sorry my spiel took so much of your time. I would be happy to chat about your questions unless you have to go."

"Thanks. I appreciate it. It has to do with what you said about your background with social language. I think I knew someone who needed your expertise." Pala sat down once again.

"Oh. Someone close?" Benita didn't intend to pry and regretted the question.

"Yes. He was my husband."

"I see. I shouldn't have pried. I'm glad to try to answer your questions. But please don't interpret anything I say to be critical--of anyone. Including you! Despite their difficulties with social cues and how hard it is for them and for those around them, I am an advocate for individuals with this diagnosis."

Pala continued as if to ignore what Benita had said. "I think the impact on me was cumulative, and I just gave up. I knew I should be more patient, but it was just so hard. Little things. For instance, he taught our neighbor to drive. Our neighbor was a teen whose father had passed away years ago.

"He took a day off from teaching to accompany this young man to his driver's test, and I asked him to send me a text as soon as he knew anything. We both cared for this young man. I took the day off from school for an appointment and had to leave before they returned home. I met them about two miles from our house. I was so curious about what happened, so I stopped; he didn't. So, I sent a text and asked what happened. The young man was driving. Instead of answering yes or no, he only answered that the young man had done very well. I was floored when I returned home that evening to discover our friend had failed the test.

"It's just unbelievable to me that he couldn't text 'no' or something!"

"You must have been so hurt and angry." Benita knew all too well what Pala was talking about.

"What would make someone act like that?" Talking about it was bringing back some or the anger Pala felt about the incident.

"I've worked with folks on understanding how rude that kind of behavior is to others, and I try to convince them what the other person needs for appropriate communication. I don't have the background to explain what is going on for them emotionally or neurologically. That's the basis for my studies this summer. I'm considering going into research."

Benita sensed that Pala needed more information, so she continued. "For years, my theory has been that someone like your husband thinks you should be able to figure out the information from their actions rather than their use of words. Ironic, isn't it? He doesn't pick up on unspoken behavior but expects you to sense what is going on without being told."

"It didn't feel like the basis for a loving relationship. I felt diminished."

Benita only nodded sadly. "Of course."

"He wasn't like that when we first met!"

Benita's emotions swelled and she shared more of her experience. "He probably didn't act like that when you first met. It's not your fault, and there was no way you would have noticed. When motivated or otherwise interested in a conversation or activity, such as a new romance, a difference might not be apparent. An individual can be warm, witty, and very responsive in those situations.

"If the situation is strange, annoying, or mundane, their reaction is apt to be more stilted. An individual might walk away from a conversation when they've said all they intended to say—ignoring the niceties of wrapping up. They might not respond to a text unless the text asks a specific question. The sender might provide information yet not know whether it was received."

Pala looked away. "Probably you think I should have put up with it."

"I would never say that. I trust you."

"Can someone like that be helped?"

"With the right confluence of awareness and coaching. In most cases, they are very capable of loving relationships."

Pala said nothing.

Benita added, "This is a vast area, and we've only touched on the surface. I understand you're hurt. I can't fathom anyone handing out advice in this situation. It doesn't sound as though you had a willingness from your husband to participate in getting help."

"No." Pala showed her exasperation.

"I'm sorry if the discussion upset you." Benita paused and added, "It's something we all struggle with to some degree. I once read a post by a friend on social media in response to what was her biggest pet peeve. She said, 'people who don't pick up on social cues.' I was alone, but said aloud, 'Yikes. How often have I been that way?'"

Despite her agitation with the subject, Pala chuckled. "I guess that helps to understand his lack of awareness. But he should have believed me when I told him the impact it was having on me."

"Yes. He should have."

Chapter Forty

Adirondacks

Benita was haunted in more than one way by her discussion with Pala. She felt she had blundered the conversation. *I am an advocate for people with communication disorders. Did Pala get that I understand her decision **and** support individuals who struggle with the pragmatics of communication?* There was something else that she couldn't identify. Deep in thought, she was startled by the landline, which seldom rang.

"The Havens."

"Hey Benita." It was Troy. "The Dean is calling a meeting of all department heads, and I don't think I can skip it. It makes it just late enough, so I won't venture up to see you tonight."

"I'm disappointed, but it's a long way. Probably just as well. I'll miss you and see you tomorrow before class?"

"You know it! I can take Friday afternoon off. Let's spend the rest of the day together." Troy suggested.

"Sounds good." She didn't say goodbye. Instead she asked a question out of the blue. "How well do you know Rex?"

"Rex? What does he have to do with anything?"

"Just curious." Benita surprised herself with the question.

"We talk. He's a good guy. Cares about the kids. Likes sports. Not a kiss-up, excuse my language." Troy chuckled.

"That part I knew!" Benita giggled a bit. "Forget I asked."

"O-kay. Bye, sweets. See you in the morning."

***

The students arrived before Troy the next morning. Troy wasn't late; the students were early. Rather than waiting for the opening bell after being dropped off, they rushed to the classroom.

"Aaron has some drawings. Let's pick one and get writing. We can publish by tomorrow!" Jake was chipper and insistent.

"Alright! This is it, then!" Benita was almost as eager as Jake.

Aaron passed around his drawings.

Benita was grateful to Aaron. "Thank you so much Aaron. You are talented!"

Aaron was embarrassed. "Oh. It's okay. I thought maybe you'd want to use photo shop or something."

"Why? Not when we have your expertise. This is perfect."

Aaron may have been embarrassed, but he was pleased.

"Shall we take attendance?" Benita knew all were accounted for, but it was her way of drawing things to order. After attendance, she added, "Are we ready to write?"

"We have an outline of every chapter, and we're ready to write the first one," Brynn said.

"Good, then! What's your production plan?"

"Nikki types really fast. Wesley, Riza, and Jake are the best writers, so they'll dictate. Aaron and I are going to proofread because we're kind of OCD." Brynn responded again.

"Before you begin, what kind of connections have you made?"

Jake fielded this one. "I have like a ton of followers on Instagram and Twitter. I've been sending out pictures 'from the chapters' with a little tease. Riza is the Facebook queen, but we all have been talking about it on all kinds of social media. So have our parents and to their email address books, too. They still use email. Ms. Townsend sent out an email to the whole school community. We all said it was going to debut on Friday, and I think we're going to make it! Wahoo!"

Secluded Summer at Hidden Havens

"Thank you, Jake. Everyone. Well done. I've also shared it with my followers. I've received many 'likes.' Far more than I normally receive! And there are hundreds of new subscribers to imprinTABl. Is that the application you decided to use?"

Jake continued, "Yep! We've been telling people to sign up! We're the studentStringers."

"People are signing up, and I'm sure it is because of your efforts. Well done." Benita was ready for this.

"So, let's get to it!"

Jake had more comments. "No adverbs, gerunds, or participles. Do not use 'that,' no prologue, and don't be afraid to use 'said' for tags. And don't say someone texted. Oh, and whom is no longer a word. Right?"

Benita laughed. "Those are the hang-ups of editors and agents. I don't think authors, readers or publishers care!"

And Chapter 1 of "Secret Trust" was published the next day.

Chapter Forty-One

Adirondacks

At the end of Friday's session, Benita was sitting at her desk with her eyes closed. She let out a cleansing breath. *Chapter One is out there. Now we play the waiting game for responses.* She opened her eyes to see Troy standing in front of her. "Oh! Don't do that!"

"I think you're going to be glad to see me," Troy said.

"I am glad to see you; I startle without much effort, if you haven't noticed!" Benita said.

"Look what I have!" He handed her tickets.

"Tanglewood! Wait, tonight? I thought you said it was a long way."

"It's a little over two hours to Lenox. We have plenty of time to get there. We will be late getting home."

"I'll stay in the apartment." Benita's eye shined. "I'll have the neighbor take care of Rackie."

"How long do you need to get ready?" Troy had plans and hoped her schedule would allow it to happen.

"I moved several outfits to Maren's apartment. What should I wear?"

"Oh. Worst question ever. Your choice, but it's a shed with lawn seating and not much warmer than the Adirondacks. So, layers?"

"Less than an hour." Benita wasn't sure she could meet that timeline, but she was going to do her best. "Would that work?"

"Sure. Heard of the Mountain Lake Inn in Stockbridge? I thought we'd skip lunch, have an early dinner there."

Troy knew he was pushing the boundaries of Benita's spontaneity, which was already stretched by her adventures so far this summer.

"Let's." *After all, I'm the one who asked for the Berkshires.*

Troy and Benita savored the time traveling together. The topic didn't matter but predominant in the conversation was the delight in listening to each other's personal stories laced with admiring comments to each other.

An unusual break in the conversation gave Benita the nerve and opportunity to explore another avenue of conversation with Troy. "I was wondering, do you know the first name of Rex's wife?"

"No. I don't think so. He may have mentioned it, but we don't chat. Most of the time we're creating adventures for students. What is this interest in Rex? Should I be jealous?" Troy was kidding yet curious.

"Oh. Right. Because he's such a flirt! Besides, he's still married."

"How do you know that?"

"Well, you said she disappeared. I thought if she took legal action, he would know where she is." She paused and added, "Besides. I think I know where she is, and she isn't divorced."

"What? Where? And why do you think it's her?" Troy scowled.

"I ran into her. Literally." She told him the story of meeting Pala.

"You know, Paula sounds familiar. What's her last name?" Troy asked.

"Her first name is spelled P-a-l-a, which is Native American for water. Her last name is Onatah, which is Iroquois meaning 'of the earth.' It is so appropriate for Pala," Benita said.

"I'm sure it is for your friend. People acquire Mohawk names. It's not common, but meaningful to folks in this area. It's a long shot that she's Rex's ex. I really doubt it, Benita. I wouldn't pursue it." He changed the subject. "Did you know that Wednesday is the Fourth of July?"

"Oh. I was thinking it was later in the week. That's the day Aunt Dilly is flying home. How odd. Well, I guess when you're retired, you don't have to be sentimental about holidays." Benita shrugged.

"I have some bad news. I have to travel from tomorrow through Wednesday."

"Why?" Benita was surprised.

"The department consults. I travel often. This was last minute because one of the instructors backed out. It's a multi-day celebration for a town's Bicentennial coupled with Fourth of July festivities."

"I didn't know you are an event planner!"

"It's Colorado."

"Ah. Enough said. Must have adventures! Well, I'll miss you." She knew he hated the idea as well, so she didn't add her thoughts to the conversation. *The timing really stinks.*

By five in the evening, they gained early seating at the Inn's Main Dining room. Both enjoyed the special, which was a seared scallop dish. Benita was delighted with the fresh flavors of the food and the inviting décor. She glanced at pictures of the historic dining room, and the current version replicated the historical pictures with a high degree of accuracy. It was bright and comfortable, with white beams and walls of windows trimmed in wide boards. Antique teapots were displayed on upper sills with transoms of leaded glass above the sills.

The couple could have lingered over dinner, but they had to make haste to get to Lenox. Opening acts had performed by the time they arrived, but they enjoyed *Earth, Wind and Fire* for their entire performance.

The hour was late when they embarked on their return trip, but they were euphoric. They chatted about their bucket list for the next visit. Benita recited her preferences. "I love to tour homes, so I want to see Jonathan Edward's home in Stockbridge and The Mount in Lenox. I love Edith Wharton. Probably you want to climb Mt. Greylock?"

"I have, but I would love a repeat performance with you. Are you interested?"

"It might be a little lower on my wish list than others." Benita then added, "Thanks for all of this." *I think I'm falling in love. Don't say it, Benita. Too soon. Too much emotional baggage from the last few weeks. Don't. Just wait.*

"I know it's cliché, but a penny for your thoughts?" He noticed her reverie.

"Someday. Maybe."

***

Rackie greeted Benita the next day with a wagging tail and a wet nose sniffing her toes. She laughed and said, "Okay, just a short walk before lunch. But you're a faker. I know you were well taken care of."

They were still on the property, with no intention to venture into the bear's territory, when they came upon Pala. Working as usual, this time she was picking strawberries from the raised beds at Hidden Havens.

Benita tried not to startle her. "Hi Pala. How's the crop this year?"

"It's been a good year so far. Some of the locals donate crops to food pantries and other events in the area. Your aunt is one of the most generous."

"What a good idea. So, what are the strawberries intended for?"

"There's a Mohawk Strawberry Festival in the next town this weekend. I'm going to attend tomorrow afternoon, but I'll drop off these strawberries on my way home for folks who to use today and tomorrow. Would you like to come? It's one of the traditional Mohawk Festivals. It's fun as well as sacred."

"Sure. Tomorrow afternoon is good. I think I'll go to the morning church service Aunt Dilly attends when she's here. It sounds like it's near the Festival site."

"It is. I know which church you're talking about. I take a lot of your aunt's crops there for their *Turf to Table* events."

"When are those events?"

"After every service when the crops start to yield. The strawberries will keep going for another week, so I'll take some to their Wednesday service and the following Sunday."

"Would you like to come with me to church? Or meet me there?" Benita welcomed the company.

"Sure. Let's meet there."

"Something else I would like to do, and I can't do it alone."

"What's that?" Pala was curious what Benita had up her sleeve.

"Water skiing. I think everything we need is in one of the carriage houses."

Pala perked up. "We should check that out. Since this weekend is spoken for, want to plan on next weekend?"

"Do you have a free afternoon this week?"

"You can do an afternoon?" Pala asked.

"Sometimes. I'll be home all day on the Fourth of July. Do you have plans?"

"I almost forgot the Fourth. It's Wednesday, isn't it? That sounds like it could work out. What time?"

"Want to grill? Noonish?"
"Sure. What can I bring?"
"Just yourself."

Chapter Forty-Two

Miami

I think this is it. Maren completed a read-through of a manuscript she considered to be the latest great American novel. Or close to it. In her excitement, she forgot the tension between Kendrick and her, and she rushed to his office.

She knocked and didn't wait for a response. "Do you have a moment, Kendrick?"

Hoping for détente, Kendrick would have interrupted anything for her. "Sure. What's up?"

"I just read the best manuscript. Maybe even better than any novel I've read. You know how many that is!" Her implication was clear. "It's a historical novel laced with politics, romance, crime and intrigue. I just need to check some historical facts, but the story she tells is fascinating."

"When in history?" Kendrick was far more interested in Maren than the novel, but if it was the medium to have an audience with her, so be it. Plus, he wasn't averse to stories per se. He didn't think Soto should be dragged into fiction, though.

"Oh, sorry. It's set during the turmoil of the Long Hot Summer of 1967. I guess some of us consider we're 'woke' to some degree, but this was eye-opening."

"What's the geographical setting?"

"She ties in several of the rioting hot spots—with artiste. It's so well-woven together. Fascinating and believable. Tragic, triumphant, tremendous. I wish you would read it."

He had to admit he was becoming interested in the story not just for the connection it provided to Maren. That was a plus.

He agreed. "I'll read it over the weekend and call when I've finished. And Maren, good work."

***

Kendrick had been reviewing manuscripts all his professional life, and in his area of expertise, the reading was dry. *Maren was right. This is superb.* He appreciated the depth and breadth of the book, and he felt a vicarious closeness to the one who introduced it to him. He couldn't decide which was better. He still longed for a real relationship with Maren.

He called Maren early on Sunday afternoon. "Maren. I knew from your apt description this was a wonderful read. And you were not overselling it. It is amazing."

"I am relieved you think so. Thanks for reading it right away. Now I need another favor." Maren hesitated.

It doesn't matter what she needs, I'll do it! He cleared his throat. "If I can."

"I want to get it published for her."

"Of course. What a strong first completed project. It's so good, I predict you can see it through this summer, unusual as that may seem."

"Will you help?"

Chapter Forty-Three

Adirondacks

The congregation at the Inselberg Worship Center welcomed Pala and Benita with enthusiasm. *So much for the cold emotional stereotypes of people from the Northeast.* The Pastor spoke on a text from the time of Israel's judges, and Maren was impressed with his ability to relate such an ancient event to contemporary spiritual experiences.

Following the service, the *Turf to Table* gathering was held as folks displayed canned goods as well as early crops outside of the building. There was no stigma; the contributions were for those in need or for those who simply wanted them. No exchanges were necessary. The event provided the best basis for fellowship Benita could remember. There was juice, coffee and muffins as well.

After a cup of coffee, they proceeded to the Strawberry Festival at the Inselberg Fairgrounds. Pala explained to Benita that to the Iroquois, strawberries were the symbol of blessing and Thanksgiving. "By the way, I appreciated the invitation to the Worship Center. They seem authentic in their faith and service."

"I was impressed as well, and I'm hard to please; in a way."

Pala continued with her explanation of Festival. "The Iroquois are focused on interconnections with nature. Part of their belief system is that everything happens for a reason." Pala explained more about the beliefs as they walked through the craft exhibits, listened to music, watched the children engaged in traditional games and dances, and sampled some of the unique dishes cooked on the premises.

"I think I like the version of strawberry fried dough the best of everything." Benita made the comment after she and Pala had tasted food from a dozen active cooks. The fried dough contained a strawberry filling. "It's sort of strawberry shortcake meets jelly donut!"

"Every tribe and nation seems to have a version of fried dough, right? I agree, this is the best I've had, even without the strawberries." Pala changed the subject, and asked, "Do you mind if I break away for the recitation of the Prayer of Thanksgiving?"

"Of course. Should I come with you?" Benita asked.

"It's fine if you do. All are welcome," Pala said as she led Benita to a seat in the Long House on one of the wooden benches arranged in a circle. The ancient prayer's origin was with the one who they revered as the peacemaker between tribes, Dekanawidah (meaning two rivers flowing). Greetings from all the natural world were recited; Benita listened.

On their way to where their cars were parked, Pala opened up about her perception of faith. "I think it's all in how you treat people."

"I've heard that, and often. It's a wonderful goal."

"And I sense there's more." Pala said.

"My faith tells me God wants a personal relationship with us. So, to me, it's how you treat God first and how you pay attention to His commands for the way to treat people."

They proceeded in silence except for when they reached their cars and reiterated their plans for the Fourth of July.

Upon her return to Hidden Havens, Benita arranged with Adele's neighbor for the launch of the boat. The neighbor's truck had a trailer hitch and Benita's rental did not. Included was an invitation to join her on the Fourth of July for boating, waterskiing and a cook-out. This family had done so much for her aunt and for her, including caring for Rackie. Besides, they would need a spotter.

***

Benita's classroom at Clear Lake Central was noisy when the workshop resumed on Monday afternoon. StudentStringers were eager to publish the second installment of their short story, and they also were excited about the holiday. Benita was able to take attendance and, as if she ever held the reins, let them loose to do their best work.

Secret Trust – Chapter 2

"Sir, you have one moment to explain before I call security." The receptionist had played her last hand in any attempt at levity with the young man.

"I am serious. If you give me ten minutes with your best financial lawyer, he will tell you that this is a bona fide emergency." Isaac tried to shake his fog and present a viable case.

"Why don't you explain this to Ms. Stiles, our security officer? The receptionist was washing her hands of him, so to speak. She dialed with the phone on speaker. "I have an incident in the lobby."

Ms. Stiles' immediate appearance made it obvious she was in the lobby as well. The receptionist made a nod toward Isaac. Stiles made a quick assessment of the young man and approached him. "May I help you sir?"

"Yes. Could you accompany me to the best finance lawyer in the practice?"

"I'm not acquainted with all of the specialties, sir. Can you tell us what your business is here?"

Stiles hadn't thrown him out yet, but he sensed it was imminent. He felt sheepish and desperate. He thought, *don't do anything rash*.

Isaac pondered his situation for a full minute with the two women glaring at him. "Could I talk to you in private?"

"Of course. I have an office. We can talk in there." Stiles led him to a tiny room, with all glass walls. "First, I'm afraid I must frisk you for a weapon." Isaac complied. She performed a thorough search and sensed he was wearing a security belt. Though it seemed strange there was very little volume in the belt, she let it go. "So, what is this about?"

"A lot has happened to me in the last twenty-four hours. I just turned eighteen, and because of being 18, I just came into a large amount of money." It was a stretch, but not an outright lie. "I need immediate help in protecting myself from vultures who want a piece of me. I would rather this firm get a big retainer than letting these suckers get all of it."

"I see. Do you have the sum on you?"

"Yes. It could be dangerous."

Stiles doubted the safety belt contained many bills. Though she supposed if the bills were large enough, it could be a tidy sum. "Thank you for telling me. We'll get you an appointment right away."

Stiles became nervous. Isaac did not know whether she thought he was wacked, or she believed him.

She accompanied him back to the receptionist. "Dolly, who is our best financial advisor?"

"Mr. Brady."

"This young man needs ten minutes of his time right away. I will accompany him to Mr. Brady's waiting area."

As the duo of Stiles and Isaac entered the elevator, Dolly dialed Melvin Brady's secretary. Dolly wasn't sure whether Isaac was a worthy client or if Stiles was in a hostage situation. But she only reported that they were on their way.

Brady's secretary greeted them and told them he had an appointment open the following Wednesday at 8:30 a.m.

Stiles countered, "We need ten minutes today. It doesn't matter how long we wait as long as it is before banks close."

The secretary was taken aback. Stiles had never intervened in this way, at least in Alma's experience with the firm. "Wait one moment, please." She disappeared for a brief time and returned to say, "Mr. Brady will be right out."

Brady appeared within ten minutes. "Hello Stiles. What seems to be the emergency?"

"This young man is carrying an inordinate amount of money and needs immediate advice. I'll remain here while you chat. He's been searched for a weapon and is clean."

"Thank you. Come in, young man. I don't have much time."

When they were seated in Brady's posh office, Brady turned to Isaac. "Please be brief."

"I think I won the Power Lotto."

Brady arose and began to walk around his desk toward Isaac as though in a trance. "Why? Aren't you sure?"

"What a nightmare. I don't want anyone to know! I just turned 18 yesterday, and I'm supposed to be in school for my senior year. My mom is way nosy. I spent all of my money getting here!"

"Do you have the ticket with you?"

"Yes. Should I?"

"Let's check it out." He picked up the phone. "Alma, cancel my morning appointments." He sat down at his desk and ran a search on the winning numbers and compared them to the ticket presented by Isaac. His voiced cracked. "Son, I am pleased to announce you just won fifty million dollars!"

Isaac sunk into his chair. It took a moment, but the lawyer grasped the reality of the situation first. This was a windfall for them both. "Isaac. You may celebrate. It's true."

Isaac started pacing. He took deep breaths. He looked up, rubbed his hands through his hair, and let out a long sigh. "I don't know how. It's been such a stressful morning." His head started pounding from the release of tension even as a new kind of tension was building. "What should I do next?"

"Shall I ask Alma for some champagne?" Brady was smiling.

"It's illegal even at 18." Isaac looked at him, annoyed.

"I know. I guess I won't put myself in the position of contributing to the delinquency of a major!" The lawyer hoped some irony would help Isaac relax.

Brady gave Isaac a few more moments of reflection, then asked, "How would you like to proceed?"

Isaac started hyperventilating. "For gosh sakes. That's why I need you!"

Chapter Forty-Four

Miami

"Have I told you how much I appreciate what you're doing for Soto?" Kendrick joined Maren early on Monday morning. "Do you wish to pursue specific publishers?"

"I do. I have a sense, I think, of the publishers who would be the most sensitive in dealing with this author and provide the best support in promoting the book. Too many would shy away from the politics and a reminder of the cultural shifts credited to that summer. The discussion of race in America is a land mine."

They worked throughout the day contacting publishers and leaving a very short window for returning calls. They made a strong team; Kendrick's reputation, Maren's years of teaching literature; and their experiences as people of color.

Kendrick's involvement throughout the day provided genuine support for the publishing effort, and he was not using the opportunity to bridge the divide between him and Maren. At the end of the day, he did venture into the personal realm. "How about dinner at my favorite food truck?"

"Yours? You don't have exclusive rights, you know!" Maren was smiling to his relief. "I think I would like a nice restaurant followed by a walk on the beach. Would that work for you?"

"Delighted." He was.

They agreed on a Peruvian restaurant. "This is the best Cerviche. Of course, you can imagine I haven't had it very often!" Maren referred to the myriad opportunities for international cuisine in Miami compared to the greater Clear Lake area. She chuckled.

"We have a wonderful selection, and I enjoy it. But I eat my favorite street food ninety percent of the time!"

The conversation was easygoing until truncated by Kendrick's dreaded question. "Is it too soon to ask if I can try again to apologize?"

Maren used her napkin, placed it back in her lap, and said, "Yes. But let's try."

Kendrick was happy and then felt a panic coming on. *What could possibly explain being a coward? That must be how she sees me.*

He cleared his throat. "You've picked up on my discomfort with Soto representing novels."

"Yes. I have. I didn't at first."

"Did I tell you about the impact of Benita departing, to an undisclosed location, incommunicado, a few hours after informing us of her plan? And that represented all of her plan that we knew about?"

"No. I didn't realize there was no preparation. And then a stranger to the agency and the publishing world appears on the scene?" Maren said.

"Yes. The only one with knowledge of Benita's location and contact information." Kendrick watched Maren for a reaction.

She responded. "Simultaneous with evidence the agency's credibility might be compromised."

"Yes. That's not all. I had an open offer to interview in New York. A much more prestigious agency. Not that it's paramount to my career goals to be in an elite agency. But …"

"You decided the time was right to explore." Maren gave him a break by answering for him.

"Exactly." He was glad for the validation.

"What did you do wrong?" Maren thought she had heard it enough, but found she needed him to acknowledge it again.

"I should have stayed. I know that. But there's more."

"I'm sorry I cut you off. Go on."

"I was falling in love. I couldn't face suspecting you. I couldn't face that it could be true. And I would have done nothing had it been true. I wouldn't do that to you. But what I did was just as bad. I should have believed in you and been brave enough to help unravel what was going on."

Maren was finding it difficult to speak. She picked up her purse and her voice was hoarse as she murmured, "You've almost persuaded me, so I can't respond now. I might do something rash. Like forgive you." She left him sitting at the table.

Chapter Forty-Five

Adirondacks

Holidays could wreak havoc on other than just the young. Benita was anxious for her day and a half of freedom to begin. The students wrote throughout the morning and the keyboarding, editing and proofreading occurred all at once. They pushed 'publish' just before the parting bell, and the studentStringers dispersed with whoops and shouts but nary a goodbye. They were on their way to the pre-fireworks and pre-bonfire celebrations.

Secret Trust – Chapter 3

"Let's talk about the first steps. Do you wish to remain anonymous?" Brady asked his newest, richest and perhaps youngest client.

"For now. Is that possible? Any attention I ever received has been negative. So, I hate being in the spotlight." Isaac seemed to shrink in his chair.

"Why negative?"

"I have a learning disability. There isn't much praise for someone who struggles. It's more usual for people to correct me."

"Is that why you were unsure of the numbers?"

"Sort of. I checked them over and over. It's the kind of thing that's hard to believe anyway. But given my history with numbers, I just had to have a different set of eyes." Isaac no longer was sheepish, rather he was emphatic.

"I can go through options. First, do you have identification?"

"No."

"How did you buy the ticket?" Brady was surprised.

"They didn't ask!" Isaac was confused.

"They should have. You said you have no license. What about a school ID?"

"Today was the first day of school. I came here instead."

"Last year's?"

"Threw it away." Isaac's eyes were wide at this point.

"Birth certificate?"

"It's somewhere at home. Probably. I don't know where."

"You have to register with the Selective Service Board."

"Just sent it in last Friday."

"It will come soon. Any routine business mail or subscriptions?" The lawyer was trying.

"No."

"I would be remiss if I didn't see some form of identification, even to set up a retainer as your attorney."

"Mr. Brady, I don't even have money to get home."

"I see. Let me give you a few more pieces of information. Don't worry, the first consultation is free!" Once again, Brady was trying to provide comic relief. It wasn't lost on Isaac, but he was distraught over the lack of ID, and couldn't muster up a smile.

Brady continued. "Some broad brush issues. The ticket isn't a winning ticket until it is signed. Once signed, your identity will become public. New York State will not protect your identity.

"That said, a way around that is to set up a blind trust. It's seldom used, and it's even more rare to set it up as revocable. That means you can withdraw the trust at any time. But it can be done. I can do that for you, we just need to name the trust. Bear in mind, the convenience store already has announced it sold the winning ticket, I would imagine."

"But they don't have my name."

"No. But, they may have closed circuit video and may be able to narrow down the purchases to a few images and publish them."

Isaac became more distressed. "So, what's the sense of a blind trust if they figure out my identity anyway?"

"No one will know for sure. It will be known that a blind trust was established, and if you're pressured, you can invoke that information. You can be innocent in your statement that you understand whoever won has protected the winnings through a trust, and it is managed by a team of financial gurus. Just put it into the words of a Gen-Z guy such as yourself." Brady smiled. He was still trying to work some levity into the day of this poor boy who had just become a multimillionaire.

"Okay. I don't know if I can do that, but I guess I will try. Do I get any say in what happens to the money?" Isaac felt as though he was pushing words at this point. He had so many questions.

"Yes. We'll have a clear contract."

"Once I turn the ticket over to you, how do I know you won't abscond with the money? It's more than you'll make in a lifetime, right? I'm sorry. I don't know where that came from."

"The trust is yours. I could no more steal it than I could steal any of my client's funds. I'm glad you're thinking this way. I don't want you to stress, but I do appreciate cogent thinking on your part."

"Where do we start?"

"I need ID."

"Chicken/Egg!" Isaac leaned forward. "What about the ticket? What ID? Do I go to school and get my ID? Even if my picture is taken today, I won't get it for a week. It's public school! If I go to the registry, they have a whole bunch of requirements that I can't meet. I might be able to find my birth certificate or social security card, but I'm not sure where my mom keeps them."

"Could you ask her?"

"I don't want her to know." Isaac used a soft voice as if she could hear.

"Because …?"

"I love my mom, but she has the biggest mouth in the Northeast! And she has more explanations for her blabbing than you can imagine. I've known her for 18 years, and I still can't stay ahead of her. That's what most of this is about, and I'm fighting like crazy to keep her from finding out!" Isaac no longer used a quiet voice. His was close to an outside voice.

"Don't tell her why you need them. Maybe your Guidance Counselor noticed your birth certificate was missing from your file?"

"She would probably march into school with it and withhold it until she inspected the file."

"You want to get a real ID at the RMV now that you're 18?" The lawyer was accustomed to manipulating sticky issues, but he was convinced he had met his match in Isaac's mother—even though he hadn't met her yet.

"She'd insist on going with me." Isaac blanched.

"Ask her five minutes before she leaves for work?"

Isaac muttered, "I'll try. Do you have a safe where I can keep the ticket?"

The lawyer sucked air through his teeth. "I've been trying to decide about that. A select few have access, so I don't think I'd go there.

Why don't we go to the bank on the corner and get a safe deposit box?"

"Don't you need an ID?"

"Yes. I'll have to set it up in my name. Do you trust me?"

"What if the bank burns down?"

Chapter Forty-Six

Adirondacks

Benita's good intentions on the drive home, besides stopping for barbecue foods and supplies, included cracking open a textbook for the first time in … *wait, I don't know when!*

Instead, Benita made her favorite recipe for hamburger patties out of ground beef, a red, white and blue topped cheesecake, and several salads. She contemplated the need to wash every pan, mixing bowl and utensil in the kitchen when the landline rang.

"The Havens."

"It's Kendrick."

She greeted him warmly. "Oh, hi!" Then it occurred to her that something might be wrong. "Is everything okay?"

"Oh, yes. Maren and I thought we'd let you know that she has a manuscript that's so good she wants to contract with the author right away. She made tentative inquiry with the author, and she is very interested in signing with us. The author is waiting for us to contact her again. So, we wanted to let you know. I'm going to let Maren explain."

They were on speakerphone, and Maren explained her passion for the book to Benita. "It is a provocative piece, though. I don't know how you feel about Soto's involvement."

Benita was convinced. "Go for it. No doubt. Move as quickly as you wish. Be generous with her terms. The truths in the story may be heart-wrenching to her. Let's make it worth the ache in her heart. I have some samples in the file. Celeste can help. Thanks for including me. What are you guys doing for the Fourth?"

They were dumbfounded. "Oh. That's right. We've been so busy we forgot about it." Kendrick spoke for them.

Maren asked, "Do we ever contact authors on the Fourth?"

Benita joked. "Would you want an agent to contact you on the Fourth?"

"Actually, yes." Maren said.

"I would too!" Benita agreed.

Kendrick added one more remark before the call ended. "By the way, we're loving *Secret Trust*. You've noticed the huge following, haven't you?"

***

Benita and Pala were sated with the appetizers Benita had prepared, so they decided to get the equipment together for waterskiing while they worked up an appetite again.

"Let's check and see if we have the equipment we need to pull off this escapade," Benita said. The door was open, and they were about to exit when the landline rang. Benita didn't recognize the number but picked up. "Hello?"

"Hi Beni. It's Adele."

"Hey Auntie. I miss you!"

"I miss you too. Though that's the case, I won't be home today as planned."

"Is everything okay?"

"Oh yes, yes. I'm going to the city with Mabel. I'll spend the night then check on my house in White Plains. I'll be back on Monday, or so."

"Do you need me to come and get you?"

"No. No. No. Mabel is coming back when I do. We must coordinate a bit to pull it together. So, how is he?"

Her voice was quiet as Benita spoke, "It's going great. He had to travel for the Fourth, but he took me to Tanglewood before he left."

"I was talking about Rackie!"

"Oh! That's embarrassing. He's great. He misses you though. Thinks I'm away too much. Good thing for the neighbors."

"I was kidding, Beni. But I would have gotten around to Rackie too. Thanks for filling me in! It's good to hear. Love you, honey."

"Love you, Auntie."

Benita closed her eyes and chuckled. She looked at Pala and smiled.

Pala smirked, "No need to explain."

The carriage house was in good order. They pulled out the ladder, skis, life jackets, and the pull rope and wiped off the dust that had accumulated. Adele's neighbor had launched the boat on Monday. It hadn't sunk, and the day was sunny as was the previous day, so there should be plenty of power. They cleaned the boat's interior, which also was dusty. They were checking around the storage area for anything they might have forgotten when Pala said, "Did you hear a car?"

Rackie was barking as well.

"Benita!" Someone was calling her name. They both headed for the exit with Benita in the lead. She saw Troy with someone behind him. After a moment, she recognized Rex just as Pala appeared behind her.

Rex stopped about ten feet away and stared in disbelief. "Paula?"

Pala was startled and looked frightened. "What is this?" Her face turned red, she looked down, rushed past all of them, started her Jeep, and drove off.

Troy looked at Benita and raised his hands to waist height, palms up, as if requiring an explanation. She thought she deserved one as well.

Chapter Forty-Seven

The neighbors arrived at Hidden Havens just as Troy and Rex drove off. The full brunt of what everyone thought Benita had orchestrated hit her full thrust. And company was arriving. It was as though she had been punched in the chest.

She had to decide what to do. The primal responses to trauma were fight, flight or freeze. The others had taken flight. Her new guests had done her great favors and had expectations for the afternoon. She froze and blocked what had happened so that she could greet Aunt Dilly's neighbors. She greeted them, but there was no warm smile. They didn't notice.

The family took over, to her relief. Ardelia, the mom, and Jasmine, her daughter, got into the boat and took on the roles of driver and spotter. Dad went with his ten-year old son to about chest deep into the lake with the skis. His son put on the skis, Jeremy, the dad and caretaker for Hidden Havens, handed his son, Benny, the rope. Ardelia trolled the boat forward. When the rope was taut, Dad gave the high sign, and the boat was off. The boy was pulled to standing but leaned too far forward and took a spill.

Benny's ride was just long enough so that putting on the skis was tricky in the deeper water, and Dad was treading water in order to help. Mom circled around so the rope came from behind for Dad to grab. They did a repeat performance except for the fall, and the boy was skiing. It was a sight deserving of celebration, and it fell to Benita to cheer for them all.

They all had a turn at skiing; some required more attempts than others. Surrounded by water in Miami, Benita had many opportunities to enjoy swimming and boating. But waterskiing was eclipsed in recent years by wake boarding, kayaking and paddle boarding. She had missed it.

Late in the afternoon the group realized how hungry they were. The family left to change, and Benita quickly changed into dry clothes, and started the gas grill. The burgers were ready and the salads on the table by the time folks returned.

The farm table was on the small back porch covered with a white cloth and a red runner with light blue napkins folded the long way and placed half on and half off the table. There was a large vase of blue and white hydrangeas in the middle of the table.

She used the gold tableware purchased during the early twentieth century for use with special guests at Hidden Havens and the blue trimmed Lenox dinnerware set purchased in the late nineteenth century when the Tavern was still open for travelers. It wasn't a busy table, but it was well-suited to an outdoor setting as well as a Fourth of July celebration.

"So, how many times did you wipe out, Benny?" His sister asked the question, and Benita almost answered before she remembered that no one present called her by her nickname.

"Just once. What about you, Jasmine? Seems like you did more swimming than skiing!"

Siblings. Benita had heard stories of what it was like. She had none of that in her life. Her parents were seldom available for conversation, say anything of banter. *It's nice.*

The food was relished given their appetites and the fact that it was quite good—except the macaroni salad. The dressing was bland and had been absorbed into the pasta. Benita tried at a save by adding seasoned salt and more dressing, but everyone was full at that point. However, they made an exception for the New York style cheesecake covered with alternating strawberries and blueberries arranged in wedge shapes.

Jeremy sat back, tapped his tummy, and said, "Benita, what a feast! Thank you for such a good day and the use of your boat."

"I'm trying in a small way to thank you for your many kindnesses. Rackie does too!" Rackie, who was relaxing not far from the table, arose when he heard his name. It was clear what he was expecting, and it induced a laugh from the group.

"There's a fireworks display tonight. Would you like to go with us?" Jeremy asked.

"What a nice offer. Do you have room for me?" Benita wasn't interested in fighting traffic or searching for a parking place.

"Yes. A van and a pick-up. No sparkle, but practical." Ardelia, the mom, answered.

"Thank you. Yes."

The whole family helped her carry food and table settings into the kitchen, but she refused to let them work beyond that task and cleaned up the rest by herself.

Every part of her being made Benita want to decline. But she needed to keep busy. There was very little time after cleanup before their arrival for the fireworks, so she resisted the temptation to call Troy. She sensed there should be time before attempting the needed conversation. Her prediction was it would not go well.

It was dusk when they arrived at Chilton Park. Benita allowed the children to show her around while their parents enjoyed some alone time relaxing on the bank they staked out with a great view of the awaited display of lights. Jasmine and Benny had worked up an appetite and purchased cotton candy. Benita couldn't look at it.

They enjoyed the swings, obstacle course, and slides that were part of the playground before returning to the blankets Ardelia provided on the bank. Benita longed to be distracted from the thoughts that haunted her. A fun day, a marvelous display. She was numb.

Worst summer ever! StudentStringers know what they're doing. They would be fine with Dirk. I should just bag it.

Chapter Forty-Eight

Miami

Celeste guided Kendrick through the files for the sample contracts Benita suggested. One was found that made sense for the *Long Hot Summer* novel. Maren preceded their telephone contact with a direct message on twitter and an email. It was a good sign that she followed Maren soon after Maren's follow of her.

Maren's prospective client video chatted at ten o'clock on the morning of the Fourth of July with Maren and Kendrick. They learned some things that were not apparent from her social media. Willow was in her late sixties but looked twenty years younger. She had the speaking voice of a teenager; they already knew she had the writing voice of a seasoned novelist.

Maren probed further. "I didn't notice a blog; have you written previous to this novel?"

Willow paused and answered, "Every day with very little exception. I have journaled my whole life."

Maren followed up. "Is there any reason you waited until now to write a novel?"

Willow said, "I have been writing that novel since 1967. I was seventeen years old."

Kendrick couldn't resist. "Is the novel your journal?"

"No. I did both. The journal is every day. The writing was occasional. But I finally retired after 42 years of social work. I worked in five cities and had to obtain a new license each time."

Maren asked, "Did social work influence your writing?"

Willow responded, "So much. Yes. Those stories were screaming to be told."

"Well, we are effusive in our praise of what you have done. I would like to offer you a contract on behalf of the Soto Literary Agency. Would you consider signing with us? I can send you a draft of the contract?"

"I would be pleased to consider it." Her delight resonated even over the phone line.

Maren was hopeful. "Please expect an email today. I have several publishers interested based on my initial contacts. May I ask, have other agents been in contact with you?"

"No, you're the first. If all goes well, maybe the last!"

They had chatted through the balance of the morning. When the call ended, Maren and Kendrick turned to each other and 'high fived.'

Kendrick spoke. "Let's celebrate. There's a holiday brunch at The Main Meal. They serve mimosas, which I think are called for."

"She hasn't signed yet. If a big-name agency that deals in fiction contacts her, she probably will consider it more reliable."

"Big fish, small pond. It can work. Besides, Soto has a good reputation with diverse authors. Be hopeful!"

"Let's!"

The Main Meal was crowded even with the attractions at the Pier several blocks away. The buffet brunch was plenteous. There were no less than four food stations, all gorgeous in their arrangement with varying heights, table coverings, flowers, and decorations created with edibles. The holiday theme's integration into the food options was superb.

Maren and Kendrick ate as much as they dared. Mid-afternoon they headed to the pier where there was a parade of boats decorated for the Fourth. Kendrick bought some sit-upons from a local vendor.

"We can relax on the grass over here and see quite well."

"As long as no one stands in front of us." Maren added, "Oh, look at that boat. It is gorgeous. No wonder it was a prize winner."

"Agreed. Ugh!" Kendrick winced. "Look at that ugly one. Who would do that?"

The beautiful boat was festooned in drapes of light blue chiffon with twinkling red lights behind it. Red roses, blue hydrangeas, and white carnations decorated the hull. The ugly boat had plastic skull and bones buntings decorating the helm.

Kendrick looked at Maren and was thankful she seemed relaxed and happy. *Maybe I have a chance. Thank goodness for that book. And it's a good book. Maybe fiction will win me over.*

Chapter Forty-Nine

Adirondacks

Benita showed up for school on the fifth of July. She wanted to think about the ramifications of running away before doing it. The list was lopsided toward the positive end, despite the negative connotations of the term. She determined not to decide until Aunt Dilly returned. Aunt Dilly would listen, advise, and take care of Rackie. No way would she consign him to more time in the kennel. Though nice, it wasn't home.

She didn't hint at what was in the offing to Dr. Gawl. She proceeded to her classroom not knowing whether she hoped to run into Troy or not. She was averse to seeing Rex, yet she had to apologize. She walked to his classroom. He didn't look up.

"Rex. I'm sorry about what happened."

"Don't worry about it. I'm not."

Benita was setting up for class when a young man entered and introduced himself. "Are you Benita Sotolongo?"

"Yes?" Benita said.

"Troy from the Outdoor Adventure Program at Cliffside assigned me to Clear Lake for the rest of the summer session. There are a few adventures during the last two weeks of the session where we could use some help. Are you willing?"

A sucker punch couldn't have more impact than his announcement. "Uh, I might not be available. Could I let you know on Monday?" Benita wasn't about to commit either way when she couldn't think.

"Sure. The biggest event is the waterfront in a week. We might have waterskiing for those who want to try." The young man who had identified himself as Carter said goodbye.

He greeted a few students as he exited, and they entered the classroom. Benita observed the students looked bedraggled.

"Are you okay?" Benita asked.

"We were up too late. I went to some fireworks last night, and then tried to catch the last of a bonfire. It's still burning! I gave up and checked again this morning." Jake sat down and put his head on the desk. The scene was repeated with most of the students as they entered.

"Do you think we can create a chapter today?" Benita wasn't concerned but did prefer goals for each day.

"I don't think we should plan on publishing. Let's make a great chapter four for tomorrow." Brynn said.

They were interrupted by a sound coming from the all-call system. Someone blew into the mic rather than say, 'testing,' and no one was surprised when Dr. Gawl's voice came on. "Attention students and faculty. There will be no afternoon session today. Adventures will resume on Tuesday afternoon. Thank you and have a good session."

Had everyone had their surfeit of activity for the week, or was it her debacle with Pala, Rex and Troy?

StudentStringers were more focused than usual. Exhaustion brought about a single-mindedness that militated against outside distractions. They created a great fourth chapter but decided to dangle a tease about it for the day and publish tomorrow.

As soon as the last student was out of the room, Benita closed the classroom, got into her rental car, and headed for Cliffside Community College. *Whether Troy is there or not, a physical presence will make a statement.*

She found out where the Outdoor Adventure Program was housed from the Information Center. There was a receptionist on duty, and she asked to be directed to Troy's office.

"He should be free soon. Would you like a seat?" The receptionist said.

"Yes. Thank you." Benita said.

She checked the messages and social media apps on her phone. After several minutes, the receptionist stepped away. What appeared to be students began to file out of the office followed by a smiling Troy. His smiled faded when he saw Benita.

Troy decided whatever was going to happen should be kept private.

"Would you come in?" He pointed to his office with his whole hand, a gesture of hospitality. His tone was not cordial.

Benita entered his office but didn't sit down.

"Troy. I am sorry for what happened. I didn't know you were coming, and with Rex?"

Troy looked pained. He finally spoke. "I wish you had never mentioned her. I had to admit to Rex what you suspected. I had no idea you were friends with her, but there's no explanation that makes this right between Rex and I."

Benita paused before responding. "I know. It's the same distrust you feel for me right now. Does it help you to see there was no betrayal in this situation? Not on my part and not on yours."

Troy countered. "I told you not to pursue it."

Benita corrected him. "I didn't pursue her identity, but we had plans together before you said anything."

Troy said, "If you hadn't told me about your suspicions, it still would be a disaster, but--"

Benita interrupted. "Just for me, not for you." She waited a moment as her guilt turned to anger. "I thought we could talk this through, but it appears to me our relationship isn't as much a priority as your need for innocence. You could have called. Though there won't be another opportunity, don't try to surprise me again!" Benita was becoming loud.

Troy countered. "I did call. You didn't pick up, so I left a message."

Benita looked at her phone.

Troy spoke again. "Not your cell; the landline."

I guess I haven't checked the landline since Aunt Dilly called.

"We were outside." Benita's tone was sheepish this time.

They looked away from one another. Troy was silent, and Benita couldn't think of anything to say.

She walked out of his office never having taken a seat. She paused in the reception area searching for another avenue of conversation to pursue, but she was lost for options. She left.

Chapter Fifty

Is that Pala? Benita parked the car expecting Pala to disappear as soon as she heard her car. Benita walked to where Pala was picking strawberries.

Benita spoke. "I didn't expect to see you. I want to apologize for yesterday."

"I didn't expect to see you either. I thought you were spoken for most afternoons, though I didn't know why. I guess I should have asked."

"I arranged an exchange of duties for the summer with Maren Scott. I'm teaching her creative writing course and she's reviewing manuscripts at my literary agency in Miami." Benita said. "My initial idea was for my location to be undisclosed for the summer; at least while at The Havens. And to be low-key at Clear Lake. Events made it impossible, but I still kept up the ruse for no good reason."

"So, you know what it's like to be exposed."

"To an extent."

Pala returned to the strawberries and changed the subject. "I just want to pick the ripened strawberries and leave them at the church. There was no service last night. But people still come by and check to see if anything is available."

"You're such a giving person." There was no response from Pala, so Benita continued, "I had no intention of letting Rex know where you are. And I wasn't sure about your identify anyway. As far as I was concerned, it was a wild hunch." Benita was sincere in her admiration of Pala.

"You suspected, right?"

"It seemed like a silly notion after talking to Troy."

"Troy? That's your boyfriend?"

"Was my boyfriend, and yes, but he dismissed it as far-fetched."

"He was as surprised as I was?"

"Both of them were. I don't think things will ever be the same between Troy and me. He feels so guilty about his part in it."

"What about their showing up like that? I don't know about Troy, but it's not like Rex to be part of a surprise."

"Troy called on the landline. We were outside by then."

Pala sucked air in through her teeth. "What a disaster."

"We all agree on that. I apologized to Rex. I teach in the classroom across from him. He wasn't a fan of mine from the start. But he was helpful during one of my emergencies."

"Not unusual. Well, I'm not gonna hide from you or from him. If he hasn't gotten the message I don't want a relationship with him by now, he never will. He puts a high premium on trust. I won't earn that back, and I don't want to try."

"I know this has opened up old wounds. Is there any chance we can still do things together? An afternoon on the lake could be fun. Healing, even?"

Pala stood up from her task. She looked at Benita. "Got an extra bathing suit and maybe ideas for a spotter?"

"Now?"

"Why not?"

"Why not indeed!" Benita was in.

Benita gathered the selection of bathing suits Adele kept on hand for guests who wanted a spontaneous swim. There were basic tankinis in a few different sizes, but as close to one size fits all as any garment could be. While Pala was sorting through, Benita called the neighbors landline. "Would Jasmine or Benny like to spend the afternoon boating?" She supposed she was talking to Ardelia.

"Benny is off with friends, but I will be right over on my bike." Benita was talking to Jasmine, as it turned out, who checked it out with her mom and was on her way.

Benita changed while Pala went to the carriage house to gather the equipment. She was in the driver's seat of the boat when Benita appeared followed by an excited Jasmine.

"May I go first?" Jasmine asked.

"Sure. There are only three of us. You have to navigate the skis and rope solo!"

"I know."

Jasmine put her feet in the skis on shore and waded with the cumbersome skiis out to where it was a bit deeper. She picked up the rope, the boat inched forward until the rope was taut, and she was up at full throttle. Pala pulled her several times around the lake when Benita gave her the sign for one more circuit. She let go of the rope and arrived near the shore as if a pro. She sank in slow motion and got in the boat to spot for Pala to ski while Benita drove.

All three had skied when they decided to swim. Characteristic of mountain lakes in the Adirondacks, the lake was clear and beautiful. A solar motor on the boat helped to keep it that way.

It was dinner time when they put away the paraphernalia and sauntered toward the house to change into dry clothes. Benita eyed the strawberries Pala left on the counter in the kitchen.

"Those strawberries would taste good on some fresh biscuits. Suppose we can commandeer them?" Benita's mouth was watering for strawberry shortcake.

Pala looked at the strawberries for a moment, looked around, and then slipped a couple of quarts to Benita. "You take yourself those strawberries."

They laughed, both getting the reference to the banana in the tailpipe caper in *Beverly Hills Cop*.

Benita changed and returned to the kitchen to prepare a biscuit mix. She had the dough rolled out and was about to cut the dough with a biscuit cutter when Pala returned. Pala helped put the biscuits on a baking sheet and while they baked, they hulled the strawberries and prepared them to spoon onto the hot biscuits.

Jasmine emerged long after the others from a changing room in dry clothes.

Benita told her they were making strawberry shortcake. "You're welcome to have some. Will it spoil your dinner?"

Jasmine quipped. "I hope so. Do you know what we're having for dinner? Tuna delight. Ugh!"

They made small talk with Jasmine while waiting for the biscuits. They knew she was witty but found her particularly funny when she described her hatred of rural life and the insignificant school district. Though the district encompassed four towns, she complained, "We only have one traffic light in the whole district, and it's blinking!"

Benita and Pala laughed. Before long there were oohs and ah's about the luscious snack. The telephone interrupted their private strawberry celebration.

"Hello. Yes, Jasmine's still here." Pause. "Okay. I'll send her right home."

"At least now I won't starve! Thanks for inviting me."

"Our pleasure. Thanks for your help!" Benita walked her to the door.

She returned to find Pala placing the dishes in the sink. Pala picked up the other two quarts of strawberries and said goodbye. "I have just the family in mind for the remaining strawberries."

"Thanks for not ghosting me, Pala."

"I'll adjust. It wasn't your fault. Thanks for the fun." Pala was off.

Troy and Rex are the ones who need an adjustment.

Chapter Fifty-One

"We are ready to publish chapter four! Wahoo!" Jake was more animated than normal.

They're still punchy from the holiday, and it's Friday to boot.

Benita completed the preliminaries for the start of class, and they went over the fourth chapter.

Secret Trust - Chapter 4

Attorney Brady tasked Stiles with driving Isaac back to Flint Loch Corners. Isaac thought of another idea after a few minutes on the road.

"I need an ID in order to work with Mr. Brady, and I don't have it with me," he told Stiles. "I can't go to the clerk in Flint Loch Corners because they'll tell my mom."

"Ouch. What kind of a town do you live in?" Stiles scowled.

"The worst, or the best, or both."

"So, what's your idea?" Stiles was willing to give him a narrow berth.

"I was born in the town that serves as the county seat. Let's try that."

"I'm game. Just give me the directions."

Isaac walked into the clerk's office and waited for a couple of patrons ahead of him. When a ten-dollar bill was presented, he realized he had no money. He hurried back to Stiles. She opened the window to the passenger's side. "What now?"

"I don't have a cent. I'll need ten dollars." He had his hand out as he asked.

"Buddy, you are a piece of work. I don't know what's going on, but Brady said you might ask and fronted me a hundred dollars in twenties. I thought you were Mr. Money Bags, so you'd better be good for it." Stiles handed him the money.

"Thanks. I am good for it. Promise. I think …" His voice trailed off and he ran back to the office to stand in line.

"May I help you?" It was his turn, and the clerk asked the question of him.

"Yes. I would like a copy of my birth certificate."

"Fill out this form and present a picture ID." She might as well have been a robot.

"I need the birth certificate in order to get an ID."

"I'm not giving whatever certificate you're asking for to just anyone who walks off the streets." Now she was just rude.

Isaac crumpled up the paper in his hand, threw it in the trash, and left. He hadn't taken two steps past the door when he regretted creating even a minor scene. He didn't want any notoriety preceding his picture being splashed all over the media.

He opened the door with force and dropped into the passenger seat. Before starting the car, Stiles inquired, "No luck?"

"You have no idea. I have no ID," he sneered. What a stinking vicious circle. Or was it a paradox? Literary terms failed him at this point.

Stiles began driving in the direction of Flint Loch Corners and asked the typical questions about obtaining an ID. He had all the answers since he had rehearsed them already with Brady the attorney. At Isaac's request, she deposited him at the Lake. He walked home from there.

"Where have you been, Isaac?" Muriel Anderson was waiting in the kitchen and was furious. "The Principal's office left a message and your Learning Center teacher called me at work. Why on earth would you miss the first day of your senior year?"

"I went to the Lake instead of school."

"Isaac. What are you talking about?"

"I wasn't feeling well enough for school, but I didn't need to stay in bed."

"You could have told me. You knew I would be called. I've been worried since before lunch."

"Did you come home from work early?"

"Yes. As soon as I could get away."

"I hope you didn't call the police?"

"No. Just half the neighborhood."

"Mom. Do you hear yourself? Calling the neighborhood about an 18-year-old!"

"Don't start. Isaac, don't you even start with that. You have another year of school, and I'm going to stay on you and make sure you don't mess up your life now."

You may not know it Mom, but we're about to start the biggest and longest fight of our lives. Before he voiced his mind, he thought better of raising additional suspicion. *Under the radar, bucko. Under the radar.* He mustered up his best fake smile and slathered it on. "Sorry, Mom. Really. I don't know what I was thinking. I guess I just dread being the oldest senior in the history of Flint Loch High." He gave her a kiss on the forehead. She was forceful, but just a tiny mite. He towered over her.

"You had me scared. Okay. I think I'll drive you to school tomorrow."

"Okay. Thanks. I hate riding the bus." He tried to put a positive spin on a situation that was circling the drain.

$$$$

And drive him to school is what Muriel did. He insisted she leave him a block away.

He was right about no sleep, and he trudged along exhausted from the time he spent searching for identification documents after his mom was asleep. His only success was eliminating places where they could be kept. He was about to enter school, when his cell phone rang. "Hello."

"It's Melvin Brady. Have you seen the news?"

"I didn't catch it this morning."

"Brook Crossings Convenience Store has been named as the seller of the winning ticket. I'll keep the news on, but I think it's just a matter of time before pictures are plastered on every screen in the region. There are about 250 million pseudo detectives waiting in the ranks to solve the mega-mystery."

"Thanks a lot."

"Were you able to get your social security card or your birth certificate?"

"I'm still looking."

"Did you ask?"

"Mom and I had a row last night. I thought it would raise too many questions. I'm trying not to drop too many clues. I'll try tonight. Maybe I can fake somethin' to do with a career program at school or college applications. I'm about to enter school."

"Good. Get your picture taken first thing."

Isaac lamented, "Yeah. I can't wait."

"Isaac, you don't sound good. Take care of yourself."
I'm not good. Isaac thought.

Chapter Fifty-Two

Miami

"Is there anything we can do to help you with your decision?" Maren's prospective rock-star historical fiction author had presented her with disturbing news.

"The firm that asked to meet with me is here in New York, and they have a long history of representing writers of fiction and authors of color. They have inroads with publishers with the most well-known imprints."

"I agree that it would be unusual if you didn't pursue the firm that you assume could provide the most book sales. Soto has a good reputation with publishers of fiction even if we're new to that market." Maren replied.

"I know. I've heard of Benita Sotolongo. I was wondering if I could meet with her?"

"I'll get back to you soon. Is that okay with you?"

"Yes. As long as it is soon. I'm meeting this afternoon with the other agents."

Maren dialed Benita with the hope that her cell would be in range. "Hi Maren. Everything okay?"

"It might not be. Our superstar is talking with another agent this afternoon." Maren told Benita about the agency.

"Oh. That's not good news. They're excellent. Truth? She's lucky. Is there anything we can do?"

"She knows your reputation. She wants to meet with you."

"She lives in New York?"

"Yes."

"Set it up for tomorrow morning, please. And I want you there. Keep track of your expenses, of course. I'll text you a hotel that is reasonable. Ask her if she can meet us there. I'll schedule a room for both of us and a conference room for our meeting. I'll get a coffee set up and pastries. All okay?"

"Yup."

Benita cleaned up the aftermath of her classroom session as she spoke, "Let me know if you hit a snag."

"You as well."

Maren made the contacts with the author and a flight for herself. She had to rush to get to the airport in time, and she told Kendrick and Celeste her plans as she hurried out of the door.

Kendrick didn't smile when he returned her goodbye.

***

Adirondacks

Benita was on her way to New York City by mid-afternoon, thanks to her wardrobe in Maren's apartment and Jasmine's willingness to take care of Rackie. She let her aunt know that she would be in the city and could drive her home if she would prefer that to riding with Rena. Adele wasn't home, so she left a voice mail message. She thought about sending a text as well, but it got forgotten in the havoc of other arrangements.

***

Adele left her White Plains home in a rush because her friend and ride, Rena, wanted to be present for last-minute guests at her summer home in the Adirondacks. Adele left a message at the Havens, where she arrived late on Friday evening. With no sign of Rackie or Beni, in that order, she called Maren's apartment.

As a last resort, Adele tried sending a text. "I'm at the Havens. Surprised you're not here. Everything okay?"

Benita was just returning from having a slice at Ray's. She loved their pizza and often ended up at one of the locations for pizza when in the city. It was a craving. She opened Adele's text as she was entering her hotel room. She furrowed her brow and crinkled her nose as she realized their messages had crossed. *We probably passed on the turnpike. How did she get a text sent from The Havens?*

She called Aunt Dilly on the landline on her walk back to the hotel, followed by a text sent to check on Maren's progress. Maren replied by text, "In the lobby now."

Maren and Benita had time to chat while waiting for the meeting the next morning. Benita was delighted with the help Kendrick had provided to Maren, but Maren cautioned her not to read romance into it. "It's an amicable work relationship. I doubt we'll achieve a full-fledged friendship."

"Well. At least you're not miserable together." Benita thought of her own love interest and their current relationship. "The idea of this exchange seemed genius, but I was insensitive to leave you alone in Miami after the debacle with Yvette, or whatever her names were, and Kendrick. I'm sorry. Do you ever wish you were in front of your students instead?"

"Truth?"

"Tempered truth."

"Every day!"

"Wow. Glad you didn't give it to me unvarnished! Do you want to bag it?"

"Do you?"

"I might, if you're willing." Benita briefed Maren of the fiasco on the Fourth of July.

"How fluky is that?"

"There are other terms for it, and I haven't resorted to any of them—yet."

"It must be as uncomfortable for you as it was for me with Kendrick."

Benita stared at her for a full minute. "I'm sorry. That is the exact situation I left you in, isn't it?"

"The prospect of working with this author will make it all worthwhile. Let's not look back." Maren did look at her watch at the end of her statement and added, "Wow, is she late! Do you think she skipped out on us?"

There was a knock on the conference room door, and Benita jumped up to answer. "Come in."

Their visitor introduced herself, and to their relief, it was the author they were courting. Their good feelings nose-dived when she spoke. "I just wanted to let you know in person that last night I signed with another agency. But thank you for your interest."

Without waiting for them to speak, she left.

Maren rested her temples in her hands, and Benita turned to her. She could just mutter, "I am so sorry. I know how much this meant to you."

Benita took a seat. There was nothing to say. Then she rallied, "Do you have any other good prospects?"

"Many."

"Any that live in the city?"

"I think. I'll log on and check."

Chapter Fifty-Three

Adirondacks

Adele grabbed her car keys and was about to pick up Rackie from the neighbors when the doorbell rang. She opened the door and recognized her caller, though she had never met him before. "Good morning. I'm thinking you must be Troy."

Troy dropped his head, looked back up and smiled. He hated the comparisons with the movie star, but he wouldn't hold it against a lady of Adele's age. "I am. And you must be Ms. Havens."

"Please, call me Adele."

"Okay."

"Come in. I've known about you for almost a couple of decades, though not always by name. It's good to meet you. Finally."

"How did you know about me?"

"A smitten teenager wandering around in a crush-induced haze for a week. I think she lost five pounds!" Adele looked like she might feel a little guilty for telling tales, so she added. "She confirmed it for me this summer, so it wasn't just my intuition."

Troy changed the focus. "Is Benita here?"

"No. I'm sorry. She's in New York meeting with a client."

"A client? From the agency?"

"Yes. I believe so. Have a seat. I haven't had my coffee yet. Would you like some?"

"Sure, I'll help you." Troy followed her into the kitchen. The china evoked the typical description of Hidden Havens over the years. "From the mid seventeen-hundreds until the beginning of the twentieth century, Hidden Havens was a stagecoach stop along the northern route to Plattsburgh, Montpelier and Canada. The carriage houses stored extra wagon parts and small replacement wagons and a stable for horses. Fresh horses were needed every ten or fifteen miles.

"Hidden Havens was busy in those days because of the guest rooms and large tavern for travelers requiring a meal or overnight accommodations." Adele and Troy carried their coffee into the tavern room. "This is the same table used in the days of the stagecoaches. And it was helpful in the heyday of summer guests too. We seldom have many guests now, though." The table appeared as something out of the world of knights, with its twelve-foot length and heavy, dark boards. "The fireplace and hearth still can be used for heat and cooking."

She walked to the original glass covered built-in cabinets, which housed the pewter used during the early days of the tavern, as well as the china fashioned after the Lenox presidential plates of the late nineteenth century.

"After the first world war, Hidden Havens was used for the summer season for entertaining friends and family on holiday. The Waterford crystal only dates to mid-century when the plant reopened after a hundred-year hiatus in manufacturing."

"Is it still in use?"

"A lovely table gives me such a lift. Yes. I use everything except the pewter. I have so few large dinner parties. But my friends and I enjoy the crystal and the fine china when we have luncheons and informal dinners. I think it strikes millennials as odd, but to us it conveys respect and enjoyment of our guests.

"Let me show you the guest rooms." They went through the foyer up the stairs that rose from the foyer and took a right turn after a few steps. At the top of the stairs was a landing with an adjacent hallway leading to a large bedroom on the left. It contained a canopy bed and antique bureaus. The walls were finished with large board panels original to the building. There was a small fireplace and mantel.

"My husband's grandmother redecorated the house in the French country style in the 1940's. The original boards were uncovered in the nineties when the house was restored to its original décor. Much of the furniture had been stored in the carriage houses and was refurbished to use in the house once again."

They proceeded to a hallway that took a right turn where the four stagecoach room doors were visible, each one with a number. Adele opened the door to number one. It was small; just enough room for a single bed, nightstand, and small bureau. There was another large bedroom to the right. It contained a sleigh bed, a peddle sewing machine, and antique dressers. The room also contained a fireplace, and Troy was sure he counted at least five in the house, including each of the two parlors.

The tour was completed, and they were descending the enclosed, paneled staircase to the foyer when the doorbell rang. Adele opened one of the double doors to find Jasmine and Rackie.

"Hello Jasmine, and my Rackie." She patted Rackie, who didn't know what to do in the excitement of being reunited with her and the house. He defaulted to making quite a racket, sniffing toes, and trotting around the house. When his excitement subsided, he found his bed and settled in feeling no need to entertain the guests.

Troy and Jasmine were introduced, and Troy excused himself. "Thank you for the tour and the coffee. It was a pleasure meeting you both." Troy left under the impression that Benita had returned to work at Soto. There was no evidence of her belongings. Of the two large bedrooms, the only one occupied contained obvious evidence of Adele's possessions. The other resembled a showcase with no personal belongings visible.

"Please, come again Troy." Adele was a little distracted between arriving and parting guests.

Chapter Fifty-Four

New York City

Maren arranged meetings with three more aspiring authors; one on Saturday evening and two on Sunday. There was time enough before and between authors for Benita to read most of the manuscripts. "I remember the pitch for this book, *"ReDefining Love."* She was reading a manuscript requested from the mother of a baby boy born with muscular dystrophy. "Even the pitch had me in tears. And her ancient quote from one of Job's comforters sets up her 'journey journal" in such a poignant way: 'Men of ease have contempt for misfortune as the fate of those whose feet are slipping.'

"It may be a targeted market but imagine how this will resonate with parents of special needs children. How in a different way they must define the success of their children—and how they must push down the pain caused by social media that harkens beauty, physical and academic prowess, and life achievements."

She recalled the pitches from the other two manuscripts as well. One was a middle age fantasy about a boy whose premonitions each evening inform him on each occurrence of bullying, by students, staff and faculty, in his school. His superpowers allow him to film each of the infractions for replay on his podcast—protecting the identity of the victims.

The novel, "Instant Replay," was written by a seventy-five-year-old former planning room monitor in a middle school. She worked with students to plan the reparations necessary for re-entry to the mainstream after they received sanctions for their misdeeds in school. Her insights into the numerous bad calls in the discipline of students and the strengthening of the power base of bullies was witty, sad, and at times, hilarious; especially as the authorities try to unravel the identity of the vigilante.

Benita agreed that Maren's choices were solid; not as edgy as the one that brought them to New York, but there would be other opportunities. "I wish every author the best, and if that isn't with our agency, I hope it redounds to their increased success." She tried to reassure Maren of the vagaries of the literary world.

"I thought only authors experienced rejection. I guess it happens at all levels!"

The interviews were successful, and they had plenty of time to enjoy the attributes and quirks of each writer. "It's typical for interviews to be set up in rapid order, so this was a luxury." Benita persisted in seizing teachable moments even though unsure whether Maren would remain invested in the agency. "Have you decided whether you want to press on in Miami?"

"Have you decided whether you want to press on with the students?" Maren mirrored her question.

"Oh, I love working with the students. It's just awkward with Rex and Troy. We don't have to un-exchange, though. I think Dirk could finish up with the summer session. The kids have this. So, what do you think?" Benita was thinking about who, if not she or Maren, would continue with the authors who had just signed contracts.

"I'm going to stay with it. I've learned a lot," Maren said.

"I think I'll stay in the Adirondacks. Either of us can change our minds. Deal?" Benita was relieved and wanted both to have an escape clause.

"Deal!"

There was knock on the conference room door late on Sunday afternoon as they were gathering their laptops to exit.

Maren was closer to the door. "Oh. Hello." It was the author responsible for their trip to New York City.

"Hi. I've reconsidered. Is your offer to represent me still valid?"

Benita said nothing and let Maren field the questions. "Yes. Of course. I still have a hard copy right here." She shuffled through the papers with her back to the author. Maren glanced at Benita and made a surprised facial gesture. Benita's face was visible to the author, so she remained poker faced.

Maren turned toward their guest with the contract and questioned her. "May we know why you changed your mind?"

"I was being impetuous going with that huge agency. I suspect you provide more personal support, and that's important. I'm so glad you're still here and still willing to work with me."

"But we haven't chatted or given you our pitch!" Maren said.

"Maren and Kendrick spent a long time with me already. You showed up, and you stayed to meet with others. That's stability and commitment. I'm in." She was signing the contract as she spoke.

"Since we're here, let's talk about next steps." Maren was on fire.

They planned and initiated contacts for the next two hours.

Maren sent a text to Kendrick. "Signed our 'big fish' and three others. I'll be back tomorrow."

Chapter Fifty-Five

Adirondacks

Benita waited until early on Monday morning to drive from New York City to Clear Lake School. Students were lively and enthusiastic but not showing the extremes of activity and lethargy as they had presented in the aftermath of the holiday. It was fun listening to their varied weekend experiences before getting down to work on the latest chapter.

"We're going to have Isaac do something unethical in his desperation. Do you think that's okay?" Aaron wanted to be cautious.

"Describe it for me." Benita said.

Jake spoke up and told her their specific plans.

"Okay. As long as we clarify somewhere in the piece that we don't support that kind of a reaction, even when the situation is drastic."

Secret Trust - Chapter 5

A lucky break. Because winning the lottery obviously wasn't lucky enough. Isaac thought. The selective service documentation arrived that day, and Isaac was the first to arrive home. Trouble was, if he returned to the county clerk's office after acting out yesterday, they would be sure to remember him when his mug shot appeared on every news outlet. He could use it to get set up with the lawyer. Or he could at least check. He hit redial from the number this morning.

"Birney-Finn-Lansner & Rockney. This is Attorney Brady's office."

"Hi Alma. This is Isaac. Is Mr. Brady there?"

"Uh, hold on."

"Isaac. What's the good word?" Brady was very informal this time.

"I had my picture taken at school. I told them to put a rush on it, and then I acted as though I was just kidding with them. But I got my selective service notice. Is that good enough to get started with you?"

There was a pause. "I would rather you get your birth certificate or, better yet, a picture ID."

"I need four methods of ID to get a real ID from the RMV." Isaac was desperate. "Maybe the school will have it ready for tomorrow."

"That would be good. After that, we're facing a weekend. Documents won't be available, but the news cycles will roll on." Brady was trying to be helpful; nothing was.

Isaac continued to tear through the files in his house and, at last, had success. Only partial success. *This is a key to a safety deposit box. Is Mom so retentive that she keeps things in a safety deposit box?* He couldn't accept that, and he kept looking. Nothing. He was ready to give up. He thought of calling his dad, who lived in California. He might know something about the documents. *That's no answer.*

His mom had portabella mushrooms in a balsamic marinade in the fridge. He grilled them outside when his mom arrived, and they ate them in hamburger rolls with a side of potato salad his mom had picked up at the deli. They ate in silence. Isaac soon dismissed himself to do homework and fell asleep on top of his comforter.

He slept through the night, though it was early when he awoke. Despite walking to school, he arrived before the first bell and waited in the Learning Center. As usual, Ms. Meyers, his Learning Center teacher, was there. She greeted him. "Hi, Isaac. You're here early. Did you have questions about any of your assignments?"

"I have some to finish up. That's why I'm here. I'll let you know if I need help. Thanks."

"Sure. I'm just going to get a cup of coffee before the bell rings. I'll be right back."

I can't. I can't look in the files. That's so not me. He couldn't help himself. He had seen her go to the files often to review goals and leave notes. Most everything was online, but she was the kind of teacher who was present with students, not in her office on the computer. She slipped notes in the files for data entry later.

He opened the drawer for his section of the alphabet, found his file and rifled through. It was there. An unofficial copy of his birth certificate. *I don't know why, but it's here!* He made a copy of the copy, slipped it in his pocket and the school's copy back in his file. Then he left.

Once outside, he dialed the attorney before he realized the office wouldn't be open yet. He put his phone away and headed for the Lake. By then, he was sweaty and tired. He could waste money on a taxi or call for advice. He called for advice.

"Hi Isaac. What's the good word? Did you get your ID from school?"

"No. But I have an unofficial copy of my birth certificate."

There was a long pause. "Ok. It's not perfect. But I'm going to make it enough for me. When can you get here?"

"Officer Stiles gave me just enough money for a taxi the other day. Should I spend it?"

"It's unbelievable we're having this conversation. Yes. I'll see you when you get here. I'll let Alma and Dolly know to expect you. I'll have food waiting. You probably haven't eaten today."

"How'd ya guess?"

$$$$

It was mid-morning when Isaac's arrival was announced at the seventh floor. Alma sent him right in.

His first act was to dive into the breakfast burrito while Brady punched some numbers on the computer. He used the napkin a final time and moved his chair closer to Brady's desk.

"Now what should we do?" Isaac felt as though he was pushing a rope.

"I think we should turn in the ticket under the blind trust and hope no one will bother with the pictures if we do that. For some reason, the curiosity loses its luster, and the store, in typical fashion, welcomes the singular focus."

"Okay, but won't I have to decide on the payout?"

"You will. Yes."

"So, this is it?"

"Yes." There was no need for Brady to elaborate.

"Give it to me straight."

"Therein lies the challenge. There's not much that's straight about it. Come around and I'll give you an overview and show you some figures." Isaac brought his chair around the desk. Brady continued. "Here are the known entities. This is your lump sum; this is your thirty-year annuity."

"Wow. The annuity seems good."

"Here is the current tax situation, federal and state. Here are the variables. You will always be in the top tax bracket. If that is lowered and stays lower, the annuity is better, in most cases. If it increases, the lump sum presents as a better option. Prevailing wisdom says that if the rate of investment return remains at four percent or higher, the lump sum is better. If it drops, the annuity could be better."

"Most people say go with the annuity, don't they?"

"Yes. You hear that from people on the streets."

Isaac looked at him askance. "That's where I got most of my information. I've heard a lot of conversations. Why? What do you think?"

"You were as prepared as anyone I've seen. Well, except for the whole adulting thing." Brady chuckled. "You may not want to hear this, but every way I work the figures, I find the lump sum is better. The money upfront will earn you a ton of additional money."

"Yeah. And I'll be all set even if the lottery commission goes under."

"Yes. Along with the bank burning down." Brady scowled and then softened his tone, "Isaac. With this amount of money, with help, direction, planning and restraint, I don't see how either decision can be a wrong decision."

"I've heard you're supposed to take all of the time you can before cashing in."

"You can. If you want to. You're young enough so that the money will have many years to work for you. But you can cash in and not spend while you take a year or more to plan. You don't appear to have ready cash. Why not start to enjoy the money?"

"People will suspect if all of a sudden I have money."

"Restraint will take care of that. It's good practice for the ensuing years anyway. And any charitable contributions will be in the name of the blind trust."

Chapter Fifty-Six

Miami

"What does Maren think she's doing with four new clients?" Polly was the latest to pick at Kendrick about Maren's involvement in the agency.

"It just happened, and Benita was with her when they all signed on. Is this a problem?"

Polly thought for a minute and couldn't pinpoint what was bothering her. So, he spoke again, "Are you getting good manuscripts? Is there anything I can do?"

"No. I guess I'm just in a slump since vacation. I'm feeling a little jealous."

"Well, I'm glad you can admit it. I think we're flooded with new work. Keep at it."

Polly left his office just as the CFO, Jett Fellows, entered. "Kendrick. Have you seen the numbers on this app that Benita launched this spring?"

"Not in the last few days. What's up?"

"It's hotter than the 'Sara Hari'!" Jett used a distorted name for the famous desert.

"Good. I thought so."

"You're too calm. Look at these numbers."

"Oh. I see what you mean. Does it generate much in revenue?"

"Yeah, some. But I think Benita's class should start charging for chapters. It isn't expensive for the fans, and it's so popular."

"I can talk to her about it. I think it's a good idea."

"Good. If you don't, I will."

"Are you angry?" Kendrick was confused by Jett's intensity.

"I'm just tired of being the only one who thinks about money."

"You aren't." Kendrick didn't wish for a fight, but it was a burden that was never far from the minds of anyone in the business. Even Benita, who hid her concerns well. "I'll be in touch with her today. Just cool your jets, Jett." It was a joke that was used too often, and Jett scowled as he left the office without voicing his thanks.

A steady stream of folks filed into Kendrick's office, and Maren was next. "Kendrick, I have publishers for two of the folks I met with over the weekend."

"What? That's too soon, isn't it?"

"We had talked to a few about the long hot summer piece, and the woman who journaled her daily inspiration about her son had a blog and was well known. I just wondered if you would review them with me and be with me when I present them to the authors."

"Ah, sure. I'll make time. When?"

"Now?"

"Sure. I just want to send a text to Benita about her students' novella. Anything I should add?"

"A quick note about what we're about to do?"

"Done."

***

Adirondacks

Benita picked up her telephone as the students noisily exited her classroom on Tuesday afternoon. They had published

Chapter 6 to her surprise. The paragraphs rolled out of their imaginations like a burst dam.

There was a text from Kendrick she knew was inevitable. Jett wanted more remuneration for the successful publications on the new app. Especially the *Secret Trust*. She took a deep breath to think about it, as she had many times.

"We're going to have about fourteen chapters. Why don't we charge for the second half to current followers and the whole thing for new subscribers? Oh, and glad to hear about the success in gaining publishers." She hit send, and another popped up. From Kendrick. He couldn't have read her response.

"A publisher wants to publish *Secret Trust* in print and digital formats???"

She waited for him to read her first response, and then sent another text. "Only if they let us finish the book on the app."

"I'll see. And congratulations."

"Thanks. It is good news. Just complicates things ... but in a good way."

She checked her computer and realized the students failed to push publish for chapter 6, so she did.

Secret Trust - Chapter 6

"Do we have time to get this done today?" Isaac had made his decision.

"Are you going for the blind trust and the lump sum?" Brady wanted to be sure.

"Yes."

"Let's go."

"Where?"

"I'm going to arrange for our White Plains branch to turn it in to the Lottery Commission Service Center in Plainville. It might throw off the scent from the Flint Loch area. We need to get going. They're alerted already. I have a draft for you to read in the car and a draft of my role as executor."

Traffic was the typical Friday afternoon nightmare on the Thruway, but the ticket was rescued from the safety deposit box, and the duo arrived in White Plains by two in the afternoon. Brady had a key for a service elevator, and they knocked on a locked door on the penthouse floor of the building without seeing anyone. The locked door was answered by the imposing figure of Wilson Rockney, who shook both of their hands as he introduced himself to Isaac.

"Congratulations, Mr. Anderson. We have the blind trust ready to be signed after we discuss any amendments you want to suggest, and then the ticket can be off to the Commission for disbursement of the funds. What is the name of the trust?"

"What are my options?"

"Myriad!" Rockney was a jolly gent. "What is important to you, and how can you create a name from that and still remain anonymous?"

"School is never out, is it?" Isaac was flustered.

"Complain, complain," Brady said in gest.

For the first time since the saga began, Isaac burst out laughing. The attorneys joined in.

"Can you give me examples?"

"No." The attorneys answered in chorus.

"Okay. May I use a tablet or computer?"

Mr. Rockney handed a tablet to Isaac. "What terms are you considering?"

"Well, I thought about Mountain Time Summit. I also thought about a mashup of epic and cash ... Epicash."

Brady was thoughtful. "Well, the Mountain Time reference will throw off the local meddlers, and a portmanteau is creative. Any other thoughts?"

"I wanted to think about Nouveau Riche. You know, from Gatsby?" Isaac was busy using a search engine the whole time. "I think this is what I want. "Paysan Parvenu."

"As in Pierre de Marivaux? Le Paysan Parvenu? The unfinished series?"

"Yeah. How do you know about it?" Isaac was impressed with Mr. Brady now more than ever.

"I'm not a scholar of the work, but I was an undergraduate literature major. How about you?" Brady was also impressed with his young client.

"I confess, I only found it when researching Gatsby."

"I like it. **Paysan Parvenu Association Trust.**" Brady said.

"Let's get this going." Rockney called his secretary, and within a short amount of time, the document was ready for signature, and the accompanying paperwork for the Lottery Commission was ready to be delivered.

Rockney dismissed the duo. "I'll have the head of security deliver this as my agent right away. Would you be willing to incur the cost of a helicopter, sir?"

"Sure," though Isaac's answer sounded unsure.

"Great! Please, exit the way you came, and no one should know you were in the building. You two can work out the details of Mr. Anderson's contract with the firm when you return to the Capital Region. It was a pleasure meeting you, Mr. Anderson. The best of luck. I think you have a good start by virtue of that ticket, young man. If I could offer one word of advice, it would be 'moderation'."

"As in the use of helicopters?" Isaac didn't intend to sound sassy, but he did.

Again, the attorneys laughed.

$$$$

Brady broke the silence that characterized the return trip. "I'll drive you to Flint Loch Corners. I promise to be in touch as soon as the funds are disbursed. In the meantime, here are a few hundred in advance and a debit card."

"Thanks. I really need to get a job."

"That is the most peculiar statement I've heard from a lotto winner."

"I was broke, and I worried that my mom would wonder what happened to my birthday money. Now I have more money than I can justify to her. So, a job would be a good front."

"Understood. Begin your spending with a real phone and get a ridesharing app."

"Okay."

"It's all going to work out, Isaac. Soon you'll have so many opportunities open to you. Spend the weekend reflecting on your values and let your values drive your use of the funds. Not the other way around."

"I will. When are we going to discuss your payment? Do you take a percentage?"

"Isaac, that was part of the agreement we signed. And, no. If you, for some reason, hire a different attorney, do not let them charge a percentage. My retainer is the same for you as for any other client. When that is gone, I'll bill you by the hour, which is $250 per hour. I hope that is acceptable?"

"I can't believe I'm beginning to think this way, but it seems like peanuts compared to the amount of money we've been talking about."

$$$$

It was late when Isaac arrived home. He realized he was about to go from Cloud 9 to the torture of Gollum. But Muriel wasn't home. The light on the answer machine was blinking. He pushed the button. "Hi Isaac. It's Nora. I didn't see you in school again today, but you weren't on the absent list. Call me. Please."

Isaac erased the message. He hadn't seen nor spoken with Nora—if he was lucky, he could call her his girlfriend--for three days. Winning the lottery was an amazing turn of events, but not thinking about Nora was a close second. Prior to Wednesday, he was obsessed with her. *Am I still?* He felt numb.

Chapter Fifty-Seven

Adirondacks

Adele greeted Benita at the door with a hug when she returned to Hidden Havens in time for a late dinner on Tuesday evening. "I was beginning to think you weren't coming back! I think that hunky boyfriend of yours was under the same impression."

"Troy? When did you talk to Troy?" Benita perked up at the mention of Troy, even in her exhaustion.

"I kept thinking I would talk to you and let you know. But I've been outside each time you called. Thank you dear for letting me know about your plans to stay in New York. Oh, and Troy came here last weekend. The morning after I arrived at home."

"What did he say?"

"I'm afraid I did most of the talking. Gave him the grand tour. I told him you were in New York City. I didn't give a proper goodbye to him as Jasmine arrived with Rackie. He was polite and said goodbye but was off rather fast. I told him I was sure you would be in touch." There was a silence while Benita considered the implication of his visit. Aunt Dilly sensed something was amiss. "Is there something wrong?"

"Aunt Dilly. I'm so ashamed to tell you what I did."

"It can't be that bad. You didn't murder anyone, did you?" It was Aunt Dilly's attempt at levity.

Benita gave the quickest version of disclosing Pala's identify to her husband. Aunt Dilly didn't want to add to her feelings of shame by having a long silence. She immediately responded.

"My goodness, dear. It wasn't your fault. But it must be one of the best plots ever! Does life imitate art or what?!"

"I can't believe this summer. Now Troy feels guilty about his part in keeping it from Rex, and I thought he had given up on me. I don't know what his appearance here means."

"It can only mean he wants to see you. A little time was all he needed."

"I'm not so sure, Auntie."

After a pat on Benita's arm, Aunt Dilly left the east parlor to answer the ringing telephone. "Yes, she's right here."

"Who is it?"

"He says it's Kendrick."

"Thanks." Benita tried not to show her disappointment. "Hello Kendrick. I've been away long enough to forget the evening hours. What's up?"

Little did she know what a frenzied afternoon it had been with Maren, the viral app, and the question of monetizing the app. "Jett performed one of his market tests and it shows that you wouldn't lose readership if you charged for the novella on the app. And the publisher is willing for you to use the app for everything except the last chapter."

"Oh. That seems rather mean to me, doesn't it to you?"

"In a way. But there's so much we don't know about an audience on this kind of app. A few thoughts. Let the subscribers know the plans—when the cost will occur and at what point it will be solely in print and e-books. After all, your students are clever. I'm sure they can have a wrap up before the ending. Maybe the last chapter is more along the lines of an Epilogue—of interest, but not central to the plot."

"I need to think about it, but you're on to something. I'll let the group decide and get back to you." Benita was amazed at Kendrick's quick thinking, and this wasn't the first time.

She rejoined Aunt Dilly in the parlor, who was worried more bad news had found Benita. "Is everything okay?"

"The best part of this summer are the students and that novella ... and the application we launched this spring. When I want to give up, that's what keeps me going."

"Have you built up an appetite for dinner?"

"Yes. I'm ravenous! What should we make?"

"There are Pad Thai Spring Rolls in the fridge all set to go. Let's sit at the counter and chow down."

"You don't want a fancy table?"

"I'm too hungry for all that falderal!" Aunt Dilly belied her claim to Troy that she loved the fancy place settings from the past century. "Maybe I'm beginning to understand the 'practical' in the practices of Millennials!"

Chapter Fifty-Eight

Adirondacks

Neither Troy, nor his placeholder, had sought her help for Tuesday's or Wednesday's activities. *I don't think Aunt Dilly's intuition that Troy wants to see me again has any merit. He knows where I am.*

She turned her attention to getting class started and sharing the good news of success with **Secret Trust**.

Brynn was thrilled. "Wow. I think our publicity paid off! Think of all the people reading what we've written."

"That's 'cause it slaps!" Jake was close at hand.

There were other self-congratulatory comments, all deserved, when Benita asked the tougher questions.

Jake was first. "Dudes! We could be makin' money hand over fist. It's almost as good as a movie deal. Maybe we will get a movie deal."

Benita smiled while holding up her hands. "Hold on. This is good news, but don't let your expectations run too high. If we offend our followers, the whole effort could tank."

Wesley spoke up. "Put yourself in the place of the readers."

Some were willing to try, but they all found they were too biased.

"My head hurts. Let's not overthink this. If Mr. Kendrick thinks an epilogue is the answer, let's do what he says. He's been in the business the longest." Nikki added. "Okay, maybe we can think about it overnight. Right now, let's start writing!"

After a few drafts during the morning, Aaron looked toward Benita. "Wait 'til you see the literary device we used in this chapter. I think you'll like it."

These students are so sophisticated. "I think I have time. Let's get to it!" Benita read through the draft, it was proofread and edited by the students, and they were ready to publish.

Jake asked, "So, should we put out word that we'll charge for the next chapter?"

Riza had a suggestion. "Before we publish this chapter, let's create a blurb explaining the coming charges after two more chapters. We can also say we're happy to be working on a book deal."

Wesley was enthused. "Yeah. We can see whether there is an uptick in readers, a drop off, or whether access is flat. Then we have time to readjust the plan."

"I'm impressed, Wesley. Very well said. I should say I'm impressed by you all. So, what do the rest of you think?"

"Oh yeah. I'm impressed by us too!" Jake joked. "Oh, you mean about the blurb. Let's."

They collaborated on a statement to precede Chapter Seven.

Jake was the first out of the door. "Gotta blast!"

Secret Trust – Chapter 7

By seven in the evening on Friday, Isaac was worried about his mother. She always called when she was going to be late. *Is there something I've forgotten?* Isaac thought. She always told him where she would be and when to expect her. *So, this is what she went through when I was missing.*

All of a sudden he wanted to talk to Nora. What will I say? Isaac questioned himself. I need to apologize. He dialed her home and got the answer machine. "Hey. It's Isaac. Sorry. Call." Then he sent a text with the same words.

I really need to talk to her. Imagine what she's been through, wondering where I am.

Isaac felt worthless. An eighteen-year old sped senior who was worthless. And a millionaire. He scoffed and said out loud, "All or nothing leaves nothing." *I am a nothing. I stole from my school records. I went behind the back of my favorite teacher. She's done nothing but help me. Probably my trust is illegal and everything. I used a stolen document to set it up with my lawyer. Probably my lawyer could be arrested for working with me.* He was tormented by guilt.

He thought about all the damage he had done by trying to keep this a secret. The secret was all about his selfishness and wanting to keep people away from his money and from having any expectations on him. *Why? What kind of a monster am I?*

He flopped down on the sofa and closed his eyes. For a moment, he thought about a different scenario. He imagined grabbing his ticket the morning after he bought it and comparing the numbers on the television screen. When he thought there was a match, he could have yelled at his mom. "Come quick. I need your help!"

"What is it? I need to be at work soon, and you need to get to school. I don't want you to be late for the first day of your senior year."

"We may not need you to work ... or for me to go to school, for that matter. Here, sit. Wait, the commercial is almost over."

"Why?" His mom was getting angry.

"I think I might have won the Power Lotto! I need your help to make sure."

"What? What are you saying! Are you kidding? Where did you get the tickets?

"I bought it yesterday at the convenience store when I bought the cola."

The news came back on, and the Chiron displayed the numbers as the newscaster chatted on about the weather forecast.

"Read the numbers to me Mom."

She did, and he still thought he was right. Isaac handed her the tickets. "Here, I'll read the numbers to you. And he waited for the Chiron to scroll to the numbers again. Muriel screamed. "It is! It's the winning ticket. Oh my ... oh my."

Muriel started dancing around the room holding the ticket. "Isaac, do you know what this means? Honey, we're millionaires. Millionaires!"

"What should we do next, Mom?"

"Let's call your father! He's going to be so sorry he left us. And your grandmother. Oh, what this is going to mean to her! And let's tell the school you can't come in this week. Why don't you run over and tell Nora? I'm going to call in to work and tell them where they can stuff that ole job."

With a start, Isaac awoke. He had dosed off. At once, he had a gnawing sense of dread one has after a bad dream as if the possibility it was true hovered like a dense cloud. Yet there was a feeling of relief that it wasn't true. *I may not have acted well in the last few days, but I was on the right track.*

The shrill of the landline startled him and he jumped up to see the caller ID displayed Nora's dad's name. "Hello."

"Isaac. Hi. So, where have you been?" Nora had an edge to her voice.

"Nora, I am so sorry I didn't tell you I wouldn't be at school. I promise I will explain, but some stuff came up. I didn't know it would be so complicated turning 18. It's complicated in divorced families. I'm glad you don't have to go through it."

"Is your dad giving you a hard time?"

"Not that. Just some things were in motion, and it's better to take care of them right away. I shouldn't have to miss any more days. Hey, I think I'm going to get a smartphone with some of the money I have from my birthday? Want to help me?"

"Sure. It's a little late to start this evening. What are you doing tomorrow?"

"Tomorrow's good. Have you had dinner?"

"Of course. You do know it's 8:30, right?"

"Nope. I didn't. I fell asleep. I haven't been sleeping all that well."

"That's bad. Hope it gets better."

"Wish I could see you."

"I know, but I've already been out tonight. I'm tired too. Let's plan on tomorrow."

"Breakfast and phone shopping?"

"Maybe that would be okay. Call me at nine."

"Thanks, night."

"Night, Isaac."

What a fool I was to ignore her. She's a little frosty. And who was she out with? Isaac was caught up in his reverie when he was startled by his mom. He blurted out an unfiltered, "Where have you been?"

"Where have I been? You have quite a nerve asking me that. In particular since I told you at the beginning of the week I was having dinner right after work with Jane Zapien. Then I needed some things for tomorrow. Isaac, what is up with you?"

"I think I'm getting senile in my old age or something." It was best to try and laugh it off. "My bad. What are you doing tomorrow?"

"I'm taking a bus tour to NYC. Zoe is going too. It's overnight. I told you this already too. But it was a long time ago. I tried to get Grandma to come and stay with you, but she can't. I guess you don't remember having a fit when I asked her."

"I remember now." Isaac's voice dropped.

"If I hadn't been so busy today, I would have arranged for someone to check on you. But I must get everything ready and then I'm headed for bed. The bus is leaving from the depot at 6:30. I think there are enough leftovers in the fridge to get you through the weekend. I'll be back by three on Sunday afternoon."

"I'll be okay. Nora and I are planning on breakfast out."

"How will you get to breakfast?"

"We can walk."

"I have too much to do to ask any more questions. I hope you'll be sensible." As she walked away, Muriel muttered to herself, "I always think these trips sound exciting when I make the plans, now I would just rather stay home."

Isaac more or less kicked up his heals as he pranced to his room. A weekend away from the watchful eye of his mother. He closed the door to his room. A thought seized him, and it felt as if every drop of blood was drained from his body; starting at his neck and spreading up and down. There seemed to be no air in his lungs. It occurred to him what the lawyer had said. Mugshots of possible winners would be broadcast in the region where the ticket was surrendered. It was the commission office serving New York City!

Chapter Fifty-Nine

The studentStringers continued to turn out chapters, and their followers continued to multiply. A publisher from a large New York City firm met with them a week after her initial contact with Kendrick. Benita reminded the students prior to the visit, "Ahem, Jake and everyone, you all are wordsmiths. There is no need to lapse into Gen Z jargon with our publisher."

Jake corrected Benita. "We haven't signed anything yet!"

But they did sign. And as the days passed, they continued to crank out **Secret Trust** after an announcement that the final chapter would only be available as trade paperback and an electronic version as well.

Secret Trust -Chapter 8

Isaac was still animated when he got ready for breakfast on Saturday morning. He sent a text to Nora. "Meet me at the Shady Grove?"

Nora replied by text. "Something came up. How about coffee at 11:30?"

Isaac was disappointed. He resisted the wave of guilt that threatened. *I did this. I've been such a jerk.* He took the high road. "Sure. Sounds good. Can't wait." He wanted to be a sweet and positive as possible. He owed it to her.

He used some of the cash Brady had given him and took a taxi to an area of town where he could find the best tech stores. He gave careful consideration before deciding on the first cell phone the guy from the tech force recommended.

He purchased a data plan, and the tech guy helped him set up some essentials for applications, including a ride sharing app. He had no idea how much money was on the debit card, and he was determined not to splurge, though, in the end, it was his money. Brady said Isaac's spending was being watched—monitored by Alma. Alma didn't have his identity, but she was tasked with reporting expenditures under a code name to Brady.

The cell phone was so much more money than his birthday money, so he would need to hide it from his mom. *I wonder how long I'll have to live like this.* He took an Uber home and searched the internet for the DMV Driver Manual. He downloaded a copy to his school tablet. Before studying, he took a practice test and passed. *I think I'll take the test on Monday afternoon. Oh no, Monday is a holiday.*

He checked his watch and saw that he had just time enough to meet Nora. He arrived first and got a booth. Just after he was seated, his old cell phone rang. "Hi Mom. Hope you're having fun."

Muriel shrieked without even offering a greeting. "Isaac. Did you know that the Brook Crossings Convenience store sold the winning Power Lotto ticket on the day we were there?"

"Oh. I meant to mention that. I saw that on the news."

"Are you kidding me? And I almost bought a ticket. If I hadn't been in such a hurry to get home to have your cake and ice cream, I probably would have. Oh my ... I just can't believe it. Of all the luck."

Coyly, Isaac couldn't help his curiosity. "Have they said who the winner is yet?"

His mother remained manic. Her voice was so loud, Nora could hear her when she arrived at the booth. "That's the thing! An anonymous trust has cashed it in. On Long Island. Someone from the city who happened to be passing through is my guess. They reported that the convenience store is going to review the surveillance tape. I hope they show it on television."

"Nice talk mom. Gotta go."

"Okay. Any trouble so far?"

"No. I'm as carefree as a baby."

"Right. Don't get into trouble. See you tomorrow."

Nora smirked. "I know who that was; the whole restaurant knows who that was. But what was it all about?"

"It doesn't need to be about anything. I don't think it sets well that I'm alone for the weekend. She actually wanted my grandmother to come and stay this weekend while she went to New York City."

"Ouch. I knew she was protective ... "

Isaac scoffed and changed the subject. "So, what do you want to eat?"

"Isaac, I'm not going to have anything to eat. I needed to do this in person. Not by text or telephone and not in school. I don't think this is working out."

She could have cuffed him and he would not have been more surprised. His chest was tight and painful. He couldn't find his voice and just stared at Nora with wide eyes. His voice was raspy as he said, "Is this about the last few days?"

"Maybe the last few days confirmed what I suspected. Most of the girls think you're super-hot and are jealous of me, but I don't think we're a match. Your mom doesn't let you do anything; you don't even have a license yet. This is the first time we haven't had to worry about her breezing in to check on us; but she did have to call!"

"That's going to change. All of it!" Isaac so wanted to tell her just how much things were going to change.

"How? Just how?"

She's the best thing that's ever happened to me. I won't let her go without telling her the truth. For a moment he considered what he had been thinking. *Was she better than winning the lottery? Why was he even comparing a person to a sum of money? I can't do this. Of all the things I let work themselves out during the last few days, this is the hardest.*

Nora stared at him for the longest time. Finally, she threw her napkin on the table, rolled her eyes, looked down and crawled out of the booth. "Sorry Isaac. Good luck."

Isaac wanted to call after her, but she exited in a burst, and he had no words. There was nothing he could think of to say that made any sense. He sat for a long time after she left. He was in a daze.

The waitress approached him after giving him a wide berth for several minutes. "Would you like to order?"

He had no appetite. To be courteous for occupying the booth, he asked for sweetened iced tea and a piece of blackberry pie. He surprised himself and ate every bite, paid the bill, left a substantial tip, and walked out. *I have the time, money and independence to do whatever I want. What do I want?*

Secret Trust - Chapter 9

On the walk home, he dialed his dad using the old phone. Otherwise, his dad might not recognize the number. "Hey Isaac. I've been expecting you to call."

Isaac had to think fast. He was hurt that his dad hadn't called him, even though it was his birthday that week. He tried to fake it. "Oh, why is that?" It sounded snooty to some degree.

"I told your mom to have you call after I didn't reach you on your birthday. Anyway, I wondered what you thought of your gift?"

"What call? What gift?"

His dad sounded perturbed. "You mean--I can't believe she didn't tell you I called."

"Why didn't you call my cell?"

"I don't know. I called the landline late afternoon."

"Oh. Well. Mom's been busy getting transportation for me to pick cucumbers in Brook Crossings the last few weeks before school started. She must have forgotten by the time we got home." Isaac was pushing words. He thought things were bad enough between his parents; he would do anything to prevent them from getting worse.

"What about your gift?" Harold Anderson was still miffed.

"I-don't-know-anything about a gift." Isaac couldn't think of any justification for that.

"Oh, for the love of Pete! I have an idea where you can find it. Your mom keeps important documents in the front of the garage. There's a fireproof box behind my old tools. Look there. I'll give you the combination."

"Is that invading her privacy?"

"It's mine too. We're not divorced, and I have things in there as well."

"If you say so." Isaac was still hesitant. He had arrived at home and proceeded to the garage, and his dad gave him instructions on opening the box. As he rifled through the box, he gasped. For the second time this week, he was the recipient of a windfall. This one didn't compare to the lotto, but there were eighteen mature bonds in his name. The grand total, eighteen thousand dollars! Not to mention the box contained a certified copy of his birth certificate and his social security card.

"Wow! Dad, are these from you? That is--I don't know what to say. Amazing! Thank you so much." Isaac was so impressed with his dad's generosity and foresight. *If he only knew. This is like carrying coals to Newcastle. But I'll more than make it up to him.* "Dad?"

"Yes." His dad was listening.

"What are you doing this weekend?"

"I have a few clients this afternoon, but nothing that I can't cancel."

"I want to come out for the weekend."

"I'll pay for your ticket, but what about traveling money? Will you use your cucumber funds? There's no place to cash the bonds until Tuesday."

Isaac's cucumber money in its entirety was given to his mom to pay for his driving course.

"Something like that." He supposed, at some point, he would stretch the truth so far it would snap back and bite him in the buttocks.

"I'll see if I can get you a reservation. I'm sorry, it will be cheaper if you fly back Tuesday. Is that okay?"

"I'll make the arrangements, Dad. Do you think I can fly without a picture ID?"

"I think we have a passport for you, don't we? Check the same box."

Isaac had wandered back into the house while chatting, so he ventured back out to the garage. His dad recited the combination once again. It took a few moments, but Isaac came up with a passport that wouldn't expire for three months.

"Here it is! This is amazing. Thanks, Dad. Are you sure it's okay?"

"I don't know what your mother will say."

"What will she say about an 18-year-old visiting his dad?"

"Right. I'll get right back to you if I can make arrangements."

"Dad. Let me. I have everything I need. I'll call you back." Isaac's implication was that he needed to grow up.

"Okay. Why don't you at least tell your mom?" Harold Anderson had learned many life lessons while living with Muriel.

"She would come home. Even if she has to take a taxi," Isaac said.

"Okay. But leave a note."

"I will." Isaac intended to do just that and only that.

Isaac got an Uber to the Capital Area International Airport. A flight was leaving at 3:30. He bought a return flight from Los Angeles for late Monday night arriving early Tuesday morning. He wouldn't miss school if the plan succeeded.

He was in the air when he realized he hadn't left a note for his mother. *I'll call and leave a message on the answer machine.* He hadn't slept well for days. He hated people who reclined their chair backs, but he fell asleep just fine while upright and wondering what Alma would think about the expenses he had incurred.

Secret Trust - Chapter 10

Harold Anderson arranged to fly out of Los Angeles to Big Sur soon after Isaac landed. They arrived late at night but arose early morning and rented a convertible to see the sites. Isaac was from the Adirondacks and thus thought he was inured to the thrill of great heights. But the impact of driving over the Bixby Creek Bridge brought a sensational combination of fear and amazement.

Later when they walked around Pfeiffer Beach, neither man could decide whether the purple sand or the stunning rock formations were more phenomenal. They spent until mid-afternoon on the beach, and then embarked on their return trip to Los Angeles. They traveled along the Pacific Coast Highway in the brilliant sun as the briny breezes of the Pacific Ocean provided the only air conditioning. There was no need for conversation; yet all five senses were filled with the excitement of the journey. No more was needed except just being together in this mind-blowing experience.

They arrived at his dad's apartment, which was just a studio, located in a large Mediterranean style building in the Los Angeles area. It was the middle of the night when they arrived, and they crashed as soon as they walked through the door; Isaac on the sofa and his dad on a bed behind a partial wall.

The morning sun was beaming in through the wall of windows on the east side of the studio and awakened Isaac. Neither man had remembered to pull the draperies closed before retiring. Isaac found the kitchen and poured himself a cold glass of milk from the refrigerator. His dad appeared from around the half-wall of his bedroom. He was disheveled, though smiling.

"I thought after all of the time in the car yesterday we'd walk along the Santa Monica pier today. What do you think?" Harold asked.

"I've always wanted to." Isaac then asked, "Do you like the Ferris Wheel?"

"I never thought about it. I guess we'd get a good view that way." His dad winked.

"Just what I was thinking."

"Let's grab a cup of coffee nearby and get going, then." Isaac's dad was in good spirits despite the lack of sleep. So was Isaac.

They had another beverage when they reached the Boardwalk—Harold a coffee and Isaac a Mock Mimosa. Included was a breakfast burrito, so they stopped at a café table and enjoyed the sights as they ate. Isaac imagined the Boardwalk was teeming with people at night, but right now it was serene. Very few people were around except those after some exercise. He determined the scenes from the media all were born out in what to him was surreal--runners, skateboarders and rollerblades. This was really happening.

They continued along the Boardwalk, and Isaac spoke first.

"I don't want to spoil my time here, but I have a lot of questions, Dad."

His dad turned to Isaac but kept walking. "I'm sure you do. Go ahead."

"Why did you leave?" It was just that basic. Isaac didn't attempt to couch it in soft terms.

"This job. It was what I was working toward all of my life."

"Was it more important than mom and me?"

"No. I can't justify what I did, but there is a history." His dad lowered his voice and continued. "Your mom was behind my plan and always voiced her willingness to go where the job took us. I think we spent longer than either of us anticipated in Flint Loch, and by the time this opportunity came along, I found out she was no longer willing to move. She used your education as an excuse; she didn't want to move you in your junior year; she didn't want you to adjust to another special education teacher, and so on. She had her arguments all lined up, and they were all about you."

"I remember telling both of you it was okay with me." It had only been a little over a year ago, and Isaac remembered the conversations well. At least, he thought he did. "But how did you decide to go anyway."

"I thought she would change her mind or that I could work here a couple of years and find something just as good but closer to you both. Son, it's what we call rationalization. I was peeved at your mom. Some time away from her seemed appealing,"

"From me too, Dad?"

"No. I came close to asking you to come with me."

"I would have."

His dad grabbed him around the shoulders from the side. Isaac noticed there were tears in his dad's eyes. They walked along in silence.

"Dad?"

"Yes?" Harold gave Isaac his full attention. He no longer was strolling.

On Tuesday, my birthday, I won the Power Lotto.

"Son?" His dad questioned Isaac when he didn't respond.

"Uh, I want to move out here for my senior year."

Secret Trust - Chapter 11

"School started over two weeks ago. You would be so far behind," Harold responded.

"Not private schools. I found a few that haven't started yet," Isaac countered.

"What about money? Private schools are expensive. And they have admission requirements."

"Don't worry about money. And we can call tomorrow morning and see if I can get in."

"I don't want you using your birthday money for high school. College, maybe. I wanted it to be a nest egg. We'll call the public schools and see how much there is to make up." His dad added, "What about your mother?" Harold grimaced.

"That part won't go well, even if the rest does." Isaac rolled his eyes.

"I want to tell her right away. What did she say when she got your note?"

Isaac raised his eyebrows and looked away while he spoke. "I didn't leave one."

"Isaac!" His dad raised his voice. "What? She must be furious."

"I sent a text."

Harold's face relaxed a bit. "Oh. Sorry I raised my voice. That was terrifying. What did she say?"

"She's been sending texts and calling. I haven't answered."

Harold scowled. "We're contacting her right now." He sent a text.

"What did you say?" Isaac was curious.

"We're going to talk face to face on Facebook."

He opened the app and waited. They were seated for the conversation and watched the activity while awaiting Muriel's call. Nothing happened, so they bought ice cream and strolled out to the pier and watched the surf. The ocean was entertaining, but the parasailers monopolized their attention until the call came.

Muriel appeared on the screen. She wasn't as frazzled as either man expected she would be, but she wasn't serene. "What's going on?" Muriel's question had more of an accusatory tone than an implication of curiosity.

"Muriel, please try to hear us out." Harold sensed how little time he had to explain. "Isaac has been through a lot the last few days. He asked to spend his senior year here."

He could have predicted her answer. "He needs to come home right now. What he's been through in the last few days is what he has brought on himself."

Harold resorted to the obvious. "He's eighteen, Muriel. We can't make him do anything. I just want him to finish his senior year."

Muriel adopted a full-on argumentative tone. "And how is he going to do that with any other teacher than Ms. Meyers?"

Harold wanted to avoid putting Isaac's special needs in the spotlight. "He will be as successful here as he has been in Flint Loch Corners."

"Oh, and you know so much about it, Harold. You, who took off on your family."

"I'm going to trust Isaac. We just wanted to let you know. We appreciate all you've done." He meant it. "You and I will talk about his birthday gift from me and my telephone call. But that will be at another time. Goodbye, Muriel." He hung up without a response.

Isaac spoke for the first time since the video began. "Thanks, Dad."

Harold pursed his lips. "This isn't over. That's for sure."

"What are you going to do?"

"Enjoy the rest of the day with you and let my office know I won't be in tomorrow. What do you want to do?"

"It's a long list. I'll let you pick."

"What are you interested in?"

"Architecture."

"Let's start there. Name something."

"Hollywood sign; Walk of Fame; Getty Center; Angel's Flight; Griffith Park and Observatory ..." Isaac could have continued, but Harold interrupted.

"Okay. Let's arrange them geographically, start with the closest, and see how much we get done. Sound okay? I've been here how long and have done no sight-seeing. It's about time I did!"

They had about eight hours before admission was closed to most places.

Harold hatched a plan and asked Isaac what he thought. If we head east on the Rosa Parks Parkway and take the 405, we can hit Greystone Mansion, the Walk of Fame, the Hollywood Sign, and Griffith Park. I think we have time for all of them. The Getty Museums are huge, and I don't know which one you'd enjoy more. So, let's plan on another day for the Getty.

Harold asked, "Do you remember anything about the Teapot Dome Scandal in history class?"

"I remember we learned about it. I don't think I know that much about it now," Isaac said.

"Well, the man who built Greystone for his family testified in the trial of his father in that scandal. He died four months after moving into the house. Apparently, it was a dispute over a promotion or a raise with an employee, so they called it a murder-suicide.

"That's not what I wanted to tell you about the place. It's now run by the National Park Service. It has beautiful gardens and it's a fifty-five room Tudor Revival. A ton of movies and shows have shot scenes there. Ones like National Treasure: Book of Secrets, Spider Man, Xmen, NCIS, Gilmore Girls. Those are the ones I can think of."

"No, really, Dad, that sounds mint."

They spent time on the grounds and had to agree with the reviews, most of which said it was amazing. When they entered the house, Isaac said, "Oh, yeah. This staircase. I know I've seen this in movies. Wow!" Isaac knew why his dad had chosen this site.

They gave it a once over, which still was a chunk of time, drove by the Hollywood sign and proceeded on to Griffith Park. Isaac's tour guide, otherwise known as 'Dad,' explained his motives behind seeing the Park.

"There's an observatory that overlooks the entire Los Angeles area. If you like architecture, you're gonna see it all. No doubt a lot of houses of famous people, but I can't point out any. And it's surprising how much green space there is, too."

Published information on Griffith Park recommended allotting two hours at the site. They were there for three hours and had to be asked to leave.

"We'll come back again." Harold knew his son would love to spend more time there.

"Why not? The price is right." He teased his dad because admission was free.

"We may have a long day tomorrow. We'd better get back to the apartment."

Harold thought about the apartment. *Two people can't possibly occupy that place.*

Secret Trust - Chapter 12

The search for a school started with the district where Harold resided—uncomfortably, now that there were two. *Will I be able to find another place in this same district? I can't move him to a third school in the same school year.*

"Come in and sign a release of records and complete enrollment forms. We'll set up a meeting with a school counselor as soon as records are received." An administrative assistant fielded Harold's call.

"But he's missed so much school. Shouldn't he attend right away?"

"Not without documents." The administrator's reply was brusque.

Harold hung up the telephone. "Let's get there soon and start the process."

"Wait. Dad. First, let's call the Canal Fuller Preparatory School. Don't worry about the money. Really."

"Even if we use your bonds, and I loathe the idea, how will we get them?"

"I have them with me. I brought all of the documents with me."

"Oh. Anyway, I'm sure I can set up a payment plan. I don't know what I was thinking. I can't let you pay for it."

Yes, you can. Isaac thought. If he only knew.

Isaac was still deep in thought when his dad called his name, twice.

"They said they have openings for the senior class, and they start tomorrow. They claim you should be able to start on time, but they want us to sign releases like right now."

A student volunteer gave Isaac and Harold a tour after they signed enrollments papers, had his picture taken, and gave them copies of his birth certificate. They waited a half hour for a school counselor, but they found it was worth the wait. The counselor explained the academic support they could provide for Isaac and recommended an introduction to architecture course they offered.

By the time they left the school, Isaac had a picture ID, a faculty advisor, and a schedule. He had an idea of how to find his classrooms, and they promised a student volunteer would be available to help if he had questions.

"Did you pick this school because of the courses in architecture?" Harold took special notice of how Isaac's eye brightened when he was offered a spot in the Introduction to Architecture class.

"Yeah. Plus, they had a one-year requirement to complete your diploma if you had enough credits. Other places require two years no matter how many years of high school you've had."

"I was glancing through the course of studies. Since it's an intro course, you could be in with first-year students or sophomores at best," Harold said.

"Yes. I don't love it. But I'm already older than everyone else."

"Speaking of age, you know where we're going now?"

"Nope."

"We're going to apply for a license."

"A permit?"

"Nope. I'm not sure they'll take your ID, but let's try."

Isaac thought his dad had lost it. But he was just along for the ride.

"Wow. I've never seen this place so empty." Harold seemed pleased. They took a number and started filling out the application.

Isaac looked up from the paperwork and glanced around. He had never seen a DMV this crowded. *I guess it's relative.*

It was near to closing time when they were called to the counter. With the combination of the school ID, Isaac's birth certificate, social security card and his dad's proof of address, they allowed Isaac to take the knowledge test.

Isaac passed, and the clerk was about to set up a date for Isaac's driver's test when an officer approached them.

"Hey, my last appointment of the day canceled. Want to take your test now?"

Isaac had his mouth open to say no, when his dad intervened.

"Sure. Let's give it a whirl."

Isaac looked at his dad with desperation on his face. How could he get his dad's attention and tell him he had not driven since his dad left for his new job. The year before he moved, Harold would take Isaac to remote areas, with dirt roads, and let Isaac drive. That was a long time ago and a long way from the California freeways.

Isaac used the DMV car. He gained some confidence from success with parallel parking on the DMV site. The officer looked at his watch and said, "Wow. I didn't know it was so late. Let's get this over with."

He directed Isaac on an easy, seven-minute drive. It was flawless. He received a temporary license and was sent on his way.

"Wow. Who'd a thunk it? Any of this. Our one-lung town at home knows my every move. But I couldn't produce an ID to save my life. Here, where there are a million people per square inch, the DMV gave me a license after living here a day."

His dad gave him a high five. "Well done, Son."

"Dad, how did you dare let me take that test?"

"You can't pass without taking the test, Son. Now you need a car to get to school. There isn't going to be a school bus."

"How about transit?"

"Um, you're from Flint Loch. What do you know about mass transit in LA?"

"What did I know about driving in LA., Dad?!"

They arrived at the apartment and saw a sweltering individual with a suitcase sitting outside of the building entrance. Isaac took a close look.

"Mom?"

Secret Trust - Chapter 13

"To what kind of a blazin' perdition did you lure my son?" Muriel was irate before waiting outside for an hour. Now she was boiling.

"Mom? What are you doing here?" Isaac was as gentle as he could be, but he wasn't calm on the inside.

"I came to bring you back to school. You're already close to violating the attendance policy for the quarter. You could lose your credit," Muriel said.

"I'm enrolled here. I start tomorrow. Flint Loch sent my records. It's all set. Look, I have a California driver's license." He held up his temporary license for her to see.

She took a step back from the document to allow for her eyesight. "How …"

"Cause, it's not Flint Stinkin' Hicksville!" Isaac was still burnt out in the aftermath of his efforts to obtain an ID while keeping his identification a secret from the Lottery Commission.

Harold brought a glass of iced tea for Muriel. "Here, Muriel. I'm sorry you were outside in the heat. Drink up. Dehydration is common in the desert. It can make you loopy. And have a seat."

Isaac muttered under his breath, "And it would go undiagnosed."

Muriel was quiet while she sipped her tea, though her eyes had a stormy look to them. Harold brought a cold compress from the kitchen. He put the compress on Muriel's neck while he motioned for Isaac to be seated on the sofa.

Harold took advantage while Muriel's mouth was engaged in drinking. "Isaac has done an amazing job. He didn't grow up overnight, but he has grown up. He's an adult. If you only knew what he's done in the last few days. On his own."

Isaac almost voiced his thoughts, *if you only knew.*

Harold brought Muriel up to date on Isaac's good choices. "Muriel, he's fine. Be proud. You've done well. He doesn't need us to do things for him anymore. Can you be thankful?"

Muriel's demeanor softened. She choked as she said, "But what about his academic support?"

"Covered. The school knows what they're doing. But more important, so does Isaac." Harold said.

"Isaac. You're leaving me, too?" Muriel went from conqueror to loser.

"Mom, that isn't the way to look at it. You could move here, too." Isaac looked at his dad, who had a sheepish look.

Three in the apartment. Harold was baffled.

His mom looked around. It's getting late. "Where am I going to stay tonight?"

Harold, still looking sheepish, said, "Well. We are still married."

All eyes appeared frozen and wide for a moment, then everyone burst out laughing.

Isaac suggested, Mom, let's give dad his space back. There's a hotel around the corner. It's cooler now. I can carry our luggage, and we'll stay there for a few days. We'll sort this out."

"What about school?"

"Oh, I'm going to school. No worries."

Isaac's mom looked askance as he paid for their first night with his debit card. His new cell rang while they were on their way to the rooms. He handed his mom her key and said he'd bring her luggage by after taking the call.

Muriel paused while he walked down the hall, but he disappeared. She didn't pursue him, though she wanted to.

Isaac answered the cell. "Hey, Mr. B."

Brady returned the greeting, and then asked a question. "Imagine my surprise when Alma turned in your expenses! A flight to California? Tuition to a private school? So, is this the moderation we were talking about?"

"I know you're just watching out for me. I'm not doing anything wrong, am I?"

"I don't know. What are you doing?"

"I moved out to where my dad lives. I didn't want to make up the work in a public school, and, I found a school that has some courses in architecture. That's what I want to do."

"It's amazing how you can make no sense one minute and explain it away the next."

"Thank you, I think." Isaac smiled.

"It's good you are considering a career, but have you considered the math component?"

"I'm sick of living in fear of math. I plan to take it where it leads me. There are so many careers related to architecture. Environmental design, computer aided design, art, landscape architecture, or landscaping or building. I know how to get my hands dirty."

"Sorry, not sorry. Good thinking." Brady was satisfied.

"It doesn't matter where I live, does it?"

"No."

"Things are so different here. I don't feel like I have to hide. I figure attending a private school, the rich kids won't pay attention to my conspicuous consumption."

"Be careful. Rich kids can be among the worst poachers. Much worse than students of modest needs."

"Okay. I'll be careful. I was wondering if I should tell my parents."

"Your parents? Both parents?"

"Yeah. Mom showed up out here. She thought she would kidnap me." Isaac wondered if she still would try.

"There's another reason why I called. The convenience store showed the video."

"What?"

"Rockney called. He said it's grainy and hard to see. He met you, but he was sure if he didn't know the backstory, he wouldn't have put two and two together. Though, if someone sees the video who knows you well, I can't say for sure they won't recognize your image. If they do and put it together with your odd behavior and escape from town, you might rise to the top as the one they're looking for."

"Was it shown in Flint Loch?" Isaac was curious.

"No. It wasn't even shown in the Capital Area. Let's hope they don't get aggressive. I can't answer your question. I can only add more. What would happen if someone does guess it's you? What impact would that have on your parents to find out that way? Conversely, what if you tell them and they can't help themselves from spreading the word?"

Secret Trust - Chapter 14

"I'm glad you're willing to have lunch with me." Harold returned to work that morning but arranged to have lunch with Muriel. They found a restaurant on the waterfront with a view from the inside where they could enjoy the air-conditioned room.

"I think we need to talk." Muriel was intense.

"I agree. No doubt we have different ideas on the topics to cover. You can go first."

"Well, I can't agree that Isaac is ready to make his own decisions. He made a series of nothing but foolish choices lately."

"I think he has explained his intentions, and he planned very well for what he needed and wanted." Harold was discouraged that they remained so far apart on the issue of Isaac's independence. "Besides, Muriel, we all make questionable choices."

"Oh?" She caught his insinuation.

"Not telling him about my call. About his gift. Not telling him where his ID documents were kept. For just a few." Harold was firm.

"You left your family. And you're telling me how to take care of what you left behind? You send a few bucks after a year, and that makes you a parent?" Muriel was furious.

"Not to nit pic, but I have given you half my paycheck all our married lives; including the past fourteen months." Harold continued, "I wanted Isaac to come with me; I didn't dare ask you. I was afraid."

"You could have stayed."

"You're right. And you could have come like you promised to do. What is in Flint Loch for you anyway?"

"Isaac's teacher. He needed his teacher."

"Well, we're going to find out, aren't we?"

"And if I'm right?"

"It wouldn't be the first time, so don't be so surprised. The same is true for being wrong."

"We're not talking about me. We're talking about Isaac."

Harold said nothing. He waited for Muriel to recognize what she said, but somehow, he knew she wouldn't.

Finally, he spoke. "Isaac will be fine. Whether sooner or later."

"Well, there's still stuff you don't know."

"Okay. Let me know, then."

"The convenience store in Brook Crossings sold the winning lottery ticket last week. Did you know that?"

"Yeah. I heard it once or twice. I didn't pay much attention. It sounds as though the vultures won't stop looking for who it was. They said it was cashed in on Long Island."

"Yes. So, they showed a surveillance tape for the time they think the ticket was purchased."

"Are you kidding?"

"No. They're showing it in the New York City area. They figure it was someone passing through."

"I imagine, so what's your point?"

"Listen. I'm getting to my point. I think I recognized Isaac on the surveillance tape buying a ticket."

"No kidding! What luck! Can you imagine if he had won?!" Harold was interested in the conversation for the first time.

"That's your take-away? Aren't you concerned? He buys a lottery ticket just because he's old enough. The very first day?"

"Muriel. That doesn't make him a serial killer."

"And you thought you should give him eighteen thousand dollars? You do not know this kid."

$$$$

Isaac muddled through his first day of school. It wasn't bad; it was just school. He so wished it was over. Not just the day; the whole year. He was still covering his tracks. He convinced the registrar and the business office that his father needed no information on his tuition or grades since he was eighteen and hadn't signed a release of information.

There was a part of the day he did enjoy. The architecture class was interesting, and he liked studio art as well. That was more than a third of his day, excluding lunch for which he had released time. When he got a car, he could take a decent break. He could do this.

At the end of the day, he was confused. Should he go to the hotel or his dad's house? They were close, so he went to the hotel. He had reserved another night for both his and his mother's rooms. He knocked on her door, but there was no answer. He found her by the pool, reading.

"Hey Mom. How was your day?"

"How was yours, is the question?"

"Good. I like my architecture and art classes; the rest I will endure."

"Lots of homework?"

"Nah."

His mom continued to pepper him with questions. Questions he could answer. It felt good to put several sentences together that represented facts.

When she took a breath, he broke in. "Should we call Dad and go out for dinner?"

"Speaking of calling, I noticed your new cell phone."

"Yup. Everything out here is connected. I do everything with it."

"Humph."

"Mom, why don't we all try to find a house together out here?"

"Why would I live out here?"

"Because dad and I are both out here?"

"You both left me. Maybe I'll just leave you both."

"Maybe you won't." Isaac was lighthearted but serious. "I want you to stay, Mom."

Muriel's demeanor softened and the corners of her mouth curved into a smile. "That's nice of you to say." She changed the subject. "Anyway, you're right. We should send a text to your dad."

Isaac did just that. "Hey, Dad. Should we go out for dinner?"

Harold replied by text. "I don't feel like going out, thanks."

"Mom, I don't think Dad's okay." He told Muriel what the text said.

"Let's go by and see what's up. We can at least get take-out for him."

At first glance it was clear that something was wrong. Harold opened the door for them, reversed direction and stared out of the living room window with his hands in his pockets.

"What's wrong, Dad?"

"Son, look at this." Muriel was holding a letter she found open on the dinette from the engineering firm where Harold was a programmer. As Isaac started reading the letter, Muriel continued. "They're closing the firm."

Isaac pursed his lips. His eyes opened wide as he looked at his mom for direction. They said nothing.

After a long silence, his dad came out of his stupor as if to spring into action. "The severance pay was generous. And I have a little savings."

Muriel stepped up to the situation as well. "I still have my job, and remember? Frasier's said you could have your old job back anytime. Would you consider it? We still have the house."

Incredulous, Harold turned to her and stared for a short time. "Yes. Yes, I would. That's exactly what I'll do. I'll call them in the morning."

Secret Trust - Chapter 15

"The funds have been released. Let's talk." Isaac received the text from Brady.

Isaac rued the timing of the long-awaited news from his attorney. Has it been less than a week? He was alone in his room. The news of his dad's layoff was still roiling in his thoughts. Should I tell them now? They're acting in desperation, but they're working together.

He dialed Brady. "Hey Alma. How's it going? Is Mr. Brady there?"

Brady came on the phone. "Isaac. The funds are in an account supervised by a financial investment firm that specializes in large inheritances. I've been informing the point person on your circumstances for some background for when you initiate ideas on expenditures and investments."

"Thanks, Mr. Brady. I have a new development." Isaac informed Brady on his father's layoff, which represented yet another predicament for Isaac.

"Oh. I see. That negates the investment expert's first idea."

"Which was?"

"When he heard of your location and interest in landscape architecture, he looked for business investments. He found a solid firm that should take off with an infusion of some money, but not much money. What they need most is a new management team. The firm has equipment and talent perfect for the Beverly Hills area."

"Hmm." Isaac liked the idea.

"Are you interested?"

"I think I am."

"Aren't you coming back to Flint Loch with your parents?"

"Maybe not."

"Are you going to tell you parents about the money?"

"Not yet."

"Ever?"

"Haven't decided. I'm still afraid of Mom moving from a helicopter mom to a snowplow parent."

"What are you thinking?"

"If I purchase the firm, I can 'work' there and earn enough money to keep my dad's studio apartment."

"That's a good ruse. What about school?"

"Landscapers are needed for overtime to meet timelines, maybe?"

"It might work. Are you going to keep going to school?"

"Yes. I've arranged my schedule of courses; most of them will be online. I just have to go in first period for CAD."

"Do you want a role in the business?"

"Under an alias?"

"It can be done."

"Good. I have something else I want you to investigate."

"Okay."

"Some charities."

"I'll talk with the financial adviser. Any particular areas of interest?"

"Children's homes?"

"Where?"

"Is there a way to find out where they're most needed and where the kids can't get a good education? Such as specialized reading support?"

"I'll get right on it."

"Thanks. I couldn't do this without you."

"It's what I do, and I'm glad it is."

$$$$

Isaac's favorite place so far was the Santa Monica Pier, and he decided to have dinner there. He drove his red vintage 1968 Mustang convertible that he purchased as soon as his parents departed. He drove along the I-10 enjoying the breeze and the sun, now that it was lowering and less intense than during the heat of the day.

He bought take out and sat on a bench people watching while enjoying tamales. A young woman stared at him as he used a napkin and dropped it in the trash. She didn't look away when discovered. Isaac walked toward her to see if she would persist, and she did. He introduced himself, "Hi. I'm Isaac. Do I know you?"

"No. I was just enjoying the scenery." She was flirting.

He felt complimented despite the fact she was joking. "I'm glad. Have you had dinner?"

"Yes. But I could go for some ice cream."

Ice cream parlors and stands were plentiful; nearly every fifth place of business. They found one that had her favorite flavor, coffee pistachio.

"I've never heard of that flavor, but I don't think I want to try. I'll have a black cherry."

They walked, went down to the beach, and strolled while eating and chatting, the latter allowing them to find out each other's names and where they lived.

"Are you a student?" Libby asked.

"Yes, and I work as well." Isaac wanted to deemphasize his school status.

"Where do you work?"

"I'll be starting with a landscaping firm in a few weeks. How about you?"

"I'm a freelance writer."

"Freelance? Do you get enough work?"

"Too much, at times. Not enough at other times." She laughed and flicked her head back. He found it endearing.

All of a sudden, Southern California became much more interesting.

Chapter Sixty

Adirondacks

"We have just a couple of sessions left in the summer workshop." Benita had some additional agenda items for the workshop. "I received notice today that Ms. Scott is a finalist for the Frederick Foundation for Excellence in Education Award, and they have invited all of us to the award dinner in early August." Benita paused while the students high-fived each other and cheered.

She continued, "And, they are asking for any supplemental supporting material we would like to submit. I will be submitting *Secret Trust* on behalf of the class."

Brynn commented, "But you taught the workshop instead of Ms. Scott."

The others were curious too and looked at Benita for a response.

"This exchange of duties is another illustration of her innovative teaching. Please don't take this the wrong way, but I am an added resource to her classroom. Right?"

"Oh, I get it. You're right." Wesley said.

"So, do I have your permission?" Benita asked.

"Sure."

"Natch."

"Of course." Each of them gave their consent.

"Good. Let's get started."

"How much money have we made so far?" Brynn was curious.

"I think it approaches fifteen hundred dollars each. And the book advance is thousands of dollars. The royalty checks are issued each month, the first one after a month's hiatus. The money could help pay for the awards dinner." Benita smirked.

"What? We have to pay our own way?" Jake sounded outraged.

"Ostensibly, yes. The Foundation wants as much money as possible to be kept in the coffers to reward good teaching. But Soto Literary Agency will pay for your travel expenses and the dinner. It's on us." Benita enjoyed the slight tease.

"Whew!" Jake, again.

"Be sure to set aside the date. It's a Saturday, and we'll leave early in the morning. Each of you will have your own room at the hotel where the dinner is held, and we'll depart after a day of sightseeing on Sunday."

"I can't wait! I wonder if we'll have time for a Broadway musical, or the museums. I've always wanted to go to Top of the Rock!" Nikki was ecstatic.

"Stop tweakin'. It's not half-way around the world. It's just New York City." Jake, again.

"We be tweakin' all we want, Jake!" Brynn had perfected the art of the chin flick.

***

Miami

Celeste handed Kendrick correspondence addressed to Soto marked 'confidential' from the Frederick Foundation for Excellence in Education. "This is for you."

"Thanks." He opened the letter letting him know of Maren Scott's nomination in the category of "Innovative Teaching Strategies and Curriculum. The letter informed him that they knew of Ms. Scott interning there for the summer with Soto Literary Agency and invited him to comment on her nomination.

I'll comment alright. Kendrick started a draft which outlined Maren's accomplishments in the weeks she had been with the agency, to include discovery and help in the resolution of the recent breach of manuscripts and finances; review of hundreds of manuscripts; contracts to represent authors; obtaining publishers for two authors and counting. Kendrick's list when on.

When the document was as polished as it could be given Kendrick's goal to have a quick turnaround, he asked Celeste to join him in his office. "Please keep this under your hat. The confidential letter was an offer for Soto to comment on Maren's nomination for a teaching award. They're considering supplemental documentation for only a few more days, so I want to send this right away. Would you look it over and let me know what you think?"

"That's nice. I wonder who nominated her."

"Does Benita come to mind, perhaps?"

"Of course. It is so Benita!"

"That's why I wanted to write the letter. I'm confident Benita's views have been well-represented. It's one of her many strengths. My voice might not have much to offer, but it is another voice."

Celeste took a moment to read the letter. "I think your letter is flawless. It emphasizes the skills she brought to the agency and her perseverance in the face of events that would have been game changers for most people. No need for edits as far as I'm concerned. You go guy."

"Thanks. I'll send it electronically, but can we send a hard copy overnight as a backup?"

"Sign it and I'll get it done!" Celeste took the signed copy and was off.

Later that week, Kendrick received an invitation to attend the awards dinner in New York City based on his letter of support. He responded right away, scheduled his flight for a few days prior to the award, and reserved a room through Monday evening. Kendrick hadn't felt this hopeful since the weekend of Maren's arrival.

Chapter Sixty-One

Adirondacks

The textbooks Benita hauled to Hidden Havens were cracked open for the second time when the sessions at Clear Lake School were completed. Her interest in them had waned. She was looking forward to the awards dinner on Saturday, but otherwise her mood was melancholy combined with confusion. This stood in contrast to her goal for her time at Hidden Havens, which was for direction and clarification.

The agency is doing well. I love my work and I have ideas I want to test out. Why do I question my involvement? Do I feel as though I abandoned my convictions to help individuals with communications disorders? If only there was a way to do both.

Aunt Dilly entered the room and observed Benita in a daydream. "Anything I can do?"

Benita shook off her trance and responded. "No. I'm just more confused than ever. That's all."

"You have a lifetime of adventure and accomplishment ahead of you. Just put one foot in front of the other, and you'll be fine. What do you want most? Say, for tomorrow?"

"To go waterskiing with you!"

Her aunt laughed. "Those days are over!"

"Why do you keep the boat?"

"I still take out the boat. In fact, I'd like to go boating. I'll pull you on the skis."

"No spotter."

"I'll call the neighbors, okay?"

Aunt Dilly was up and dialing without waiting for an answer. Nor did she receive an answer to her call. She returned to Benita. "No one answered. I have an idea. Why don't you invite your friends up for a visit? You said Maren is leaving Soto to return to Clear Lake any day now. I think a retreat is what is needed for everyone."

"That's not a bad idea. The agency can get along without Kendrick and Celeste for a few days. At least, I hope so."

"What about Troy?" Aunt Dilly hadn't asked again until this moment.

"Not Troy," Benita said.

"Have you given up on him?"

"Maybe. But we reunited after more than a decade once. I don't know, I would rather hold out hope for the distant future rather than take a chance right now that could torpedo things for good."

Aunt Dilly muttered under her breath. "I think you're both far too sensitive."

"What?" Benita heard her mutter.

"Nothing, dear. Except, let me just say… no, forget it. It's none of my business.

***

Benita called and left a message on Maren's cell inviting her to Hidden Havens for a visit. They spent some time chatting when Maren returned her call, and Maren addressed the question.

"I've been nominated for a teacher award, and the ceremony is in New York City. I'm way behind on things around here, too. I would love to come, though." Her voice drifted.

"What? Are you back in Clear Lake? And congratulations on your nomination!"

"I'm sorry. I thought Kendrick told you when I was returning."

"No worries. But I hope you can come. Even for a day visit. We need to have some time on the lake."

"I could use some fun, but I want to be back at my apartment and prepare for departure on Saturday morning."

"Yes. What an honor, and you are very deserving." Benita sensed there was no suspicion on the part of Maren about the involvement of studentStringers.

"Thanks. I have no idea how I got nominated, but it's overwhelming. In any event, a day on the lake sounds inviting. I'll call you if and when, is that okay?"

"Sure," Benita said. She then called Celeste.

"I'd love to, but I have plans. Rain check? I'm so curious about Hidden Havens."

Benita assured her there would be other opportunities and placed a call to Kendrick's cell. She left a voice mail.

Benita and Aunt Dilly picked veggies from the garden, washed them, and made a salad for after their boat ride on the lake. They had tethered the boat and were still in their bathing suits enjoying their salad on the dock sitting in, of all things, Adirondack chairs when they noticed Pala walking toward them.

"Hey stranger. Where have you been?" Benita shouted out to Pala.

Pala moved closer before speaking. "The crops have kept me so busy. And, I've been revamping my curriculum. I'm going back to teaching."

Aunt Dilly replied to Pala without giving Benita a chance to respond. "Congratulations. I'd like to offer you some salad."

"Thanks. I think I will." Pala helped herself and took a seat in what had been the only empty chair until Benita stood up in response to Pala's news.

Benita finally got in a word. "Congratulations, indeed. Where?" She was animated and a bit annoyed that the others were so nonchalant. "How did this happen?"

"Clear Lake."

"What? What about Rex?" Benita blurted it out.

"I contacted him after I was discovered. I admired his restraint, and I wanted to tell him I wish I had found a way to make the separation easier on him. We had occasional contact at first and then it became more frequent.

"Anyway, he mentioned to Dr. Gawl that we are in touch. She wasn't happy with the way I disappeared, but we always got along well, and they need a part-time biology teacher. I wasn't interested at first. I told her I want to pursue the language studies and pass along my knowledge. Dr. Gawl contacted me again after consulting with the school board. They are interested in an overview course on Iroquois culture and languages in the fall and an introduction to speaking and writing the Mohawk language in the spring."

Benita was thrilled. "That's perfect. I hope the students respond."

"I couldn't resist. The school committee sent out a request for parents to ask their children about any possible interest. Sometimes parents say their kids want something parents want *for* them. I hope they were honest, but there seemed to be a positive response."

"I hope so. What an opportunity for everyone involved. Kudos. Let me know if I can help. For instance, if you create a two-year sequence, I believe colleges would accept it as their world language requirement for admission." Benita was impressed with Pala.

"I'll look into it and be in touch. I'm interested in ideas that would make it a viable program. Think of the impact it would have on preserving the language."

"I know this isn't my business, but how are things going on a personal level with you and Rex?"

"We're okay. Right now, I can say I'm glad he's in my life again."

Benita and Aunt Dilly used their discretion and probed no further. They were thankful with things as they were.

Pala stayed long enough to finish her salad. Benita suspected the purpose of her visit was to inform them of the news about her return to Clear Lake. Aunt Dilly faced Benita on their walk from the dock to the house and said, "See, dear. The summer isn't a complete disaster."

Benita smiled, but didn't voice her response. *I know. But I still miss my Adirondack crush.*

Chapter Sixty-Two

Maren's and Kendrick's visits to Hidden Havens would overlap by a little less than twenty-four hours if all went as planned.

"Do you think they'll resent me? As if I'm throwing them together?" Benita told Aunt Dilly about the vagaries of their relationship.

"Well, you could have asked me that before you invited them." Aunt Dilly chuckled, touched Benita's arm and gave her a reassurance. "They've been working together. I know a setting like this suggests something more personal, but how much romance can the situation suggest with us present?" Aunt Dilly's long life had imparted a knowledge about circumstances—time and contact were key to resolution.

The duo of aunt and niece spent the morning preparing food that could be enjoyed on hot summer days and evenings. The fridge was stuffed with deviled eggs, chicken-chutney salad, washed greens, snow peas, Caesar gazpacho, seafood salad, and three-bean salad. They were just cleaning up the kitchen when Maren arrived. The afternoon flew by at the waterfront. Aunt Dilly commandeered Maren for the formal tour of the grounds, which she usually conducted upon a visitor's arrival, and then Maren and Benita enjoyed another ride in the boat.

Kendrick arrived late in the evening and was thrust into a conversation on the porch where he determined the story commanded 'you had to be there.' As the women described their day on the water and the associated mishaps, they giggled to the point where all communication ceased. He laughed at them and with them. He enjoyed the iced tea and bruschetta; the scenery, especially Maren; and the company, especially Maren.

The group chatted as they walked upstairs to retire, both new guests electing one of the stagecoach rooms, an unwitting reflection of Benita's consistent choice of Room 4.

Kendrick remarked, "I think I'll elect to paddle board tomorrow and refrain from waterskiing."

They all laughed, and Maren spoke, "Don't let our stories scare you away. We're harmless."

The group enjoyed a full breakfast of eggs, biscuits, bacon and pancakes; the sole meal of the day when the house and its inhabitants would be exposed to the heat of the stove and oven. Kendrick received his personal tour of the house, conducted by Aunt Dilly, of course, followed by a leisurely walk around the grounds.

Kendrick suggested they have some more fun on the paddle boards, and the three young people, as Aunt Dilly described Benita and her colleagues, headed to the carriage house to fetch them.

Aunt Dilly finished up the chores. She had insisted she wanted to perform them alone and arrived in time to see most of the hilarity. The women received their just deserts as their villainous splashes with the paddles resulted in the loss of balance on the boards. Kendrick remained upright until very late in the game. He, too, became seduced by the urge to use the paddles for other than their primary use. His aim was off, and Aunt Dilly received the inadvertent shower. At this point, Maren and Benita lifted the front of his board and dunked him in the lake.

He came out of the water with a nose full of water, and after sputtering and coughing, apologized to the shocked, but amused Aunt Dilly. They three 'young people' enjoyed the lake until lunch, which was on the porch and consisted of an array of the cold entrees prepared earlier.

As the hilarity was loud enough for the neighbors to hear, Benny and Jasmine appeared after lunch to check out the source. Benita invited them to waterski. "Please, join us. Besides, we need you. Mr. Kendrick has withdrawn due to cowardice."

Kendrick refuted her statement. "Not true. I've reconsidered. I since have developed strategies in dealing with these two."

Maren and Benita snickered. Maren said, "Yeah. By taking it out on Ms. Adele!"

Kendrick smiled despite their ridicule and waived them off as he headed toward the storage area.

The scene was a repetition of the last two skiing episodes, even with the complement of Maren and Kendrick. There was an abundance of fun, sans the frivolity for the sake of safety.

Maren left in the early evening for her return trip to her apartment. Kendrick said he was ready to change as well and escorted her to the house. On the way, she mentioned the teacher award nomination. He sensed she was starting to become excited about it. He was genuine in his congratulations and felt no guilt in hiding the tangible support he provided. He added, "Good luck. You deserve to win."

Maren blanched and said, "Thanks," as she ascended the stairs to change. The others had toweled off and gathered in the foyer waiting to say goodbye when Maren returned. Kendrick changed more quickly than Maren and was chatting with the others in the foyer when he heard Maren emerge from her room. He climbed the stairs to help with her luggage and carried it to her car. She stood with the car door open, embarrassed and humbled by the proverbial toasts she received from the adoring crowd of water buddies … and Aunt Dilly.

As she drove out, Benny turned to the others and said, "That was fun! But we gotta get home, Jasmine." They hopped on their bikes, wet bathing suits and all, and headed up the dirt road.

Kendrick turned toward Benita and Aunt Dilly. "It was fun. We all needed this. Except for Ms. Havens' shower."

"Call me Adele. And I loved it. What a joy for me to have you young people around. This place had been a little lonely before this summer." There was a pensive look on her face. "If you'll excuse me, I'm going with Rena to Reed's. You remember Reed's, don't you Beni?"

"Reed's the department store? Is that still in business?" Benita said.

"It sure is."

"Still five floors with three departments on each floor with a clerk and checkout in every department?"

"Almost. They've consolidated to three floors. And dropped the formal china, crystal, and silver items. Come to think of it, if the whole county suddenly wanted that stuff again, I could probably supply them." She pursed her lips, and her gesture was understood to combine humor with a smattering of regret.

"Have they updated besides that?" Beni had good memories of the store.

"Not much. But they'll have to if they want to survive. However, dear, they don't come to me for advice." She left with her typical pat on Benita's arm. "Oh, here's Rena now. See you two later."

Kendrick and Benita were left alone. It was a bit awkward, and Benita asked, "Ready for some tea?"

"Is it teatime at Hidden Havens?"

"It is." Benita smirked.

She brought back the tea service to the west parlor and poured in silence. She sat down and then it dawned on her that it was hot tea. "I'm sorry. I didn't ask if you would prefer iced tea."

"This is fine," Kendrick said.

"I thought it was time to debrief the events of the summer. I remember a comment from the *Gilmore Girls*. 'Things can seem less awkward with something in your hands.'"

"Sure. If you think we need to." Kendrick didn't want to ruin his mood with a rehash of his misdeeds.

"I wanted to apologize for how I initiated this exchange with Maren and my escape to Hidden Havens. If it's of any comfort, most of it blew up in my face. At least it seems that way." Benita furrowed her brow.

"Thank you. I need to correct what you said. This summer was very successful. My reaction was the lowest point of the summer as far as I'm concerned. I let down you and the agency and for that I'm truly embarrassed. I also lost my chance with Maren, which is a big personal loss."

"My actions here this summer caused me to lose someone I've been fond of since I was a teen."

"Our love lives do eclipse some of the successes. We know how to mess things up in that arena." He smiled.

Benita rallied a bit. "But we have Maren's nomination to look forward to. I think the school community presented a strong case. She was an unwitting contributor given her accomplishments."

"I know. The letter I wrote for her was the easiest I ever composed."

"You wrote a letter?"

"Yes. A request came to the agency, so I praised her for all she did there."

Benita was surprised to find out about the request at this late date. She said nothing.

"Benita? Are you upset that I responded?" Kendrick was worried.

"No. I'm sure the more support the better." She was still processing what it meant but didn't want to cast a pallor on what might be the second-best thing to happen during the summer. *Well, maybe it was the highlight of the summer.*

Chapter Sixty-Three

New York City

"Jake, Nikki!" Benita turned around and saw the remaining member of studentStringers. "You all look wonderful." It was nice how well they cleaned up.

"I hope she wins!" Brynn scrunched her shoulders and giggled. "Is she going to sit with us?"

"I didn't tell her we would be here. Our involvement is still a surprise, as far as I know." Benita added, "I think she is just expecting Dr. Gawl to be here. I'll see if I can find her."

The students milled around while Benita wandered off to find Maren. She stopped looking when a reporter who had been lurking spoke to her.

"The nominees are on either side of the dais on the stage." Melodi Sims, the news reporter spoke to her having overheard her mission. "Do you have time for a short interview?"

Benita agreed, and the camera rolled for a minute while Benita answered questions about Maren. She gave up on her mission to find Maren when she noticed Kendrick. "I didn't know you were coming."

"What? I didn't mention it?" Kendrick asked. "I thought we talked about the awards dinner when I told you about my letter of support for Maren's work at Soto."

"I don't seem to be myself. It's crazy it didn't come up. Well, I'm glad you're here. Let me introduce the Stringers!" Benita introduced Kendrick to the students.

Jake, in his inimitable manner piped up. "Oh. You're the one who arranged to make us all that capital!"

Benita tried at mitigation. "I've told you about Jake."

"Yes. It's a pleasure to be in the presence of such famous authors! Congratulations! No matter what happens this evening, your renown should be celebrated." Kendrick meant every word. He continued, "Have you enjoyed New York City so far?"

"We took a hop-on hop-off tour. The streets were so crowded, we almost didn't get back in time for the dinner." Aaron was unimpressed.

"Well, how many hop-offs did you do?" Kendrick was enjoying their enthusiasm, whether negative or positive.

"There was a lot to see. We had to see Ground Zero. And we wanted to walk in Central Park," Wesley offered.

"We bought the tickets in Hell's Kitchen, so we ate lunch there. I had sushi. It was a lot better than in Clear Lake," Riza said.

"You've seen a lot of Manhattan already. Any plans for tomorrow?" Kendrick asked.

They all spoke at once. "A Broadway musical."

"The Empire State Building."

"The Museums."

"Madam Tussaud's."

"St. Patrick's Cathedral."

"Park Plaza Hotel."

Riza added. "I don't know about the Empire State Building. Seriously, sorry about the l-y-word Jake, but that thing is scary tall. And I've been on Whiteface Mountain!"

The list continued, but Kendrick broke in. "Wow. You can do one of those things. Maybe two! But don't hesitate to come back. You're not that far."

"Yeah," Jake said. "I have my license, now."

"Yikes. Way to drag down the conversation," Brynn said.

"I have a surprise for everyone." Kendrick hadn't intended to lose control of the conversation, but it happened, and he needed to pull it back.

Benita looked at him. "What do you mean?" She dreaded what he might say. The culmination of her summer work was at hand, yet she felt so out of control. Was another shoe about to drop?

"Well, what is it?" Grover asked.

"Yeah. What?" Riza was eager for a surprise. The weekend seemed rife for them.

The conversation was interrupted. No one noticed the salad plates had been distributed, and their waitperson hinted that they should be in their places. They looked for their name cards. They were surprised at the size of their table. There was seating for twelve, yet Benita could account for no more than ten. As they were taking their seats, three people joined them who looked like a family.

The young man, who was late teens or early twenties, nodded and spoke as he pulled out his chair. "Hi! Are you the studentStringers and their teacher?"

"Yup. That's us. And our principal. Who are you?" Jake came through again.

"I'm Isaac. This is my mom, Muriel, and my dad, Harold."

Chapter Sixty-Four

No one spoke. Not even Jake. The studentStringers, Benita and Kendrick were stunned.

"Our real names aren't Isaac, Muriel and Harold though. But we are like the characters in the story," Wade, aka Isaac, said.

"I had left the family and took a job in the Silicon Valley in California." Milo, aka Harold, said. "I counted on Bridgette, aka Muriel, to follow me. But she didn't. She was afraid for Wade. He has a medical condition, and she was so afraid of moving him away from his doctor."

"But as soon as my back was turned, and after his dad sent him the mature life insurance policy he had been building up until his eighteenth birthday, Wade took off for California to join his dad. Just like the story, I followed. Before I left, I started reading **Secret Trust**. I saw so much of myself in each chapter. After Milo got laid off, he came back, and we're rebuilding our lives together," Bridgette said.

"Wade stayed in California. He found a job with benefits right away, and a good doctor, but we flew him home when we found out about this event for the teacher nominated by studentStringers. We wrote a recommendation to support her candidacy." Milo said.

"So, our story is the story of *Secret Trust*, except for the lottery, of course," Bridgette added.

Wade looked at Benita and winked. She caught her breath. It was audible and she glanced around hoping no one had noticed. *I wonder how much he won.*

Dinner was underway. The waitstaff seemed a little annoyed when they returned to Maren's table of supporters to clear the salad dishes and every one of them was still full. The group set their salads aside and made room for their dinner plates. Out of the corner of her eye, Benita noticed the reporter hovering.

The eating part of dinner never took off. There was so much discussion because of the many questions they had for each other--'Isaac's' family of the studentStringers and the student-Stringers of the family. Dr. Gawl said little; she could only mumble about her nerves. Benita regretted Sylvia's inability to attend. She had done so much to assemble the documents and make them presentable.

Their plates were taken away with little notice, and the President of the Foundation stepped up to the dais.

"Greetings friends of the candidates and a special welcome to our teacher award finalists. The happiness and successes of our youth are the reason the Frederick Foundation for Excellence in Education exists. We thrill at their accomplishments for their sakes and at once are aware of the wondrous bounty as our recipients of their continued contributions to our future.

"Tonight, we extend our humble efforts to acknowledge those whose remarkable methods of reaching young people is expressed in myriad ways in and out of the classroom. Every finalist on tonight's stage has received the accolades of their school community. The lavish praise in all cases was backed by evidence of teaching and learning through a variety of outcomes, products, and modalities.

"Thank you first to the teachers and your dedication to the profession and continued efforts to improve your methods. Also, thank you to all who provided support through nominations and supporting evidence.

Secluded Summer at Hidden Havens

"Tonight, we want to par-tay!" The audience roared as their attention was wrenched from the formal discourse. "So, we are going to announce the third and second place winners in a moment, followed by our amazing winner."

He did as he promised, and the third and second place winners were announced to individual deafening applause for each in turn. When things had settled down, he began his overview of the best teacher among the array of finalists.

"Every teacher here tonight is amazing, and all have received an enormous outpouring of support from those who know them best. That is true and magnified for our winner. This individual was nominated by a group, and supporting statements and evidence were provided by no less than 327 people.

"As our panel review continued, this candidate rose to the top in all categories and was almost sure to be the winner. And then a letter was received that bumped her scores off the charts. A teacher who works as a practitioner in his or her field, especially in the year leading up to the award date, receives additional credit. Let me make this easier and read an excerpt from the letter.

"**Within a few days of becoming a member of our agency, this candidate had read and reviewed hundreds of manuscripts. This was no cursory reading, for her acuity in the world of fiction caused her to discover forgeries submitted as original works. Within days of that discovery, accounting discrepancies, not necessarily those in the wheelhouse of many English Language Arts teachers, were detected as well.**

"**She could have ceded to perceived defeat and returned to the familiar environs of her creative writing class in the Adirondacks. Instead, her alacrity in addressing the forg-**

eries and graft led to the apprehension and arrest of the culprits, and the agency's loss was recovered.

"Further, her sustained efforts to find the great American novel came to fruition. In a few short weeks, she has offered contracts to six authors with four of them receiving advances from publishers.

"I am excited to see the many ways her summer experience will inform her teaching and redound to the increased engagement of students in her discipline."

The table of Maren's supporters found it difficult to contain their delight. Everyone remained on their best behavior waiting for the crescendo of the speech.

"There's more news. On the dais tonight is the public debut of the product of her summer experience. Our winner engaged a literary agent, with whom she exchanged roles for the summer, who led the students of Clear Lake Central School in an innovative publication of a novella on the internet. The book was picked up by a New York City publisher, and the first copy is here."

The President held up the book, and the studentStringers held their peace no longer. They whooped, stood, and cheered. In a flash, they rest of the crowd joined them. It was obvious to Maren's group who the winner was; no announcement was necessary for them. For the benefit of the rest of the attendees, the winner was named, but the thunderous roar of the crowd precluded any audible statement. The President didn't fight it. Rather, he walked over to Maren, took her by the hand and escorted her in front of the table of finalists. As the victor, he held up her hand. Though not thought possible, the crowd resounded louder. The applause was sustained for over a minute.

StudentStringers rushed the stage but didn't ascend. Instead, Maren came down. There were high fives, hugs, and more whooping and applause. The exhilaration didn't settle for a long time. The eventual resumption of order was followed by an announcement from the dais.

"You may have a passing interest in the details of the award, Maren Scott, whose name has yet to be announced ...

There was more applause at the mention of her name and a delay in additional announcements. He resumed when the excitement died down. "Maren Scott will be the recipient of a $10,000 personal gift and $10,000 grant for her school, to be used at her discretion." There was more applause, and Dr. Gawl looked pleased for the first time since Benita met her.

The President spoke again. Two more announcements, only two. We are going to dance the night away in this ballroom, and the friends of Maren Scott may proceed to the adjacent ballroom to revel in private! Celebrate!"

Additional applause ensued but of a shorter duration. Pala and Rex entered from the adjacent ballroom to the surprise of everyone who knew them. They congratulated Maren and escorted her next door. More thunder! Any interested parties were invited at the last minute. They weren't informed of the winner, but most of them suspected. There were parents, students, local business owners, the mayor, school committee members, and people who would attend a party just because. Though there wasn't enough room for them in the main ballroom, all were able to watch the proceedings via closed circuit video.

Melodi, the reporter and the camera operator struggled to get a word with Maren. Failing that, she interviewed the studentStringers, Benita, Kendrick, 'Isaac's' family, and Dr. Gawl. Wade, aka Isaac, seemed to avoid the camera.

Melodi cut in on Maren's dance with Rex in order to obtain an audience with her. They turned toward the camera, and the reporter asked the question, "Do you have a reaction to what has happened here tonight?"

"After working with millions of words for the past few weeks, I am amazed that I am at a loss for even one right now to describe how I feel. Thank you. Everyone. I am thrilled."

The reporter, never at a loss for words, took full focus from the camera and put her own spin on the events.

Kendrick caught up with Maren. "Congratulations. The best woman won."

"Thank you. And thank you for that letter. There is no mistaking who wrote it."

"Why do you say that?"

"I know your work. I know you. And I'm glad I do."

He gave her a quick kiss on the lips.

Her voice was soft. "We're getting together just as there will be fifteen hundred miles between us."

"Not quite."

"What?"

"A little over two hundred."

"Why?"

"You are in a struggle for words tonight, are you?! I agreed to join the agency that's been pursuing me."

"You'll be in New York? That's such good news. We'll have weekends! And school vacations and summers!"

"I can't wait. I wish it wasn't August already."

"I still have a little time."

"Your place or mine?"

She laughed. "Do you even have a place?"

"No. Just a figure of speech."

They were silly and enjoying each other.

Maren thought of something else. "Does Benita know?"

"No. I was about to tell her when we were forced to our table for salads."

"How do you think she'll take it?"

"I sense our paths started to diverge a long time ago, and it's time to succumb before we lose our friendship."

"I don't think you're right about that. But I hope it's a good move for you. It is for me, that's all I know."

"And this is all about you," he teased.

Chapter Sixty-Five

Miami

The ocean breeze did little to cool the air. It was a sweltering mid-August day, and Benita was thankful to enter the air-conditioned Basin Quay. She greeted Celeste and filled her in on the discussion she just enjoyed with a prospective author over coffee.

Her office landline rang as she entered. "Hello. Benita Sotolongo."

"Ms. Sotolongo, this is Hamilton Crawford, I am the attorney for your Aunt Adelaide Havens."

"Oh. Is she okay?"

"Yes, yes. Everything is fine. She wanted me to inform you of her plans for some real estate. It is her wish for me to determine your honest reaction."

"Okay."

"When she and her husband, Glonn Havens …"

Benita thought, *Glonn. No wonder he wanted to be just Havens.*

"… talked about their will, they planned to leave Hidden Havens to you."

Benita interjected. "Oh. You know of course Aunt Dilly has a stepson … Uncle Havens' son from a previous marriage."

"Yes. Yes. He inherited after Glonn died. All taken care of. In any event, Ms. Havens is finding the estate difficult to keep up, and she wants you to enjoy it now. If indeed you would enjoy it."

"Oh. How generous of her. I am so grateful for her thoughtfulness."

"But are you interested?"

"Oh. Of course. I love Hidden Havens. I just need time to think about how this will affect my business here in Miami, and whether I have the wherewithal to keep up Hidden Havens."

"I understand. Should I inform Ms. Havens?"

"I'll call her. Thank you so much."

She pondered what had just happened. An immediate idea came to mind, but she needed time to process. She placed the call.

Her Aunt Dilly picked up. "Beni. Hi! How is Miami?"

"Hot, Auntie. Very hot. I miss you and The Havens. And I'm calling to thank you. You are the most special person in the world."

"Oh. Sweetie. That's nice of you. You belong there. It's you. Does this mean you accept?"

"There is no question I love that place and would love to own it. But can I take care of it?"

"I understand. Your Uncle Havens left an endowment for that. I guess the attorney left that part out. He's wily. He wanted to gauge whether you valued the place."

"Oh my, I can't accept any more. I shouldn't accept The Havens. It's worth so much."

"Knowing you will have it is priceless to me. And I wanted to tell you that I won't miss the lake. I'm selling the house in White Plains. I bought a small place in the Hamptons."

"I didn't know there was a small place in the Hamptons."

Aunt Dilly laughed. "There are. You'll like this one. Though small, there's plenty of room for visitors."

"I can't wait."

"Beni, is there any chance you would move to Hidden Havens?"

"I'd have to think about that. It's always been a summer home, so that is how I see it."

"I thought maybe you could telecommute."

Benita laughed this time. "If I made some changes to the agency, and the data access at Hidden Havens, there are parts of my job that would allow for that. It would be easier if Kendrick were still here. You've given me a lot to think about, Auntie."

"There is no better thinker than you. I'll let you know when I'll be turning over the keys, which I could do at any point regardless of the deed. It's beautiful in the late summer and fall."

"I've not been there in the fall. I look forward to it. Auntie, I don't know how to thank you."

"You already have, dear."

Benita was still daydreaming about possibilities for Hidden Havens when Celeste knocked on the door jamb. "Beni. Someone's here to see you." She paused. "It's Troy."

Beni jumped up and went to the reception area. Celeste pulled back and let her pass.

"Troy. What are you doing here?"

"I came to talk to you, if you will."

"Of course. My office? Or should we go out for some coffee?"

"I have an appointment soon, so, your office if you don't mind."

"Sure. Come on in. Welcome back to the agency. You've met Celeste before."

"Yes. Nice to see you again." He nodded toward Celeste.

Benita tensed as he brushed against her arm and entered her office. "You came to Miami for an appointment? Not to see me. So, what can I do for you?""

"I have a job interview. I want to be in Miami because of you." Troy had sweat on his brow despite the cool air of the air-conditioned room. I've been miserable without you. I'm sorry for how I reacted to the situation with Rex and Pala."

"Everything about the summer worked out ... except us."

"And that's my fault. I know that now. Tell me it's not too late."

"I think you are the one who could have fixed it, yes. Even if I am the one that unwittingly put in motion the elements that collided at The Havens."

"I came back to The Havens to talk to you, but you were seeing a client in New York. I thought that meant you had given up on us and returned to the agency."

"It was an emergency meeting to help Maren with a prospective contract. I came right back to the Adirondacks. I was looking for you every morning at school. When that didn't happen, I didn't know what to do. But, for some reason I thought you would show up at Maren's award night. When you didn't, I thought we were over."

"I heard about it after the fact. It was incredible of you to nominate her and, given your efforts, it's not surprising she won. Congratulations. And the book is like, who would ever accomplish that with a bunch of kids in summer school. It's unbelievable."

"Thank you." Benita wanted to get back to the discussion about their relationship. "What now?"

"Can we try again?"

"I don't need to try at all. It's what I've wanted all along."

"I have too." He drew her close and kissed her gently. She broke away just as gently.

"Oh. And I don't know about that job. I'm thinking about a move to Hidden Havens, which I just inherited."

Troy's eyes got wide. "Nice. Congratulations. What about Soto?"

"I'm thinking about an agency structure where I could, as Aunt Dilly said, telecommute. I would be more confident if Kendrick hadn't taken another job."

"Oh. Kendrick left? Sorry. But the Miami job I'm applying for has ties all over, especially Adirondack State Park."

"So maybe both of us could end up in both places?"

"As long as it's at the same time."

"I think I know what I want to do with The Havens, besides live there part time."

"Tell me." Troy drew her close as he listened,

"I want it to be a retreat for families with autistic children."

"I think that is a great idea. I have another great idea, too." He said.

"What's that?"

"I have to go now, but I'll tell you when I get back from the interview." Troy kissed her and left.

Chapter Sixty-Six

Miami

Troy sent a text to Benita, "Meet me at the pier near our beach. I'll be waiting."

She replied, "I'll be there in thirty minutes. How was the interview?"

He didn't reply.

Benita finished a DM reply about a YA fantasy pitch and bid Celeste goodbye. "I think I'll be back, but I'll be in touch."

It'll be so hot at the pier. I wonder what's up.

She was glad that she had dressed as comfortably as possible that morning in a black and white striped dressy linen jumpsuit. It was sleeveless with cropped pant legs. She arrived at the pier and scoured the area without seeing Troy.

"Benita. Over here!" She looked in the direction of Troy's voice. He was on a yacht tied to the dock. *A yacht? In the middle of a workday?*

He helped her board, and their skipper powered the vessel out of the inlet. The deck of the yacht was decorated with garlands of white rosebud sprays and green leaves draped from accent poles. A table in the center of the deck was set for lunch with a white hydrangea bouquet, and the table linens were white as well with green china—a perfect accent for the leaves of the flowers.

Benita looked at Troy with curiosity as they were seated in chairs covered in the same white linen as the table with large green bows tied on an angle. Troy pulled a tiny velvet box from his pocket, got down on one knee and said,

"Benita Sotolongo, we already know that life involves the eruption of high seas, the challenges of white breakers, the dangers of deep waters, and the rare but welcome wave to ride. But if you let me join your voyage through life, I will do everything in my power to make even the most unsettled waters an adventure to savor. May I marry you?" His hand was shaking with excitement. "Like, soon?"

Benita was ready. With a broad smile and misty eyes, she replied, "Yes! I will marry you. And soon."

They kissed, and when they parted, Troy whispered, "How soon?"

"How about fitting in a summer wedding at Hidden Havens?"

"Just what I had in mind."

Adirondacks

"You're getting married at a kid's camp? Leonie Rayne returned from Paris to arrange her daughter's late summer wedding. The interrogation took place as they walked to the dock on the lake at Hidden Havens.

"Li, it's a chapel, and it's where Troy and I met. And, it's close by Hidden Havens. We'll have the reception here." Benita called her mom by the nickname given to Leonie by her dad.

"I just don't know how you can plan a wedding in four weeks." Leonie groaned.

"We're getting married. The when, where, and how aren't paramount in our minds."

"You have to think about the comfort of your guests. It can be cold in September up here. The parlors aren't big enough for a wedding."

"A tent is scheduled with the capacity to provide heat. Technically, it's still summer."

"What about food?"

"The cafeteria manager from Clear Lake Central School where I worked this summer is catering. The kitchen at The Havens is perfect."

"A cafeteria manager? Really, Benita!" Leonie was more repulsed with each added detail.

"He is an excellent chef. Even the kids say so. You know how fussy they can be." Benita tried to reassure her; without any confidence it would work. *What she wants is two years to plan the event of the decade.*

"A dress? Flowers? Invitations? Attendants?" Leonie continued.

"Wait until you see the dress. Reed's Department store, you remember that place? They ordered a couple of dresses for a bride to be, and they were about to send this one back. It's perfect." Li's nose scrunched but Benita went on undeterred. "It's sleeveless, but the chapel train is a sheer shawl that cascades over the shoulders and down the arms. The bodice is fitted with ornate details, and the fitted skirt flows to a flare at the bottom. I don't even need alterations."

"I could have had a Paris original for you, and you bought a reject? Under her breath she muttered, "C'est bete."

Benita quipped. "Li, I can hear you ... and understand you! That bride-to-be couldn't wear both dresses, and they were both beautiful. We invited anyone who wants to come, and people understand we don't have time to send formal invitations. An e-vite went to the school community, everyone at Soto, Troy's former department and his new colleagues, and each of us called our friends."

"I've never heard of such a thing. Who are your attendants?"

"I don't have specific attendants. I going to keep with the theme of Troy's proposal, which was white. We were surrounded by white roses. I'm going to have something more durable, but white flowers made into sprays will cascade from the end of each of the center aisle pews. The stage area will have the urns of roses, and there will be urns filled with rose bouquets tied with green ribbons in the foyer. Anyone who wants to serve as an attendant may grab a bouquet and stand with us. We can accommodate as few or as many as volunteer."

"It sounds like something out of the sixties. They won't wear the same gown?"

"Any color is welcome! I don't care if someone wears white." Benita attempted optimism, but she was unsure whether her mom would ever warm up to this wedding.

"I hope you have a long wedding march. What about ushers?"

"Not per se. But don't worry," Benita knew just what her mother was thinking. "You and Aunt Dilly will be ushered in."

"Tuxes?"

"Optional." Benita took a deep breath to brace herself against her mother's attempts to interrupt. "Troy attended several formal functions through the community college. He has one. You mentioned music. That is where I am very traditional. Pachelbel's Canon for the attendants' procession; "Here Comes the Bride" when Kendrick and I march; and Mendelssohn for the recessional. Did I tell you Kendrick is escorting me?"

"Is he giving you away?"

"We're working on the wording of that."

"Who is officiating?" Leonie still wasn't resigned to this unorthodox occasion. "I hear anyone can these days."

"The pastor of the church Aunt Dilly and I attend when we're at Hidden Havens. Let's see if I can anticipate the rest of your questions. No rehearsal, so no rehearsal dinner. No breakfast the next morning. No bachelor or bachelorette parties. Dinner for guests staying at Hidden Havens of course will be the night before the wedding."

Chapter Sixty-Seven

Adirondacks

Jasmine, the neighbor from Hidden Havens; Pala, Celeste, Maren, and studentStringers Brynn, Nikki and Riza, as well as two of Benita's closest friends since college led the procession down the center aisle of the Finney Memorial Chapel at Chain Mountains Extreme Camp. The sprays of white flowers and baby's breath cascading on fresh green leaves created a half wall along the path they followed.

The piano and cello transitioned to the traditional wedding march as Benita seemed to float down the aisle on the arm of her honored friend, the very debonair Kendrick.

Troy had eyes for no one but Benita and thought she looked like a vision through the involuntary mist that filled his eyes. Taking a series of deep breaths, Troy endeavored to convince himself this moment had come.

That man is so easy to look at, and I get to do just that for the rest of our lives together.

Benita and Troy were rapt by each other. After the ceremony each retained a faint memory of the beauty of the attendants; Leonie and Adele seated and content; and the suave men who volunteered to escort the lovely ladies in the recessional after the bride and groom were married, had kissed, and retreated from the chapel.

They circulated through the crowd that gathered outside of the chapel and invited each person to the reception. Soon they were on their way to Hidden Havens.

The mid-September sun warmed them in the cool sixty-degree weather. To add to the good fortune of the day's weather was the fact that no frost had touched Aunt Dilly's prolific hydrangeas, and they decorated the boundary of the lawn from the road to the water's edge on both sides of the property. Few took refuge in the tent even after the food was served and chose instead to mill around the beautiful grounds as they carried various cool-weather comfort food. There were antique soup tureens filled with broccoli cheese and Italian wedding soups. The main course was shrimp with cilantro cream over rice, la empanada, and sweet caramelized plantains.

The photographer facilitated the bonding of guests by taking small group pictures on the dock; something that most people resisted yet, in the end, engendered fun and conversation among the guests who didn't know one another.

Dancing became the bonding agent after the bride and groom initiated the fun by dancing to the song Troy insisted on ... "Could I Have this Dance for the Rest of My Life?" Their dance was followed by Benita's dance with Kendrick, where they spoke about their journey together as colleagues and friends.

"I hope you love your position in New York City. You're perfect for that job." Benita had assured him of their continued friendship at the moment he told her about his resignation from Soto. "And I wish you and Maren all of the best."

"I wish the same for you and Troy, of course. You are one of the most beautiful brides I have ever seen." Kendrick offered his own reassurances to her. "I've told you how honored I was to escort you down the aisle.

Troy split his dance between Leonie and Adele. Leonie was a superb dancer, and she had no trouble leading his six-foot-two-inch frame around the dance floor. She stared at him for several seconds in silence. She broke the silence with, "Benita has done well. She made a success of the agency, this event is one of the nicest weddings I've attended, she owns Hidden Havens, and she's landed you, a kind man who resembles a movie star."

Troy uttered, "Thank you?" He was relieved that the disc jockey announced he would also dance with Adele. He embraced her and whispered, "Thank goodness. Leonie scares me more than a little. It's a pleasure to be dancing with you. Thank you for all you've done for us and for being a wonderful aunt."

Adele laughed. "Benita is one of my favorite people on earth! And you're right up there as well. I am overwhelmed with joy now that you're beginning your lives together."

Other dancers joined them on the parquet. Before long, the studentStringers devolved into the "Cupid Shuffle Dance," with most of the wedding party joining them.

Benita attempted a conversation with Maren, but she and Kendrick were inseparable after his dance with Benita was over. So, she sought out Pala.

"It's complicated seeing Rex every day," Pala admitted. "I love him, and I have to resist falling back into his orbit until we've had a chance to work on the traits that could drive me away."

Benita understood. She asked about teaching. "It's early to say, but the Native American classes for both semesters are full. I just hope they go well."

"I believe they will."

Troy wrapped his arm around her waist. "Are you hungry for some cake?"

"Yes. Let's go!"

They tenderly fed each other, with forks, and then served the cake to each of their guests and thanked them for coming. Benita grabbed Aunt Dilly and Leonie and requested their help in changing out of her dress into her a grey silk blouse tucked into matching palazzo pants.

Benita met up with Troy in the upstairs hall by room number four. He took her breath away in his jeans and plaid buttoned-down shirt just as he had in his tux. His desire for her was so strong, he couldn't decide whether to drink in her beauty or embrace her for a long kiss. He did both in that order.

The party was in full swing when they left for their honeymoon to the Berkshire's Mountain Lake Inn. It was difficult to decide where to travel. They lived in two of the most desirable spots in the country. Rather than travel far, they returned to where they shared fond memories and a mutual bucket list of things to do.

One of the most important events had just been checked off that list.

Epilogue

Southern California

There's another parallel between fictitious Isaac and real-life Wade. I'd bet money on it. News reporter Melodi Sims studied the few images she stole of Wade from the video taken at the teacher awards ceremony. *I think there was security video of the Adirondack's big winner in June.*

She found the grainy images of people who purchased lottery tickets from the Brook Crossings convenience store. *I knew it. Wade is a match to one of the customers.*

Leaving her internship at WKVN was no problem since it was the end of summer, and she flew to LAX near where she lived and attended college. Melodi had big plans to bust this story wide open. How many sophomore communications students uncover a story this big?

She found a residence in the name of Milo, the dad. She registered at a hotel within walking distance and watched the studio apartment as soon as the morning light dawned.

She observed Wade leave about an hour after her vigil began, and he returned a couple of hours later only to reemerge in a few minutes. This time she followed him. He parked in front of a large office building. She hadn't followed closely enough, and by the time she entered the building, she had no idea of his destination.

"Excuse me. Did you see that young man enter the building?" Melodi asked the woman at the Bean Counter. She ordered coffee to encourage cooperation from the barista.

"You mean Edward? Yes. He comes every day at this time. He's on the planning board for the On-Location Landscapes."

"Thank you." *Edward? But it has to be him.*

Melodi found the floor listed for the firm and proceeded in to the elevator. Before pushing the button for the correct floor, she changed her mind, pushed "door open" and went back to the coffee cart. "Do you know what time he leaves every day?"

"Edward? He's very predictable. He leaves at 5:00 o'clock almost every day."

"Thank you again." Melodi hadn't lost her savvy for getting information from people. But anyone could get information from this barista.

Melodi returned at 4:00 o'clock p.m., ahead of Wade's expected time to quit for the day, to be more confident of catching him. He was out of the building when predicted, and she followed him in his vintage 1968 Mustang convertible. He took the I10 west, and stopped at the Santa Monica pier, ordered dinner, and sat on a bench.

Melodi caught his eye as he tossed away his napkin in the rubbish while on his cell. "Nah. They didn't recognize you, bro. They didn't pay attention to many of my hospital roommates. Ah, I gotta go, Wes. Someone's trying to get my attention. Call ya later."

"Do I know you?" Wade was sure he had met her before.

"I just finished an internship at WKVN in New York City. I think you were at an awards dinner I covered. I'm entering my sophomore year at the College of Arts and Communication."

"Oh yeah. Hi. What a coincidence."

They bought ice cream, strolled on the beach, and talked. They returned to the bench and talked late into the night.

"I'm afraid I need to go. I have a morning class." Wade was the first to suggest the evening had to come to an end.

Melodi had a good time. She would ask him about the lottery in time. Her reporter instinct told her that he was still hiding it from the world, hence the alias. Melodi's heart told her there was no need to ask about his winnings right now. *Eventually. Perhaps.*

Inspiration for Secluded Summer at Hidden Havens

Inspiration for the 'Hidden Havens' Inn and Tavern in *Secluded Summer at Hidden Havens* is this 280-year-old M. Root Inn and Tavern on the property adjacent to the home of the author. The above structure was built by Captain Joseph Root, a co-founder of the quaint New England town of Montague, and served as a stagecoach inn and tavern date from the mid-1700's to the late 1800's along the busy Kings Highway.

Milton Keynes UK
Ingram Content Group UK Ltd.
UKHW031831300124
436988UK00013B/916